PLASTER CITY

A JIMMY VEEDER FIASCO

ALSO BY JOHNNY SHAW

Dove Season: A Jimmy Veeder Fiasco

Big Maria

JOHNNY SHAW

PLASTER CITY

A JIMMY VEEDER FIASCO

THOMAS & MERCER

Published by Thomas & Mercer, Seattle

www.apub.com

Amazon, the Amazon logo, and Thomas & Mercer are trademarks of Amazon.com, Inc., or its affiliates.

ISBN-13: 9781477817582
ISBN-10: 1477817581

Cover illustration by becker&mayer! LLC

Library of Congress Control Number: 2013915800

Printed in the United States of America

For
Bob Hunt

The Imperial Valley represented in this novel is an entirely fictional version of a real place.

While Plaster City, California, and the other desert towns depicted do exist, the real Plaster City, Indio, Thermal, and La Quinta bear little similarity or resemblance to the ones in this book, beyond shared locations on the map.

As I've stated in previous works, a hometown is like a younger brother. You can tease him, knock him around, and give him a hard time, but you'll always love him and stand up for him.

I might take some liberties and do some name-calling, but this novel was written with the greatest respect and admiration for the people of the Imperial Valley.

PART ONE

ONE

Ceja Carneros hit me so hard he broke his watch on my head.

His thick fist cranked my jaw and loosened my molars, but it was his chunky fake Rolex that did the real damage. You get what you pay for. The cheap Malaysian knockoff shattered on impact. Shards from the watch face tore my skin. The minute hand pierced my cheek.

I didn't know people still wore wristwatches. As the old saw says, you really do learn something new every time you get punched in the face. Here's another pearl of wisdom: When walking through a door, make sure there isn't a giant Mexican with one eyebrow and a vicious haymaker on the other side. A crucial life lesson.

My next educational tidbit came as a straight jab to the bridge of the nose that jellied my legs and drained a sinus-load of brain juice down the back of my throat. The sour taste of all the weird ick that lived in my head brought back the worst kind of memories. All the fights I'd ever lost. It tasted like humiliation and defeat. More literally, it tasted like pickling brine.

Ceja stood six feet away when I stopped backpedaling, and the stars quit spinning around my head. I gulped down more vinegar, feeling a tooth go down with it. The big ape panted from his two-punch combo, hands on knees. He let a line of spit trail to the ground, keeping his eyes more or less on me, too drunk to fully focus.

I had no idea why Ceja coldcocked me. I couldn't remember doing anything to piss him off. Hell, the last time I had seen him was over a month before at our buddy Lansing's Mormon wedding. If something had happened then, beyond sneaking into the parking lot to take pulls from a much-needed bottle of Southern Comfort, I would have known. To Ceja, revenge was a dish best served straight out of the oven. He was only physically an elephant. His mental capacity and memory were less advanced.

A quick aside about Mormon weddings. No alcohol. Not even coffee or soda, because of the caffeine thing. An alcohol-free wedding reception is like masturbating for an hour without reaching orgasm. It's fun at the beginning, but after a while it's just exhausting and depressing and you want it to be over. Like that, but with dancing.

"Kill dead on you," Ceja Yoda-ed. His alcohol breath queased me as a cloud of sour murdered the air between us.

I didn't want to hurt the big moron, but I wanted to get hit again even less. I needed to use my sobriety as a strategic advantage. I could think faster, move faster, and exploit my cleverness. I devised a devious and intricate plan.

I kicked him in the balls.

Call me old-fashioned, but I prefer the classics.

It took a lot of booze to ignore a steel-toe to the grapes. Ceja's eyes watered and he let out a death rattle of an exhale, but he didn't go down. Instead, he charged, dropping his shoulder and driving into my gut. My back slammed against the brick wall.

I'm not proud of what happened next. To be honest, I'm not all that proud of the nut-kick either, but you got to work with the tools in your shed. And the closest tools at that moment were the cues in the wall rack. When Ceja stepped back to throw another shot, I cracked the pool cue over his head. He didn't exactly drop. He eventually hit the floor, but his descent was more of a slow, sad crumple. Like his limbs surrendered to gravity, a modern dance version of a Peckinpah death scene. When it was over, he curled up on the ground, fetal. Eyes open, snoring. I thought about giving him an insurance kick, but we were buddies.

"Rack 'em up," Bobby Maves said, toasting me from behind the bar. "No, wait. Nice rack! Or, I think that's my cue—dot-dot-dot—to kick your ass. Get it? Cue. Or something with the word *pool* in it. I pity the pool?"

"Why didn't you help me?"

"Laughing too hard."

Bobby looked closer to the end of his night than the beginning. An even split between Swiss and Mexican, Bobby favored Latin in his look, but identified as white. What we called a Rednexican. A very drunk one. His trademark bone-white pompadour drooped to one side, clipping three inches off his height. Five eight and wiry, Bobby had always relied on his ivory coxcomb to boost his physical stature. His eyes were only slightly redder than his face. If I squinted, he looked like a photo negative of Elvis. Bobby set a glass on the bar, poured a shot of tequila, and slid it toward me as I approached. As I made no move to catch it, the shot glass slid off the bar.

"Jest ride into town, Hoss?" Bobby twanged, ignoring the broken glass.

3

"Bar towel," I said.

Bobby reached under the bar and tossed me a damp towel. It didn't smell too beery. Dabbing at my cheek, it came away bloody, but not much more than if I would have been shaving on a rollercoaster.

"Now that you're here," Bobby said, "have a drink with me."

"Fuck this," I said, turning toward the door. "I'm going home."

"Come on. One drink."

"I'm tired of this bullshit, Bobby. It's late. My face hurts. You're laughing and I'm bleeding."

"All right. Don't drink. But hang out."

"Why the hell did Ceja attack me?"

"I kept calling you. Even before the bar closed," Bobby said. "Left you like twenty messages. You didn't pick up."

Bobby poured another drink and slid it to me. I caught it, liquor spilling onto my fingers. I licked the tequila off, but I left the glass on the bar.

"It's three in the morning. As soon as I saw it was you, I turned my phone off."

"What if it was an emergency?"

"I could live with that. Seriously, I'm out of here. This is stupid."

"Some friend you are."

"Quit being an asshole. I can't come out every time you want to play." I dug my finger into my mouth. "I swallowed a goddamn tooth. If it was my new gold crown, you're paying for it, digging through my shit to find it. Cost a grand I didn't have."

"Ceja did it. He can do the prospecting."

"Take some fucking responsibility."

"If you didn't listen to my messages, how'd you know I was here?"

"Pinky called Angie," I said. "You got to quit harassing that sweet old lady."

Pinky Gruber owned and operated the bar we were in, Pinky's Bar & Grill, the toughest bar in Holtville. That's saying something, considering the Top Hat Saloon and Portagee Joe's were nightly Thunderdomes. My bar, Morales Bar, would be a contender, but it was outside city limits so it didn't officially rank. The men and women that frequented Pinky's knew what they were getting and came back for more. At that moment, an hour past closing, the place was empty. But on most days, regulars filled the shadows for a night of competitive drinking, hobby fighting, and some occasional backseat stinkfinger. It was desert local, border fighty, and Bobby's Tuesday bar.

The interior of Pinky's was what every great bar aspired to be. No frills, all function. A two-pool-table dive's dive with a long bar and plenty of Johnny Cash on the juke. The sawdust that carpeted the floor was gray and furry from spilled drinks, vomit, and tobacco juice. A few faded Cinco de Mayo beer posters sporting curvy Latinas in bathing suits and sombreros were the only adornment. If Pinky's Bar & Grill had a decorative motif, it was darkness and a healthy dose of what the fuck are you looking at.

"Pinky said you wouldn't leave," I said. "She said she was going to call the cops. I thought if I came down here, I could put out a fire."

"She wanted to close and I wasn't done drinking."

"You can't drink at home?"

"I'm a social animal."

"I can see that." I motioned toward the empty—save for the passed-out Ceja—bar.

"That's why I called you, drinking buddy." He nodded toward the drink in front of me. "Catch up."

I slid the glass back to Bobby, most of the liquor spilling out.

"Where's Pinky? Please tell me she's not locked in one of the bathrooms."

"I wouldn't do that to Pinky. I love Pinky. She eventually surrendered, left me the keys, and told me to lock up."

"You're paying for those drinks, yeah?" I asked.

"I'm keeping track." Bobby held up a dog-eared pad of paper covered in columns and tick marks. There were a lot of tick marks. He made another mark and poured another shot.

"How many have you had? You look like you're about to pass out," I said.

"The night is young."

"No, it ain't. And neither are we. I'm worried about you, bro. It's fun when it's spread out, but since Griselda and you split, this shit's happening on the regular. You can't keep it up."

"Sure I can," Bobby said, grinning.

"Let me rephrase. I can't."

"Have a drink. Let the alcohol decide."

"Seriously, Bobby. You're a bender away from an intervention."

Bobby laughed. "If you're going to throw an intervention, give me a couple days' notice and I'll cater the fucker. I'll pit a pig, get a pony keg, maybe hire a stripper clown. Do it up."

"I'm serious."

"That's what's so adorable. Fuck off, okay? I ain't hurtin' no one."

"I just got hit in the face. Twice. Lost a fucking tooth. What did you say to Ceja? Why'd he attack me?"

"I might've kinda had something to do with that. I got pissed you were ducking my calls. When Ceja showed up, we got to drinking and bullshitting and reminiscing. This is his drinks." Bobby held up the pad, pointing to a column with a dozen marks. "I don't know how we got on the subject—right around my twentieth call—but I told Ceja that his little sister blew you in the backseat of your car after Junior Prom."

"You what?"

"Yeah."

"That didn't happen."

"Wait for it."

"I was with Darlene What's-her-face, not getting any. Spent all night boner-stabbing the inside of my tux zipper. I still have a scar."

"Wait for it."

"I drove Pop's Chevy LUV then. It's a pickup. Doesn't have a backseat."

"Wait for it."

"Quit saying, 'Wait'—Oh, hell no. Ceja doesn't have a sister, does he?"

"There it is." Bobby howled. "That's the best part. At first he didn't believe me, but after all them drinks. You spin a story right, anyone'll believe anything."

I turned on my stool and looked at Ceja. He snored, his hands in fists jerking slightly, still fighting in his dream. I regretted not giving him that insurance kick.

"What are you going to do with him?" I said.

Bobby shrugged. "We can't leave him here. He'd catch all kinds of shit mañana. I'd drive, but I'm in no condition. I know he gave you a beating, but as his friends, we need to throw him in the back of his squad car and get him home."

"I'm not feeling like a Good Samaritan."

"He could get in real trouble, especially after the last time."

"Pinky really called the cops on you."

"Yeah, but only because she knows I don't like to drink alone."

Two years. Give or take. That's how long I'd been back in the Imperial Valley, my stretch of desert between San Diego and Yuma, as far south and as far east as you could go in California. Life on the Mexican border. Life below sea level. A whole new life.

As strange as it was on most days, I had settled into a routine, become an active member of the community, come to terms with my new present. I had a farm, son, and live-in girlfriend, which made me a farmer, father, and live-in boyfriend. I'm not sure how good I was at any of those things, but I tried like hell and put my everything into it. If caring got things done, I'd be golden. Unfortunately, caring don't dig a ditch. So I did the work.

I was poor but happy. When you'd lived by the seat of your pants as long as I had, the edge of bankruptcy wasn't stressful, it was daily life. On the border, I was often reminded that while things might be tough, there were plenty of people worse off. It sucked to eke out a living, but it sucked more when you had to tackle it alone. With my girlfriend, Angie, we had each other. We had our family. We made sure that Juan, my son, had everything he needed. We figured out a way. But for all the love I had for my family, going from sixty to zero hadn't been easy. For the previous twelve years, I couldn't have been further from the pace and responsibility of farm living. Twelve irresponsible, insane, fun years. Twelve story-filled, don't-tell-your-kids-ever, I-remember-eleven-out-of-the-twelve years. I had drifted around the world. Saw cool places, made cool friends, and did cool things. I had spent time in Europe, Asia, South America, and most of the US. Now I was farming one hundred and sixty acres of alfalfa and driving my son to T-ball, right before I ran to the store to get tampons for my girlfriend. I had slammed on the brakes and jackknifed into a straight life.

Bobby was the chaotic ballast that held it together.

Every time things felt crushingly dull, when life wasn't as Norman Rockwelly as it appeared, when the bills piled up or the crops died, I'd get a call from the one and only Bobby Maves, my best friend.

Every three or four weeks, I would end up at a bar or a strip club or an open field that would represent the launching pad for what Bobby would refer to as an "official Mavescapade." I would hate to see what an unofficial one looked like. A Mavescapade was hard to explain. Slightly dangerous, always childish, and frighteningly irresponsible. But when it was all over, I only remembered the laughing and the bruises. A Mavescapade meant raising seventeen kinds of hell and then eating menudo and drinking Clamato and room-temp beer the next day to mute the hangover.

With the help of the irregular Mavescapade, I could live the straight life. Knowing there was fun-danger around the corner kept my itchy feet scratched. On the toughest days, the promise of a Mavescapade kept me from jumping in my car and heading out of town screaming from the tightening responsibilities and pressures a grown-up endured.

I wouldn't call it a healthy balance but it was a balance. One that even Angie had reluctantly come to accept. Not at first, but it didn't take her long to see the positives of the dynamic. She knew me well enough to know that it was something I needed. And it was all going well. Until Bobby and Griselda broke up.

They had been a couple since I had been back. A strange pair to be sure, with Griselda being a Deputy Sheriff and Bobby being a—well, Bobby. But it worked. I don't know what happened between them, but it hadn't been good. When I asked Bobby, all he had said was "Didn't work out." And that was the last he spoke of it.

After the breakup, the Mavescapades shifted from monthly to weekly to all the time. Bobby lived in a constant state of madcap mischief. He went from a fun-loving loose cannon to a monkey with a machine gun. Sure, it's cute, but eventually someone's going to get hurt.

Bobby drank every day and raised hell every night. Inevitably I would end up getting a call from some bartender or bouncer or friend begging me to drag Bobby out of their bar or house or barn. It's hard to admit that your friend is an alcoholic when he's a fun drunk. Bobby made it easier with each day.

The problem was I owed him. Bobby had been there for me when I needed him—no questions asked—when anyone with sense would have turned his back on me. Bobby hadn't flinched when I had asked for help. So I wasn't about to. Even if he pushed limits that I didn't know I had. There were times I wanted to bail on him, and I felt like shit every time I considered it.

It might sound hokey, but Bobby was a man of action. Denied action, he created it. Fun, dangerous, exhausting—you never knew what you would get. But beyond my sense of duty, it was always an adventure hanging out with the funniest guy I knew, doing the stupidest shit we could think of, and opening up that release valve to let off all that fucking steam.

———

Beyond Bobby's innate ability to get me to do stupid things, I couldn't resist fulfilling a childhood dream. I had always wanted to drive a police car. Been in plenty, but never behind the wheel. It was too good an opportunity to pass up.

Bobby and I tossed the unconscious Officer Ceja into the back of his squad car and we hit the mean streets of Holtville.

Ceja lived out in the country north of town, which gave us a chance to see what his cruiser could do. Well over 130 miles per, was the answer. And smooth, even on some of the washboard roads. Cop shocks.

Bobby insisted on running the lights and the siren. It was a bad idea. I knew it. But I couldn't come up with a good argument, because I wanted to run them, too. Sometimes bad ideas were the best ideas. I'm sure we didn't make any new friends along Holt Road.

Bobby and I took turns pretending to talk into the radio.

"Strike Force Delta 8, Strike Force Delta 8. We got a 957 on Chell Road," Bobby said, making static sounds with his mouth between sentences. "What's your 10-11, Officer Veeder? Roger. Over."

"Can you give me a spelling on the location of that Niner-Fiver-Sevener? Roger Dodger. Over."

"A 957. An illegal sheep-fighting ring. Chell Road. Chell. Um. Charlie. Hepatitis. Elephone. Lumbago. Luggage. Over."

"You used two different words for L. That's not how they do it. And did you say Elephone? Not a word and way confusinger."

"How else would elephants talk to each other? On the elephone. And you forgot to say, 'over.' Over and out."

I threw some donuts in a flat lot used to store hay bales. The car spun in a tight circle, kicking dust that sparkled in the moonlight. Ceja's torso flopped to the floor in the back with his feet still on the bench seat. If he could sleep through it, it couldn't be that uncomfortable.

"Speaking of doughnuts," I said. "It's practically breakfast time and I got the hungries. Could really go for one or a dozen glazed."

"Fuck doughnuts, man. Fucking carne asada. Let's hit that roach coach outside of Paloma's. Two dollar burritos. Might be open. Throw ourselves a spicnic."

"Spicnic? Really?"

"I'm half-Mexican, so it's okay."

"Only half okay. Ten-four on the carne, good buddy. I'm on it."

I pulled the parking brake, sending the car spinning. Bobby and I scream-laughed. After doing a full 720, we came to a stop perpendicular to the road. I made a slow seven-point turn that took forever. Incredibly anticlimactic. But not more anticlimactic than what happened next.

We ran out of gas on a ditch bank six miles north of town and three miles from Ceja's house. It occurred to us at that moment that we hadn't thought things through. We had gotten so excited about driving a police car that we never considered how we were going to get home with both our vehicles back at the bar. Planning wasn't really our strong suit.

"Who can we call?" I asked.

"You're the only one I call this late."

"Buck Buck or Snout?"

"Don't get back from San Felipe until tomorrow."

"Not Angie. She's already going to give me shit when she sees my face bruise."

"Maybe there's a gas can."

We popped the trunk. No gas can. We did find a spare and a jack. A scattergun. Road flares and a first aid kit. Little Debbie boxes of Zebra Cakes, Nutty Bars, and Banana Pudding Rolls. Two dog-eared pornographic paperbacks titled *Wet Cheerleaders* and *Balling on the Ballboy's Balls!* Three gallon jugs of water. A case of beer. And two collapsible frog gigs.

When you get dealt a ten-high, you can't change it. I decided to play the cards I was dealt, not because I was overly excited about them, but because it was what was in my hand. I used the contents of the trunk to determine the next chapter in this still-unfinished misadventure. As if the Fates themselves had left me and Bobby with beer, dessert, and frog gigs.

I woke up the next morning in a sugar beet field covered in mud. Sadly, it wasn't the first time. My head hurt, my mouth tasted like artificial banana, and I was missing a shoe. The mud felt cool against the already triple-digit heat. The low sun stung my eyes, but that pain was just the preamble. I knew it. When a Little Debbie and beer hangover kicked in, it was a dilly of a doozy.

Mud oozed between my fingers as I pushed myself into a sitting position. Five feet away, Bobby sat Indian-style, as peaceful as a Buddha. The mud on his face and clothes had set, already dry, deep brown fading to gray. He grinned, nodded, and tossed me a can of beer. It bounced off my shoulder and landed in front of me.

"Ow," I said. "We should go. Angie's going to be worried. And pissed."

I stood up too fast, got dizzy, and slipped in the mud onto my ass. A karmic lesson in impatience.

"Take it from a man with experience," Bobby said. "Never rush. It's not natural. Life is harsh sober."

I scraped fresh mud off my arm, the clean areas only highlighting the overall mess.

"How do you get me to do this shit?" I said.

"Don't blame me. You wanted to drive a cop car."

"Fucking stupid," I said and cracked the beer.

Fifteen minutes later, Bobby and I plodded through the field, hopped the ditch, and circled the police cruiser like we were examining a crime scene. Looking through the back window, the previous night's activities came back to me. Ceja remained passed out in that strange position. But now he was covered in dead frogs.

After we had run out of gas, Bobby and I had knocked back some beers and frog gigged in the ditches. Without a bucket, we shoved our bounty through a crack in the car window. Stranger things had seemed like a good idea to a drunk mind. Sober and in the light of day, covering your buddy in dead animals wasn't nearly as funny.

Bobby gave the window a knock. The heavy ring on his pointer finger—the one he called Knockout Charlie—clicked loudly. He held up his phone, poised to take a picture.

Ceja's eyes opened. It took a second. Then the screaming started.

Click. "Oh, man. That's a keeper."

One hundred percent pure panic. From sound sleep to what he must have perceived as an amphibian takeover of the world. His body flailed, slipping and sliding and swimming in the blood and slime of a sea of dead frogs. Ceja started crying.

Before anyone brands me cruel, remember that Ceja knocked out my tooth for corrupting a nonexistent sister. And while this wasn't a conscious revenge, I'd take it. One man's cruelty is another man's justice.

As Ceja tried to get up, the bloody frogs flopped around the back of the squad car like popcorn. Ceja looked like he was in a serial killer's version of an amusement park ball pit.

I opened the back door. Frogs spilled to the ground. It smelled like the men's room in a bait shop. Ceja darted out, dancing and rubbing at his clothes.

"Where am I? What happened? What are you guys doing here?"

Bobby answered calmly. "We're in Texas. Outside Laredo. You were drugged last night by an operative working for the

CIA, the PTA, and Amazon. We are here from the future. Come with us if you want to live."

"I don't understand. Why frogs?"

"Exactly," Bobby said.

Ceja looked from Bobby to me and back to Bobby. Confusion and fear. I thought he was going to start crying again.

"Take it easy, Ceja. Bobby's screwing with you," I said. "Except the part about the CIA. That's true. They put a tracker up your ass. Way up there."

As an accidental punch line to my joke, Bobby's phone farted. He answered.

"Yello," Bobby said. "Hunh? Slow down, Beck."

His expression stopped me cold. With every second, his face grew more serious. His eyes stared at a dead spot in space. He was focused entirely on listening. Bobby didn't do serious that often. Something big was happening.

"Why did you wait until now?" A hint of suppressed anger in his voice.

Ceja looked at me. He looked worried too. We waited. Bobby hung up.

"Bobby? What is it? What happened?" I asked.

It took a moment, but Bobby finally looked at me. It was like he'd never seen my face before.

"What?" I pleaded.

"Julie ain't been home for five days. Nobody's seen her, knows where she's at. Cops got nothing." He looked down at his phone like it was the phone's fault. He turned back to me.

"My daughter is missing."

TWO

Angie watched me from the bedroom door. She hadn't said more than ten words since picking me up, not even a snide remark about the fist-shaped bruise on my forehead or my mud-caked clothes. I would have preferred a scolding to the fatalistic scenarios in my head.

I pulled my big gym bag from the closet and chucked it on the bed. I opened the bottom dresser drawer and threw a random stack of T-shirts in and around the bag.

The neutrality of Angie's expression gave me no gauge. Her silence, even less. It made me infer emotions and thoughts that probably weren't there. In film theory, it's called the Kuleshov Effect. A blank expression taking on whatever emotion the context implies. A neutral expression looking at food. Hungry. A neutral expression looking at a clown. Amused or terrified, depending on one's opinion of clownkind. The things you retain from the easy-A classes in college.

When I couldn't take the silence anymore, I let words leak out of my mouth to fill the void. "I read somewhere that a good thief starts on the bottom drawer. So they only have to open them, but not close them. If you go top to bottom, you got to close 'em as you go. Saves valuable stealing time."

"Or you can pull them all the way out," Angie said.

"Yeah, I suppose you could do that."

A handful of socks joined the pile. Angie walked to the bed and refolded the shirts, placing them one at a time into the bag.

I shook my head. "I ain't seen Bobby that messed up since we were kids and his old man made him shoot his dog, RoboCop. It had attacked some sheep, got the taste for blood. Bobby's confusion was scary then, and he was thirteen. I can't imagine what's going through his head."

"He should've waited for you," Angie said.

"If it were Juan, I'd've—you'd've done the same. I'm only a couple hours behind him."

"Anything I can do?" She set another freshly folded shirt into the bag.

"Hell, I don't know if there's anything I can do. It's not like he even asked me to come along—to help. I just know this isn't a thing anyone should do alone."

"Hopefully it's normal teenager crap. Road trip with a boyfriend. Running off to become an actress. Finding-herself shit."

"Julie's somewhere around sixteen. I'm thinking how wild we were. Must've freaked out our folks plenty."

"It's a teenager's job to torture their parents. Wait'll Juan grows up. You'll see."

"Let's hope it's something stupid," I said.

Angie nodded, but I could tell by her face that her thoughts had drifted to the other possibilities.

"You going to be okay with Juan?" I asked.

"We'll be fine, but try not to be gone long. You know how he gets. Even this morning, he woke up and you weren't there. He got real quiet. Wouldn't talk to me."

"He's got to start getting used to me being gone. He starts kindergarten soon."

"You concentrate on finding Julie. And keeping Bobby out of trouble. Which is no simple task. Longer than a few days, we might have to figure something out. See how he is. At least we got Mr. Morales. Who knew he would be such a good babysitter. Now run across the road and get your son. I'll pack the rest of your shit."

"Rudolph El Reno de la Nariz Roja" played on the jukebox of Morales Bar. Since I'd been raising Juan, Mr. Morales (or Mr. More-Or-Less, as Juan said it) had been the go-to babysitter and all-around grandfather figure for the boy. Right across the street, Mr. Morales and his bar were our only neighbors out in the country. I had known him my whole life. Notoriously stolid, I almost saw Mr. Morales smile for the second time when Juan went nuts for the pocketknife he gave him on his fifth birthday.

Without prompting, Mr. Morales had added a half dozen kids' songs to the bar jukebox. The first time one of the regular campesinos made some noise about "La Itsy Bitsy Araña" replacing his favorite banda tune—well, it was also the last time one of the regular campesinos made any noise about any song selection.

When I was growing up, Mr. Morales had raised his grandson, Tomás. I think he missed it. In recent months, Mr. Morales's relationship to Tomás had all but dissolved. He didn't discuss it with me, but I had to guess that it was mostly due to Tomás's role as a prominent Mexican crime figure.

Two years ago, it had been pornography and prostitution, which Mr. Morales had no moral reservations about. But if the scuttlebutt and bar-whispers of the last few months were to be believed, Tomás was attempting to expand operations north. And that level of crimelording—and the violence that came with it—rubbed Mr. Morales the wrong way.

Mr. Morales had Juan in the middle of the empty bar, both of them crouched in a boxer's stance. From what I could figure, Mr. Morales was demonstrating proper technique for throwing an uppercut.

"You want to really feel these two knuckles hit," Mr. Morales said.

Juan nodded intently.

"Are you teaching my boy how to fight?" I asked.

When Juan saw me, he dropped his hands and ran to me. I knelt down and lifted him as he leapt into my arms. With Juan in one arm, I gave Mr. Morales an awkward handshake with the other.

"Someone has to," Mr. Morales said. "If I leave it to you, Juanito will sissy slap, kick shins, and pull hair."

"He's five. And you forgot eye-gouging."

"That bruise on your face is all the reason I need."

"I got sucker punched."

"Don't blame the punch. Blame the sucker."

I set Juan down, got on my haunches, and held up both hands to him. "All right, grasshopper. Show me what Mr. More-Or-Less taught you."

Juan nodded and, with textbook timing, turned and punched Mr. Morales square in the nuts. The old man let out a deep exhale and took a knee. Like father, like son. Juan had my moves.

"What was that lesson called?" I asked.

Mr. Morales silently rose. He cowboy-walked to the bar, put a handful of ice in a towel, and gingerly held it to his groin.

"I punched him good. Like Mr. More-Or-Less teached me," Juan said, smiling broadly.

"You sure did." I put my arm around him and concentrated on not laughing at Mr. Morales. No reason to add insult to injury. Especially not to someone who had a shotgun within reach.

———·—·———

Back at the house, I set Juan in front of a big box of crayons and some coloring books. I joined him, trying to get Wonder Woman's costume just right. Really working the curves.

I looked at my boy, his tongue sticking out of the corner of his mouth in concentration. I wondered what I would do if he went missing. I couldn't fathom it. I didn't want to.

As much as I loved Angie, Juan was the thing that made everything make sense. The reason I kept my feet planted and took whatever shots came my way. I had never thought I'd become a father. Did so reluctantly. But two years later, I couldn't imagine my life without him. As Pop would say, it doesn't matter what we want, it's what we do with what we have.

"I have to go away for a little while, a couple days maybe. Okay?" I said.

Juan stopped coloring and screwed up his face. Not tantrum-angry, but definitely mad. "I don't want you to."

"I have to. Uncle Bobbiola needs my help."

"Why?"

"His daughter Julie is in trouble. Nobody can find her. I have to help Uncle Bobbiola look."

"Maybe she's playing hide-and-seek and she's a real good hider."

"Maybe. I won't be gone too long."

Juan's brow wrinkled with concern. "How do I know you'll come back?"

"Of course I will," I said. "I've gone away before. And I came back those times, didn't I? I'm your father. I'll be back as soon as I can."

"You promise?"

"I promise."

Juan thought about it for a moment. He picked up a crayon and squeezed it in his hand. He didn't look happy, but he said, "Okay."

"Listen to your mom and Mr. More-Or-Less. Do what they say. Be good."

Juan nodded and returned to coloring Batman's cape a blasphemous lime green. But he had lost his passion for it, going through the motions of filling the blank spots with random color.

I chucked the gym bags in the passenger seat of my truck. Angie gave me a quick kiss, more of a see-you-soon kiss than a come-back-in-one-piece kiss.

"Could be overnight, could be longer," I said. "Depends on how things shake out. I'm only an hour and a half away. I just irrigated, but I'll have Mike check on the fields if I'm longer than a day or two. I know money's tight, but we'll figure it out."

"I wish Buck Buck or Snout could go instead of you," Angie said.

I laughed. "Even if they were in town, you know that wouldn't work. Becky called Bobby to look for her. Buck Buck and Snout would be gasoline on whatever nuclear explosion he sets off while searching. I can keep Bobby from getting into trouble."

"No, you can't. When have you ever? That's like trying to rope a tornado."

"Everything's going to be fine," I said, not selling it. And from the look on Angie's face, she didn't buy it either. Something told us both that this was going to get bad.

———

Bobby Maves and Becky Espinosa met in kindergarten or first grade. Like most of the people we graduated high school with, we all went to grade school together.

It wasn't love at first sight. If I remember the story correctly, Becky beat the shit out of Bobby on the playground over a game of marbles. A few choice words and punches were exchanged over whether or not blocksies, jumpsies, and no-takesies could be used in conjunction with each other.

Time passed and the fight was forgotten. With a graduating class of eighty-five at Holtville High, the dating pool ran shallow. Everyone knew everything about everyone, making everyone less attractive as the years went on. But nobody liked to dance alone and sex was more fun with a partner, even one you didn't like that much. Eventually Bobby and Becky found each other in the rotation. They didn't date for very long. Just long enough.

Becky's parents both worked as migrant field hands. So when they moved the summer after junior year, nobody thought anything of it. A lot of families spent half the year in the Central Valley or in Arizona, depending on what crops needed picking.

Five years later, Bobby found out he had a daughter. A shocker for a two-kegs-a-week college student studying Ag Econ in San Luis Obispo. Becky needed cash and Bobby had access to student loans. She didn't ask him for anything more than the financial commitment.

Somewhere in the roughly ten years since, Becky had decided that Bobby should play a more active parental role. Not knowing how to handle the situation, Bobby made a weak effort to become involved in Julie's life. He already sent money, what was left after the child support payments for his younger daughter—she's a whole different story. He sent presents on birthdays and holidays. Those grew to occasional awkward visits.

Becky and Julie had lived in Twentynine Palms, which was far enough to make it an effort. But a move to Indio a little over a year ago had brought them close enough to nullify most excuses. The problem was that Bobby was Julie's father, but he was never going to be her dad. Julie had become a young woman, his absence already felt. She was who she was going to be.

I had only met Julie once. A quick stopover on our way to a boxing match at Pechanga. She had no interest in meeting her father's friend, so our interaction was brief. I wanted to tell her that the Misfits shirt, tongue and nose ring, and super-short shorts really played into a predictable stereotype. Individuality through conformity. A look that screamed, "I'm different in the same way this gigantic group of other people are different." But teenagers have to be teenagers. As long as trouble didn't become permanent in the form of addiction, a kid, or death, that rebellion was a part of becoming a real person. Kids have to act grown up before they grow up.

Hopefully Julie was acting out in a predictable way. But it was hard not to think of the other scenarios. Too many news stories and movies of a kid gone missing to not expect the worst. All those loonies that made a parent's skin crawl. They were out there. And the desert was like a psycho-magnet to the worst predators. The nefarious potential of wide-open spaces, no neighbors, and unmarked graves.

———·•·———

The drive from Holtville to Indio took less than two hours. Through Imperial, Brawley, and the US Immigration checkpoint in Westmoreland, the route ran along the western shore of the Salton Sea. I took in its aroma: the smell of anchovies mixed with rancid cottage cheese. I would've taken the odor as a bad omen, but it always smelled that way. I didn't even bother to play the radio, letting my mind wander. I went over the last conversation I had with Bobby before he headed out without me.

"Becky said Julie's been gone five days already. She'd done it before—never more than a day or two—so she didn't think much of it. Called the cops two days ago. Me, today. They're on it, she says, but forgive me if I don't show a shit-ton of confidence in the Indio PD or Riverside Sheriff or whatever group of country cops got the case.

"Julie's gotten wilder in the last year. Back sass. Coming home drunk. Tats and piercings. Loser boyfriends. Older boyfriends. Pot in her underwear drawer. Fights. Like father, like daughter, I suppose. Except she's straight-A's. Smart as shit. Don't know if that makes it worse or better. Worse probably, because it means she does stupid shit, but she ain't stupid. Smart enough to know better."

"Lots of us manage to be smart and stupid at the same time," I said. "When's the last time you saw her?"

Bobby didn't answer for a moment. "Six, seven months. How fucked up is that? I don't barely know her."

"It's always been an impossible situation."

"If you think that me not being around's got nothing to do with that bad girl shit, you're a dumbass who slept through college."

"When did you crack open the Freud? She's independent, does her own thing. Sound familiar?"

"Except her keys, clothes, phone, all her stuff was still at the house. She hasn't posted anything on Facebook or Twitter or any of that teenage shit. Her last message on Facebook said, 'He treats me like a woman. Knows I can take a punch as hard as I can throw one. That's all I need.'"

"Shit."

"I'm going to find out who the fuck that fucker is and fuck him up. Pardon my fucking French."

That's why I was driving north. Bobby's sentiment was solid. It was his plan of attack I worried about. To talk to Becky. See what she knew. Go through Julie's stuff for clues. Talk to

Julie's friends. Find out who was who. Then fuck up the fuck-ing fuckers. I felt sorry for anyone in Bobby's path.

Indio might be known for the Coachella Music Festival and a stretch of Indian casinos, but the bulk of it is lower-class resi-dential neighborhoods filled with people who work for a living.

Becky's house was a nondescript, salmon-colored box in a concrete brick neighborhood. Squat, mostly dead palms passed for topiary along the walkway. The rest of the front yard was dirt, a big swath of uneven brown. Three cars filled the driveway, the third poking into the street.

The man who opened the door was in his early forties. More Palm Springs than Indio, he was tall, tan, and in shape, easy to picture bounding over a tennis net. He wore an apron that said "Kitchen Bitch" on the front. The apron, his pants, and his hands were all dotted with flour.

The aroma of cookies or brownies, something sweet and chocolaty, wafted from inside the house. Not exactly the smell I was expecting. Although, to be honest, I wasn't expecting any smell except a general house smell.

"Everyone's in the living room," the man said. "I have cookies in the oven."

And on that, he went back into the house without saying anything more, leaving the door open. I heard voices, the muffled hum of a small crowd.

There were eight people in the living room, evenly divided between men and women. They organized stacks of fliers with Julie's picture on them.

Becky Espinosa stood up and gave me a quick hug. She wore jeans and a halter top and didn't look much different than high school. Other than her eyes, which revealed she hadn't slept in days.

I realized that I only really knew Becky from back when. I didn't know who she was anymore, if I ever did. In school she had been a cheerleader, smiling and nice. But her chipper demeanor was like a politician's promise. You wanted to believe it, probably some truth in there, but you knew it was mostly bullshit. In addition to being on the cheerleading squad, she had also been a Precious Girl. The Precious Girls were a lipstick and razor chola gang that frightened the whole school—girls and boys, students and teachers. Even the hard-core hairnet and top-button vatos stayed clear of the Precious Girls.

"Christ, Jimmy," Becky said. "What happened to your face?"

"It's nothing. At least, nothing worth talking about."

"Bobby didn't tell me you were coming. Thanks. We can use all the help we can get."

"Of course. Is he here?"

"He's in the back, looking through Julie's things. I can go get him for you."

"In a bit," I said. "How you doing? I mean, considering. Shit, I don't know what I mean."

"Worried, pissed at myself that I didn't take it serious sooner. But what can I do now? Trying to do whatever helps find her. And hope that brings her back." She turned and spoke to the flier crew. "When you get done with those, pull out that stack of maps and break each map into neighborhoods. Last thing we need is all of us canvassing the same place. We got ground to cover." She turned back to me.

"Don't know if any of this will help, but if I don't do something, anything, I'll lose it. I want to cry, punch someone, and give up, but none of that will do any good."

"When was the last time you saw her?"

"It was nothing special. I was leaving for work. She was eating breakfast. Nothing strange. Nothing memorable. We'd had plenty of fights, but not this time. I can't figure it. Every few minutes I look toward the front door and imagine Julie walking through it. I wouldn't even ask where she went, what happened. I don't care. I'd hold her."

Becky gave my arm a squeeze. "I'm going to go find Bobby for you." She walked down the hall into the back of the house.

The flier crew seemed to have the flier situation under control, so I looked around the room. My eyes immediately went to the framed school photos of Julie on the TV. Maybe a little heavy on the eye shadow, but she didn't have the full raccoon that some kids go for. She was even smiling in what looked like the most recent photo. Julie was light-skinned Mexican, pretty like her mother, but with the same mischief in her eyes as Bobby. No doubt she was his daughter.

The rest of the room felt as spare as a jail cell. No art on the walls. No plants. A couch, a table, the TV, and a bunch of folding chairs. An air-conditioning box unit in the window cranked full blast. It had the feel of a squat. Not a home, but a place to get out of the heat.

When two people finally looked up at me, I decided to engage. "Hi, I'm Jimmy. Friend of Becky's and Bobby's. From high school."

The crowd said hello or gave a nod, then went back to the fliers. From what I could tell, they were taking some from one stack and putting them in another stack, but I know next to nothing about fliers. I got the sense they were doing things just to do them. Better to be busy than idle, even if busy wasn't productive.

The man in the apron came into the room with a plateful of brownies. The flier crew gave theatrical moans and held their stomachs.

"No more, Russell," one said. "We're full up."

"You?" Russell said, offering me a brownie.

I never turn down free food.

"Thanks," I said, taking a brownie off the plate and shoving half of it in my mouth. I made mmm sounds and nodded.

"I should have introduced myself at the door, but nobody likes burnt snickerdoodles. I'm Russell. I'm Becky's boyfriend."

I shoved the rest of the brownie in my mouth, wiped my hand on my pants, and shook his hand. "I'm Jimmy. Friend from high school."

The introductions out of the way, neither of us had anywhere to go with the conversation. We stood in silence, both of us staring at the platter of brownies in his hand.

"Any news?" I finally asked. "About Julie?"

He shook his head. "We're going to flier tonight. Be sure to grab a stack. The police are talking to her school, but it's summer, so I doubt that's going to help. I teach there, so if the other faculty knew something, I would know. The police seem to be taking it seriously, but how much can they do?"

"Any leads at all?"

Russell shook his head. We went back to our awkward silence, watching the group do their flier-stacking. Seriously, what the fuck were they doing with those fliers?

Becky popped her head out from the hall. "Bobby's back in Julie's room. Second door."

I grabbed another brownie and headed toward the back of the house.

———•+•———

Julie's room didn't look like the stereotypical teenage girl's room. Or maybe it did. What the hell did I know about teenage girls or their rooms? Was I expecting stuffed animals, unicorn posters, and a frilly bed skirt? The room looked more like my college dorm room, down to the Iron Maiden *Killers* poster. Unlike the stark living room, the walls were covered to the ceiling. Heavy metal and punk posters. Stolen street signs. Some police tape trimming. Original drawings, mostly of birds, but one of an insect, close-up and creepy.

The furnishings were sparse: a bed, a desk, a desk chair, and a dresser. All very used with chipped edges and corners rounded by wear. Cables and wires snaked from the back of the desk where a computer must have been.

No photos. Not a single picture of Julie or her friends or any boyfriends.

If I were a TV detective, that might've meant something. But I was an idiot, so it only made me more aware of the limits of my ignorance. The lack of photos felt significant, but I didn't have the experience to work it out. Or maybe it was nothing. Do kids print out photos anymore? Or do they just store them digitally on their phones and computers?

Bobby sat on the edge of the bed, reading from a spiral-bound notebook. The same dark pen drawings of birds adorned the covers—crows or ravens. Like the drawings on

31

the wall, the artist had really pressed into the paper, the pen digging deep furrows. Bobby glanced up, set the notebook on the bed, stood, and stretched his back. A plate of cookies sat on the desk. He took one, stuffed it in his mouth, and paced the small room like a tiger in a cage.

"Want one?" Bobby nodded toward the cookies.

I shook my head.

"Dude, eat some. There's like five more plates in the kitchen. Russell's going to graduate to pies soon," Bobby said. "I'm keeping an eye on him. Don't know if I trust him. But the fucker can bake. Science teacher, so I'm sure he measures real exact."

I grabbed a cookie and ate it. "I thought Becky was the cook. Didn't you used to call her 'Betty Crocker' in high school?"

Bobby shook his head. "A bad joke. Nothing to do with baking. Not really funny now. Probably wasn't then."

"What was the joke?"

Bobby shook his head, disappointed in himself. "I called her 'Betty Crocker' because she was 'ready to spread.'"

Whatever the opposite of laughing was, that's what we did. We stared at each other, feeling the weight of a bad joke in the room.

"Yeah, not so funny now," I said.

"You mean because she's the mother of my missing daughter? Yeah."

"We were idiots then."

"Not like now."

I gave Bobby a weak laugh. "Cookies make the house smell good."

"I was out there, helping with the fliers, but not my thing. I mean, it's cool that the neighbors and Becky's friends or whoever the fuck those people are want to help, but, man alive, they're annoying."

"What about Russell? What do you know about him?"

"Becky says he's all right, been together a year or so. I'll admit it, I want to take him out behind the shed and see what's what. Ain't no secret a piece of wood can't get out of an ironed shirt. But I know I'm suspicious 'cause of all the flicks I've seen. In a movie, the more straightlaced the person, the more likely he's a perv or freak or whatever. But for real, no reason to think he's more than what he seems. It's not like the cops are grilling his ass. He's just the dude that bangs Becky. And she ain't stupid or a victim. If she says he's okay, I got to trust that. Still, I got my eye on him."

"Is the real Bobby here somewhere? That sounded almost rational."

Bobby stopped his pacing.

"Don't get me wrong. I want to bust some heads. A lot. But I can't waste my time busting heads for the fuck of it. I need to bust the right ones. Russell gets a pass for now."

"For now."

"Nothing's pointing toward him. Fuck, nothing's pointing anywhere. I'm reading these journals. Cops looking through her phone and computer. I need something, anything, pointing me in some direction. Then, watch the fuck out."

Becky poked her head in the open doorway, holding another plate of cookies. Bobby waved her in. She set the plate on top of the other one.

"Russell finally ran out of sugar, thank God. This is the last one," Becky said. "I know the baking is crazy town, but it calms him down. Russell's as frantic as me. So if cookies relax him, cookies it is. They keep."

"We all deal with stress in our own way," I said, feeling lame as I said it.

"The group's heading out in a few to put up posters," Becky said.

I grabbed a cookie, still soft from the oven, sweet and smelling of cinnamon. I shoved it in my mouth and chewed through the heat. I had a feeling cookies were going to be my dinner.

"That Julie's journal?" I asked through chews.

Bobby nodded. "It's from six months ago. Means there's maybe one she has with her, one that's missing. Cops breezed through it for names. Don't got high hopes that I'll get any clues. But won't hurt. Considering how much I know about Julie, I'm at least getting a look into her head. Who she was—is."

Bobby softly cursed from his mistake. He avoided eye contact, looking toward the open closet door. "Reading these journals, the girl seems pissed off a lot. Mad as all hell. Really hates being poor. Like it hurts to live that way."

"She was angry. Lately, all the time. Just an angry girl," Becky said, her all-business veneer disappearing.

"She's a teenager," I said. "Isn't that part of the deal?"

"Julie's different," Becky said. "When she gets real mad, it's like she's capable of anything. I got my own issues with anger, so I know."

"Yeah, didn't know when to bring it up," Bobby said, "but she writes about you hitting her. Only a few times. She's casual about it. Is that something we need to talk about?"

"I didn't beat her. If that's what you're asking. But Julie's felt a slap."

The way Becky said it with a slight quiver in her voice ended that thread of the conversation. The room fell silent.

I stared at the drawing of the insect on the wall. Growing up, we called that particular bug a stink beetle. I tried to remember the insect's real name. One of those black, scarab-like little monsters that roamed the desert floor. It was different than the bird drawings, the pencil was light on the paper. Odd that the birds were drawn angrily while an insect whose primary defense was spraying skunk juice out its ass was drawn so daintily. Then I saw the signature.

"Who is Angel?"

Becky looked up. Bobby turned to her, expecting an answer.

"From what I can see," I continued, "Julie drew birds, like on the wall and on that notebook. She didn't sign all of them, but a couple have her signature and they're in the same style."

Bobby picked up the notebook and looked at the drawing on it. He ran his finger along the rough texture.

I pointed at the drawing of the beetle. "But this one. The bug. It's drawn different. And it's signed, 'From Angel.'"

"You know any Angel, Beck?" Bobby asked, hope in his voice.

"I don't know any of Julie's friends," Becky said, shaking her head. "Since we moved to Indio, I haven't met one. She has them. I think. She must. Talks to people on the phone, texts, but never had one over. If this Angel is a friend of hers, I don't know him—her. Damn it, I don't even know if Angel's a boy or girl."

I said, "I know we don't have her phone or computer, but is there another computer in the house?"

Becky nodded. "Russell's laptop is in my bedroom."

"Bobby said she was on Facebook, Twitter. Even if we can't get into her account, we should be able to browse her friends. Maybe there's an Angel in there. We get a name, we go old school, pull out a phone book, find the address."

Bobby clapped his hands once loudly, "Fuck yes. Let's do it. Putting up fliers don't play to my strengths. And if I sit around anymore, I'm going to break shit. Get on that computer, Jimmy. Give me something to do."

THREE

According to Facebook, Julie only had one friend named Angel. The profile picture on the account was a drawing of an insect. He (we found out it was a he) had a last name unique to the area. Which was a minor miracle, considering it could have been Ramos or Garcia or Lopez or any other common Mexican surname.

Twenty minutes later, Bobby and I were south of Indio in the town of Thermal, parked in front of the address of the only De La Cueva listed in the Indio & Vicinity phone book.

Thermal, California. No irony in the name of the almost completely Mexican suburb of Indio. Thermal is always hot. Death Valley hot. Year-round. Hot, shadeless, and fucking miserable. One of the reasons is that Thermal is one hundred feet below sea level. Closer to hell than most any place on earth. When you live in Thermal, you can't get any lower. Unless you dig.

The buildings looked like they had always been a part of the desert landscape. White stucco structures the color of bleached bones. Red terra cotta roofs the same deep hue as the clay ground.

The sun had set, but it wouldn't be dark for another hour. The De La Cueva house sat on the edge of a residential area, the backyard bleeding into the bare desert. Brown Bermuda grass died in the shadow of the building. Light glowed from inside the house, visible behind the closed curtains. A sun-faded burgundy Chrysler LeBaron sat in the driveway. A bungee cord held the dented hood down, the driver's side door was primer gray, and duct tape kept one of the mirrors in place.

"So what's the plan?" I asked.

"Plan B," Bobby said.

Bobby pulled his Plan Bs from under the seat. That's what he called the two fifteen-inch long, one-inch thick steel pipes that he kept in his Ranchero. Each had an end wrapped in electrical tape for grip.

"Are those necessary?"

"You rather I bring a gun?"

"We don't know nothing about this Angel. Probably just some teenager. He's artistic. No reason to go in hard," I said. "We're here to talk. At least, until we know something."

Bobby turned to me. "When it's your daughter, Jimmy, you can run the show. You can make the plans. You can even tell me what to do. But it's my girl. We'll do this whichever way I think will bring her home. Whichever way."

"Fine, so long as you remember that's what we're trying to do. You go vigilante, bust down doors, stir shit, and you'll end up in jail. We're here to find Julie, not get arrested. Not prove anything. Not even punish anyone involved."

"You're wrong on that last one. We're definitely here to punish. If someone took her. If that's what's going on. If something squirrelly's going on. Then they'll pay," Bobby said. "I know you're sensitive, cry when you step on a bug, but this ain't baby seals or whales or unicorns. This is real life."

"Do you even listen to the shit you say?"

"How could I listen to it? I'm saying it. I'm going to put this out to you straighter than Lee Marvin. If you're not up for some mayhem, I can't have you here, can't have you hesitating when shit goes sideways. I need to know you got my back."

"You know I do. I just don't see why you have to bring those fucking things. It's overkill. Someone could get hurt."

"As long as it's not me, you, or Julie."

I didn't say anything. There was nothing to say, because there was no way to win the argument. Bobby's stubbornness was an immovable force.

"It's my show," Bobby said. "You can wait in the truck if you're not up for it."

"I'm in. If just to make sure you don't kill no one," I said.

"Now if I didn't know any better, I'd think you were stalling. So unless you need to paint your toenails, can we get on with this?"

Bobby banged on the door with a Plan B. Each knock left small indentations in the cheap wood. He stepped back a foot, the pipes behind his back.

The door opened. Bobby tensed.

A five-year-old boy wearing only white underwear, one hand still on the knob, looked up at Bobby and then me and then back at Bobby. Mexican with a bowl haircut, he didn't look that much different than my own son.

"Your hair is like a Santa," the boy said to Bobby, "but your face is like a butt."

A quick laugh slipped from my mouth. Bobby shot me a look. I shrugged. "Kid's got timing."

"Your face is a butt, too," the kid said to me. "A punched-up butt."

Bobby snorted out a thin laugh. "Cute kid."

I got down on one knee, eye level with the kid. "My name's Jimmy. Santa here is Bobby. What's your name?"

"Miguel." He eyed me suspiciously.

"Nice to meet you, Miguel. Is Angel home? We're friends of his."

"No you're not."

"Yes we are. Can you get him for us?"

"You're not Angel's friend. Angel doesn't have friends. Not buttface Santas and not stupidhead liars."

Miguel slammed the door in my face.

I looked up at Bobby. "Do you have a Plan C?"

———

I knocked again. This time a squat Mexican woman answered the door. Low to the ground with Indian features, she was one of those women who was definitely over forty, but beyond that, it was anybody's guess. Maybe forty-five, maybe seventy-five. She dried her hands with a kitchen towel and looked at me with complete neutrality.

"Hi," I said with a smile so big my face hurt. "My name is James Veeder. This is Robert Maves. We're looking for Robert's daughter, Julie Espinosa. She's missing. We were hoping to talk to Angel De La Cueva. He and Julie are friends. Is he in, by any chance?"

"Qué?" the woman said.

"Fucking hell," Bobby said. "As sidekicks go, you suck."

"I'm used to being the hero. You're usually the sidekick."

"Stop the stupid train," Bobby said. "I have never been a sidekick in my life. I'm too awesome for sidekick status. I am the everyman hero of my awesome movie, a badass NC-17 action comedy with heart called *Bobby Maves: The Art of Asskickery and Woman Conquesting.* You, on the other hand, are the main character for some arty-farty Eurotrash indie flick, one of those three-hour borefests that you're always making me watch with a lot of shots of rainy sidewalks and nothing happens, but at least there's tits. Something called *Leaves and Sorrow* or some equally shitty title. If this is *True Grit,* you're Glen Campbell."

"Qué?" the woman said again.

Bobby handed me the Plan Bs. He pulled Julie's school photo out of his back pocket and held it up for the woman. "Esto es mi hija. Es ida. Soy preocupado muy. No la podemos encontrar. Me puede ayudar? Debemos hablar con Angel."

"Sí, sí, sí. Mi hijo está en la casa," the woman said, waving us inside. We followed her into the house. Every few steps she turned and gave us a little wave, making sure we were behind her.

The house needed some repairs, but it was impeccably clean. Cracks in the walls and some water stains on the ceiling, but no visible dust and a lemony smell. The home of someone who was doing their best despite what they had to work with. We walked through the living room where Miguel played a video game and down a short hall. The woman stopped in front of a closed door.

"Aquí," she said. I reached for the knob, but the woman put a hand on my forearm, stopping me. She held out her other hand. I gave her a confused look, and then looked down at my hands, which held the two tape-wrapped fighting pipes.

"Lo siento," I said, handing over the pipes. Bobby and I both looked appropriately embarrassed to have brought such vicious weapons into anyone's home. She turned and walked down the hall. As she turned the corner, she gave one of the pipes a surprisingly lithe ninja swing and a high-pitched "Hi-yah!"

"Am I getting my pipes back?" Bobby asked.

"How the hell should I know?"

"Anything else of mine you want to give away?"

Bobby pushed me aside and opened the door without knocking. In the bedroom, a thirteen-year-old kid looked up from a drawing pad. He lay on the bed lit only by a desk lamp. He didn't look scared. He looked like he was used to a lack of privacy.

"Hi, Angel," Bobby said, "I'm Julie Espinosa's dad. You're going to talk to me."

Angel didn't stop drawing. From my angle, it looked like it was a grasshopper or maybe a praying mantis, something leggy with bulging eyes. Cute and fascinating from afar, but a monster up close.

The room would probably be referred to as the master bedroom by a real estate agent. But with two beds pushed up against opposite walls and a folding table covered in engine parts taking up most of the central floor space, the room felt cramped. It smelled of grease and armpits.

Unlike Julie, the kid didn't hang his drawings on the wall. Only pages torn from lowrider and motorcycle magazines, featuring topless or bikini-clad chicas and white trash models pulled straight from their double-wides. Models in those magazines were like no other. There was something about the girls that was hard, surly, and working class. Girls that ate ribs, chewed tobacco, fought dirty, and had no idea what Pilates was. My kind of women.

Bobby sat down on the corner of the bed. He spoke in a soft, even tone. "Look, Angel. Nobody has seen Julie in five days, almost six. I'm worried about her. Her mom is worried about her. Have you heard from her, seen her, know any of her other friends? I need your help."

Angel looked up at Bobby, but his pencil continued to draw. "Julie hasn't been over in a while. I don't know where she is. I hope she's okay. Really."

"Do you know any of her other friends?" Bobby asked.

"We're not friends. Julie would never be my friend."

"You're friends on Facebook."

"Facebook isn't real friends."

"She has a drawing of yours on her bedroom wall."

That made Angel smile. "Really? She put it on her wall?"

"Yeah, a stink beetle," I said, happy to contribute.

"Pinacate beetle," Angel corrected.

"That's right. I've been racking my brain trying to think of that bug's real name." I'm sure he was right, but I had never heard the word *pinacate* in my life.

"Jimmy, you're killing me here," Bobby said, giving me his shut-the-fuck-up look. He turned back to Angel. "Were you in a drawing class together or something? Study buddies?"

"She used to come over a lot. We talked sometimes. But she never came to see me."

Loud motorcycle exhaust shook the walls and drowned us out. The headlights from the bikes flashed over the closed curtain.

"Julie comes over to see my brother Gabe and his friends. That sounds like them." Angel set down his pencil and drawing pad. He got up and lifted a corner of the curtain to look out. "You need to go. Come back when it's just him. You need to run."

It won't come as a surprise. Running wasn't in Bobby's playbook. Running was the thing the other guy did. Running and bleeding. Too many John Ford movies had etched their way into his psyche, developing a clear—if skewed—definition of what it was to be a man. I, on the other hand, while an avid fan of classic Hollywood cinema, understood the difference between real life and make-believe. That it wasn't unmanly to be civilized. To avoid confrontation rather than start it. At least I told myself that when my fight-or-flight instinct screamed flight.

Or maybe my face still hurt from getting pummeled by Ceja. I still hadn't passed that tooth, and I wasn't excited about the thought of it.

Bobby marched out the front door—and like an asshole, I was right behind him—as the three men got off their motorcycles. Or I should say, boys. Ranging from seventeen to twenty, their faces all had smooth, boyish looks. They tried for something harder, but the softness of youth betrayed them. Mexican or mixed Mexican, each boy sported a stylishly shaved head. I wondered if bald men got angry when they saw kids with obviously full heads of thick hair shaved off on purpose. Like tap dancing in front of a man with no legs.

They were all ripped in that way that only the young can be. Defined muscles covered in tattoo sleeves, though they would have been more intimidating if one of them had been taller than five seven. Two wore wifebeaters and one—just because—was shirtless. The two with shirts had sleeveless jackets, Los Hermanos patches on the back. They could have been a boy band, if their expressions didn't telegraph the enormous chips on their shoulders.

"Should've grabbed my Plan Bs back," Bobby said under his breath. "If this uglies up, the one on the right is yours. You handle that?"

I wanted to say no and get the fuck out of Dodge. Instead, I nodded.

"Don't go back on your heels. Balls of your feet," Bobby said.

"I've done this before."

"I know. I've seen you. Thought a few pointers couldn't hurt."

I glanced around the yard for a potential weapon. Hoping for a shovel, garden hoe, or even a decent-sized rock, I found nothing. I mentally prepped myself for some eye-gouging and ball-kicking. Unfortunately, with their shaved heads, hair-pulling was off the table.

"Hey," Bobby said, "how you doing tonight? Which one of you tough guys is Gabe?"

The alpha of the pack broke off from the other two and strutted toward us. He would have had a baby face, except for his eyes. The distrustful eyes of a kid who grew up poor. The look of unkept promises and abandoned dreams. Santa had stiffed him one year too many.

For a long while, Baby Face didn't say a word, only tilted his head as if asking a question. Fronting, I think the kids called it. I don't think he blinked. His boys took a couple steps forward to remind us they were there. I hadn't forgotten, but I appreciated the gesture. I took a step forward, too. I had no idea why.

"Hey, Gabe, you order a shitty Mexican Elvis?" Baby Face never took his eyes off Bobby. "Who the fuck are you, *ese*?"

"I ain't going to fuck around, waste your time. You obviously got important gangster shit to do," Bobby said, eyes laser-pointing back at the kid. "I'm Julie Espinosa's dad. I think you know her. I think Gabe knows her."

Baby Face stared back, his eyelids dropping to half-mast in exaggerated boredom. A bit more head tilt.

The shirtless boy separated himself from the other one. "Julie don't got no dad."

"Cállate," Baby Face growled.

"But Chucho—"

"Shut the fuck up, Gabe." Chucho, aka Baby Face, had spoken. Gabe looked down at his feet.

Bobby gave me a nod toward Gabe, but I had already spotted his neck tattoo. The tattoo of a bird. Similar—if not identical—in style to the drawings in Julie's room. Down to the rough scribbling of an angry artist's ballpoint.

"Nobody knows where Julie's at." Bobby looked past Chucho to Gabe. "Nobody's seen her for almost a week. Maybe you know where she's at. Or maybe you can help me find her. Not looking for trouble, just my daughter."

Gabe opened his mouth to speak, but Chucho got words in first. "Don't matter you wasn't looking. You found trouble, bitch. Gabe ain't telling you shit."

Chucho was itching for a fight. At three against two, he must have figured an easy win. A little bit of fun. In Thermal, like most small desert towns, violence was entertainment. Better to be bruised than bored.

"I'll tell you why you're going to talk to me," Bobby said through gritted teeth. "Because if any of you knows something and doesn't tell me—right now—and let's say, God forbid, something bad happens to Julie, it'll be your fault. And I'll punish the fuck out of you. You'll have a new enemy. I don't know if there's a good kind of enemy. But I ain't that kind. I'm the worst kind.

"But that's later. Look at now. Don't matter there are three of you and two of us. I'm a father. My daughter is missing. I'm frantic and scared and angry and have a lot of other weird feelings churning inside me. I am Vesuvius. That's a volcano, if you ignorants don't know. And I'm ready to fucking erupt. You pretty-boys might think you're badass, but you ain't tangled with Bobby Maves. Fuck with me and I'll destroy you."

"So much for diplomacy," I said.

"Fuck diplomacy in the ass. If we can't get information, at least we can get a workout."

Chucho had no idea what to do with that. These boys were used to being the intimidators, not the intimidated. They were young, muscled, tattooed, and Mexican. Ninety-nine percent of the people they came in contact with crossed the street to avoid them. Bobby didn't just not avoid them, he asked them to dance. And from their faces, they knew it wasn't a bluff.

I stepped in, seeing if I could salvage peace. "Look—Chucho, right?—it's okay to back off. You're not pussing out. You don't got to prove nothing. It's all cool. Let's crack open some cervezas and talk. We didn't know you three minutes ago. I didn't even know there were Mexican bikers. We're just trying to find the girl."

I felt good about my succinct, logical argument. But moron trumps logic every time.

"Fuck you and fuck this white-haired fuck," Chucho said fuckingly. He telegraphed his punch. Bobby slipped it and snapped a quick jab that broke his nose with a wet crack.

"Fuck me," I said, turning quickly. As Bobby had assessed, I got the Mexican biker on the right, who I will refer to as Cold Sore. The name is not ironic.

I didn't have time to duck Cold Sore's punch, but it was a wide, lumbering thing. I tucked my chin into my chest and shifted slightly to my right. The result had Cold Sore hitting me square on the top of my head, all skull. His fat biker ring cut me, but I heard at least one knuckle pop. He reeled back, cradling his damaged paw.

I stomped down on his foot and gave him a hard punch to the center of his chest. The face is overrated. I'd rather punch a fucker in the body any time. It's a bigger target and I won't hurt my hand. I also didn't like the look of that cold sore.

Cold Sore stumbled backward, slamming against his motorcycle and tumbling over it. He scrambled to his feet quicker than I thought, but he was still off balance when I kicked him in the shin, spit in his face, and slapped him with an open hand. The angrier people got, the dumber they fought. I wanted him seeing red.

"Quit fighting like a little bitch," Cold Sore said.

I evaded his left easily. His right didn't appear to be in his arsenal anymore. A broken finger will do that. The swollen hand looked like an inflated rubber glove.

I ducked his next punch, pushed myself against him, grabbed his broken fingers with my left hand, and squeezed. He screamed. With my right, I threw body shots, whaling on the same spot again and again. He had no leverage to hit back effectively. He made an effort to get an arm around my neck, but his ribs must have been jelly after the fifth or sixth punch. When I let go of his hand, he folded to the ground.

I kicked him in the face. He fell back against his bike again. This time, he stayed down.

I looked to Bobby to see if he needed any help.

Yeah, right.

Holding onto Gabe's belt, he dragged the shirtless kid over to the Ranchero. Chucho was laid out on the ground like he fell asleep making a dirt angel in the front yard.

That's a common sight when you tangle with Bobby Maves. People on the ground and Bobby walking away. Bobby had warned them.

"That your blood or his?" Bobby asked.

I rubbed my hand across my wet forehead and looked at the blood. I felt the top of my head and found where Cold Sore's ring had struck.

"Kid's ring cut the top of my head. Doesn't feel deep."

"Yeah, heads bleed more than anywhere. You look like a Sissy." Bobby laughed. "Spacek, that is. You know, in *Carrie*."

"I got it."

"We need to skedaddle," Bobby said, leaning the kid against the Ranchero's back tire. "When these dumbasses come to, they're going to be pissy. Might find some weapons. Punks like these can't take a beating and learn from it. Mexicans love revenge. It's cultural. They always got to be a dick about it. Escalate the violence. If we had time, I'd teach them a few more lessons, but we got to talk to Gabe."

Bobby picked him up by the belt with one hand and grabbed him by the thigh with the other. With some effort, he threw the kid into the bed of the Ranchero. Gabe rolled against the wheel well and groaned, his eyes fluttering open.

"Fuck," Bobby said, looking at the house.

"What?" I turned quickly, expecting a Mexican biker to jump me.

"My fighting pipes."

I let out a relieved breath. "It's not like they're hard to make."

"Those ones got memories. Sentimental value. They're my favorites."

"You'll have to make new memories."

Bobby looked at me like I couldn't possibly understand. "Hop in back and make sure the kid don't escape. I know a place we can chat. It ain't far."

"Quick voice of reason. This is close to kidnapping. And when I say, 'close,' I mean it is kidnapping. You know that, right?"

"He ain't no kid. You really want to stick around?"

I looked at the two Mexicans starting to stir. "Yeah, okay. Fuck that."

I jumped in the bed of the Ranchero with the kid. He looked at me, not scared but drained of any tough veneer.

"Angel, Miguel, and Gabriel?" I said. "Your mom must have a thing for angels. Consider yourself lucky. You could have been named Metatron."

He blinked at me. "I don't get it. That like a Transformer?"

"Never mind. Sadly trying to justify a semester of Religious Studies. Still paying the loans, might as well get some use."

"Whatever. Don't let that crazy albino hurt me no more and I'll laugh at all your shitty jokes."

Bobby pulled away and headed down the road. In the dying light, I watched Gabe's two pals slowly get to their feet. They didn't look like they had any interest in following. Behind them, I caught a glimpse of Angel looking out his bedroom window. It almost looked like he was smiling.

FOUR

"How's everything going?" Angie asked on the other end of the phone.

I had no idea. We had beaten the shit out of some young Mexican motorcycle enthusiasts. The fact that that felt like a step in the right direction really illustrated how little we knew about what we were doing.

Driving in the back of Bobby's Ranchero with the kid, looking at his face, at the unnecessary violence, my brain told me to go home. Bobby didn't need me and if I wasn't careful I could get in real trouble. And that trouble would have consequences. Then, just as quickly, I felt like an asshole for even thinking about going home.

Talking to Angie, hearing her voice, reminded me of the real life waiting for me. It felt like days, not hours since I had been home. Probably what it's like when you first arrive to the battlefield after being drafted into a war.

"We've got some leads. Talking to some people," I said. No reason to mention certain violences. Avoiding details wasn't officially lying.

I glanced over my shoulder to check on the action. Bobby stood over Gabe, who sat on the ground and listened to whatever Bobby was explain-yelling at him. I was too far away to hear, but Bobby's hand gestures were animated. From the distance, it looked like he was doing his orangutan impersonation (which was very good). Gabe tried to act tough at first. He now looked resigned to having been bested.

According to the rusted sign out front, we had ended up on the edge of Thermal in Toro Cemetery. One of those desert cemeteries that had three tall salt cedars, no grass, and gravestones faded to the color of chalk. This cemetery sat next to a park and a baseball field, some of the gravestones overlapping into centerfield. I assumed they were in the field of play, but it would take a brave outfielder to dive for any ball for fear of a concussion or ghost.

"We still got no reason to believe anything other than she's run off. Which is good," I said. "How's Juan doing?"

"He's been real quiet, kind of brooding," Angie said, "but he usually gets like that when you go away. He called me Angie at dinner. Not Mom, but Angie. He's never done that before."

"Just another way to act out."

Headlights lit up the gravestones. I turned to see a Honda Civic bouncing down the dirt road leading to the cemetery. Moonlight lit the wake of dust. A hubcap flew to the side when the car bottomed out in a deep rut. The Civic slid to a stop twenty feet from Bobby and the kid.

"Oh, shit. Angie, babe. I got to go. I'll call later if it's not too late. Sorry. I love you." I hung up and quick-stepped over.

Becky leapt out of the Civic, slammed the driver's door, and fast-walked to Bobby and Gabe. In an act of mercy, Bobby stood between her and the kid, one hand on Becky's arm. He whispered something in her ear. She nodded and Bobby let her go. Becky took a deep breath and leaned down to Gabe. He looked scared. Smart kid.

"Listen, kid." Becky spit-sprayed Gabe's face. "I don't care what kind of teenage shit you and Julie are up to. I want to talk to my daughter. Know she's safe."

Bobby cut in. "If the two of you are thinking about running off or shacking up or whatever the fuck, we'll deal with that another time. Right now, me and her mother, we need to talk to our girl."

Becky took over. The poor kid was being tag-teamed. "Wherever she is, whatever she's doing, we need to know that she's there because she wants to be. I'm scared for her."

Bobby put a hand on the kid's shoulder. He flinched. "Think about it, Gabe. We got no interest in messing with you or your life. I ain't the kind of dad that gets wood from intimidating the prom date. I'm here to make sure Julie's alive and unfucked with. That's all I care about. You help, I'll thank you. You get in the way, I'll hurt you."

Bobby looked to Becky to see if she had anything to add. She shook her head. I watched from a distance, definitely not my show. I felt like a bystander, a Peeping Tom.

Gabe looked up with fear in his eyes. "I ain't seen Julie. For real. I know her good, but I ain't seen her. Not in a long time. I swear. I don't know where she's at."

"You're her boyfriend?" Becky asked.

"Was, I guess. Not no more. I liked her a lot. We used to hang out, nothing special. She liked riding on my bike. Or she'd come over, we'd drink some beers, do stuff."

"Stuff?" Bobby asked, menace in his voice.

"Come on, man, her moms is right here. You really want the play-by-play? Shit, you already kicked my ass once tonight, I don't want to get buried up in this graveyard."

I looked around at the aged and chipped headstones. Whether on accident or consciously, Bobby had chosen an effective and intimidating setting.

"How old are you?" Becky asked.

"Nineteen."

"Julie's sixteen. Did you know that?"

Gabe shrugged and grinned. Not his best choice. Bobby cuffed him on the side of the head. Gabe nodded. He knew he deserved that one.

"She's like sixteen on paper. But she's mature and shit. Smart, you know. She reads books. Like for fun. And even the ones for school, she liked some of them too. Not like any of the chicas 'round here, not even the older ones, ones at the junior college. More interested in their hair. She might've been born sixteen years ago, but she's grown up."

Bobby pinched the bridge of his nose and shook his head. "She hasn't called you?"

"Nothing. I told you. I ain't seen her—talked to her—in like a month. I don't know how to tell it better, she was done with me. Real cold, you know. Not even like I was a toy she didn't like playing with. More like she didn't play with toys no more, and forgot she ever did."

Becky snorted and said, "Maybe she just didn't like your ass no more. Or are you like God's gift?"

"I ain't nothing. She changed, got different. When we met, neither of us had any bread. So we'd just hang out. She'd draw with Angel while I cleaned parts. Shit like that. But once she got some money, that shit was done. Once she started working, it was different."

"Where'd she get the money? What was she doing?" Bobby asked.

"Chucho told me she started working for some dude in La Quinta. Some rich dude. Said he drove a camo Hummer. Had an aquarium and works of art. A big pool in the backyard. She never talked about it, and when I asked she didn't tell me shit. Sometimes she'd be gone a couple days. One time she came back, had a fucking shiner."

"A black eye?" Bobby said, turning to Becky.

Becky nodded. "She said she got it in gym. About a month ago."

"Your friend Chucho tell you what she was doing for this guy?" Bobby asked.

"No. You'd have to ask him."

"Even if I find his ass, I doubt he's going to want to chat."

"Oh, Christ," Becky said, pacing a little, her hands moving without her control. "What the fuck are you doing, Julie?"

"Beck," Bobby said, "there are tons of things she could've been doing. Cleaning house, doing the books. None of them got to be bad."

"She's missing, Bobby. House cleaners and personal assistants and pool cleaners don't disappear. It's the other people that do. Girls that do things."

And without warning, Becky lost it and started kicking Gabe. I don't think she knew it was going to happen, just needed something to attack. She kicked him three times hard in the side.

Gabe rolled up in a ball. "Get her off me. Get her off me."

Bobby and I pulled Becky back as she kicked air. I got an arm around her chest and held her tight against my body. She slowly calmed. Bobby helped Gabe up. "You know this rich dude's name? Where he lives?"

He shook his head, keeping one eye on Becky. "La Quinta is all I know."

La Quinta was Palm Springs Light, all golf courses and rich people and snowbirds, but without the class. A place where old white people and Mexicans could live together in peace, as long as the Mexicans were doing the dishes and mowing the lawns. Merv Griffin used to live in La Quinta. Merv fucking Griffin.

"You done?" I said into Becky's ear.

She nodded and I let her go, my sidekick duties complete. She eyeballed Gabe. He cowered, but Becky kept her distance.

"Why didn't you talk to me back at your house?" Bobby said to Gabe with honest bewilderment. "We didn't need to do all this."

"You got me wrong, Julie's Dad. I ain't no fighter. That's Chucho. Chucho's an asshole. Rides with Los Hos. They think they're the Mexican Hells Angels. I ain't one of them. I fix their bikes, that's all. Chucho's always starting shit. He's a fucking estupido. But what can I do? Known him all my life. He's my boy. I got to have his back."

"You need better friends," I said.

Gabe looked at me, like he had forgotten I was there. "You're here with your boy. Got to back your homies, no matter if they're right."

"I ain't doing nothing he wouldn't do for me," I said. "But if your buddy is always starting shit, always needing backup, and never's got your back, that dude ain't your friend."

"What is this? *Sesame Street?*" Gabe said. "Learning about friendship and shit."

Bobby tossed me his keys. "I'm going to take Becky's car. She's too amped to drive. We'll take the kid back to his house, then I'll take Becky home. Your truck's over at her place. Give me your keys. We'll meet up later."

I handed my keys to Bobby. "Christ, we even make arranging cars complicated. I'll grab a motel room somewhere. You staying at Becky's?"

"Too weird. I'll crash with you. We can have some beers, make some kind of plan of attack."

"How we feeling about the kid?"

Bobby and I looked over at Gabe. He leaned against the Civic, a watchful eye on Becky. But she just sat in the passenger seat and stared out the windshield.

"Not sure," Bobby said. "Felt like truth, some punk Julie dated, but that crowd he's running with—what did he say, Los Hos?—they've got to be involved with more than only riding their scooters around. Have to talk to that Chucho. Those boys might not got nothing to do with Julie, but you don't do that outlaw shit as a grown-up and stay spotless."

"Bad boys aren't always that bad. Could just be their look, trying to get laid."

"You've only been back a couple years, Jimmy. You forget living in the desert puts you at ground zero of the War on Boredom, a never-ending fight to stay awake. People do the stupidest shit when they're bored. And don't think I don't realize I'm talking about myself, too."

"I'm fine with letting Gabe go home. We know where he lives," I said.

Bobby kicked a rock. "I fucking hate this."

"We'll find your girl, Bobby."

"Yeah, maybe. But it don't sound like she's a girl no more."

I was on a lean budget, so I found the cheapest motel in the vicinity. And that's saying something when you're on the out-skirts of Indio, California. I checked into the Date Palm Motel, a by-the-hour motor court whose denizens appeared to run the gamut from bathtub meth cooks and their part-time prostitute girlfriends to four generations of Mexicans living together in a single room. But it was nineteen dollars a night and I was eighty-five percent sure I wasn't going to catch chlamydia or scabies from the toilet seat. Maybe more like eighty percent. Let's split the difference and say eighty-two and a half.

The cut from Cold Sore's ring had stopped bleeding, but dried blood painted my forehead and matted my hair to my head. The bags under my eyes and the bruise on my face made me look like a George Romero extra. The guy who gave me the key didn't bat an eye. Whether professionalism or apathy, it was nice not to have to answer any questions.

Using only the tips of my thumb and forefinger, I pulled the bedspread off one of the two twin beds and threw it in the corner. The sheets and pillowcases joined the bedspread. I'd put my own pillowcases and sleeping bag on when Bobby showed up in my truck. I've stayed in a lot of places like the Date Palm. When in doubt, use your own gear.

The TV had an antenna, which meant it only got channels broadcasting from Mexico. It was news on Canal Cinco, so I turned on Canal Tres and watched the beginning of a movie called *Intrepidos Punks.*

Bobby arrived before I caught the end, but without a doubt and speaking without hyperbole, I can say for a fact that *Intrepidos Punks* is the greatest movie ever made and that will ever be made ever for all time ever in the history of cinema. It's like an insane package filled with awesome wrapped in crazy paper.

"What the fuck is this?" Bobby asked, staring at the TV. On the screen, the scene cut quickly between a Mexican with a mohawk that looked like Shel Silverstein playing the drums and some violent sex between another punker and a woman in her fifties. "And how much did I miss?"

Bobby sat down on the corner of the bed, his eyes locked onto the lunacy on the television, a welcome distraction.

"Oh, man. It's hard to describe and I'm only catching half the Spanish, but there's this biker gang that includes some Mexican wrestlers. Luchador masks, the whole megillah. And the biker chicks, they rob banks dressed as nuns. They have to bust the leader of the gang, I think, out of prison by having sex with the guards and some other guys— I don't know who they were. Wardens, maybe. Do Mexican prisons have more than one warden? And then every once in a while the gang rocks out. That's where we're at right now. It's like a game of telephone. Like someone described what punk rock was, what Sid Vicious looked like, and then that person told someone and that person translated it into Spanish, reverse-engineering it. Some parts are kind of Mad Maxy, too."

Bobby pulled a beer out of a cooler he had brought, tossed it to me, grabbed one for himself, and plonked down on the other bed.

"They don't clean the bedspreads, Bobby. Seriously, if we had a black light it would look like Jackson Pollock's drop cloth."

"This blanket'll be lucky I don't give it a disease. Shit's all bullshit, anyway. Germs aren't real, man."

"I don't even know how to respond to that." I cracked my beer. "But I assure you that germs are real. Scientists say so."

"I mean, germs are out there, yeah. They're things. But they aren't trying to kill us. They're being germs, germing around, you know. They're all over, right? You touch 'em, breathe 'em, eat 'em, all day. We grew up drinking ditch water out of the hose, playing under that crop duster spray—remember that weird, sweet smell?"

"I think that was DDT."

"Smelled like burnt cabbage-flavored candy. I grew up eating street food in Mexicali. And I'm not talking the good places. I'd eat in the alleys. I can't digest food unless it has some *E. coli* in it for flavor. All this nutrition nonsense is horse-shit. There weren't such thing as antioxidants, electrolytes, or superfoods ten years ago. Now I'm supposed to be afraid to sit on the shitter at the park toilets, eat an unorganic apple, and not lie down on a hotel bed. Shit, man, I ain't the kind of guy that dies of old age. And I'm damn sure that someone else's dry cum or piss or whatever else is on this blanket ain't going to kill me."

"Okay, you convinced me. Lie down on your spermy blanket," I said.

"You smoke. I could run my tongue across this entire blanket and it wouldn't do as much bad to my body as one Winston."

"I quit smoking."

"Really?"

"Ten days."

"I ain't discouraging, but don't you got to stop for at least a month to call it quitting? If I quit drinking for ten days, you'd say I was taking a break."

"Fine. I'm taking a break."

The remote didn't work. Of course. So I got up and turned off the TV by unplugging it. The dial was missing, too.

"How's Becky doing?" I asked. "Any news from the cops or the fliers?"

"Nothing. Becky's a fucking mess, all over the place, but she's got people around. I want to not like him, but Russell seems to be a stand-up guy. He's probably still putting up fliers."

"How you doing?"

"Sitting around, thinking maybe Julie's lost or scared, drives me apeshit. I've been here five minutes and I'm ready to pop. Fucking up those punks felt good. Maybe I should put up some posters. Do something."

"We spent last night in a sugar beet field. You need rest. You need to be sharp when we got something to do. Tomorrow we'll hit La Quinta, maybe get lucky, find the rich dude Julie was working for. Maybe she hooked up with him and they went on some trip. Something—while not innocent—harmless."

"Don't really want to think about it, but yeah," Bobby said. "There's only so many ways to make fast money out here. And they're all fucked up. Don't matter whether it's drug stuff or sex stuff, it puts her around bad people. People that use people." Bobby drained his beer and dug into the cooler. "If we keep talking about his, I ain't never going to sleep."

"How many beers we got left?"

"Five."

"I'll run out, get some more."

Bobby gave me a weak smile and toasted. I plugged the TV back in and *Intrepidos Punks* came back on.

"Don't tell me how it ends," I said, heading out the door in search of a liquor store. "I want to experience the insanity myself."

———·•·———

I stared at Julie's smiling face. The flier team was on its shit. Taped at eye level to the door of the mercado, I almost walked straight into one of their fliers. I lingered for a moment, realizing that I hadn't really studied it. Julie could've walked past me on the street, and I might not have recognized her. That's a problem when you're looking for a person.

An electronic bell rang as I entered. I went right for the beer cooler and pulled out a twelve of Coors Light, enjoying the refrigerated air. I lingered in the snack cake aisle, considering some of the Bimbo offerings, but managed enough self-control to pass. I was still Little Debbied out from the night before. I set the beer on the counter and pointed at the big bottles of Jack Daniels.

"A handle of Jack."

I glanced over the cigarette selection.

Fucking Bobby. I hadn't even thought about smoking. Now I really wanted one. But I had promised Angie that I'd try to be healthier. Because it's better for me. Set a better example for Juan. But mostly because it limited Angie's playful—yet pointed—barbs about my physical conditioning, or lack thereof. I'd been exercising. I'd cut out fried food. I'd been eating non-potato vegetables. (I put chard in my mouth for the first time days earlier. Chard!)

I didn't buy any Bimbos. Fuck it.

"And two packs of Winstons. And one of these NASCAR lighters."

The counter guy tossed the smokes onto the twelve. He rang me up.

"You get mugged or something?" the guy asked, more curious than concerned.

"No, got one of those faces people like to punch."

As soon as I stepped outside, I set the beer and Jack down and lit a smoke, inhaling deeply. The first drag made me light-headed, nauseous, and pukey. It was glorious. In a slow suicide kind of way. I missed you, old friend.

As I enjoyed the shit out of my first cigarette in ten days, I looked into Julie's poster eyes. I wish that I could say that I saw something in them, the windows to the soul and all that. But I didn't. Little more than the face of a stranger.

"You better be okay."

———————

Back at the Date Palm, Bobby and I drank like we had received federal funding to study the impact of beer and Tennessee whiskey on the human body. We talked a little, but mostly we drank. The talk would come, after the booze got us slippery. Drinking was what we knew. The simplest and most effective way to avoid our grown-up problems. I'm not saying it was healthy. I'm saying it was.

I flipped through the channels, but since there were only the two Mexican stations to flip between, that got old quick. After the greatest movie ever made was over, Canal Tres showed the highlights of some politician's speech. And on Canal Cinco, there were music videos. Mexican music was too happy for the occasion. The lyrics might have been the saddest in the world, telling the story of a mother's grief for her baby in a well. But once you throw in a tuba and an accordion, it's got all the seriousness of a circus.

"I got to do better, man." Bobby said after I turned off the TV and cracked a fresh beer.

"Sure, we all can."

"Julie's my daughter. She's an hour away. And I didn't make an effort. None."

"It's more complicated than that," I said. "And it's more like an hour and a half."

"That's not what I'm saying. I'm not saying her going missing is on me. We don't even know what happened yet. I'm saying that me being a shitty father is. I messed up. With Julie. With Griselda."

"You talk to Griselda?"

"No. I told you, Gris and me are over."

"You brought her up. I was thinking in terms of Julie. Griselda is a cop. She might be able to help is all."

"If I thought she could, I'd call her. I ain't got that much pride. But all she'll tell me is that the cops here got nothing and until there's evidence of otherwise, they'll treat her like a runaway. I call Gris, I'll dig up old shit. I've hurt her enough."

"You want to talk about what happened between you two?"

"No."

Bobby shook his head and poured himself another splash of Jack. "You got one kid," he said. "Hell, he's not even really yours. And I see you being ten times the father I've been to my flesh and blood. I got two kids I don't never see. And I don't barely care that I don't."

"With Julie, it was always a weird deal."

"Quit making excuses for me. Call me a piece of shit. That's what you're thinking. I can see how fed up you've been with me."

"Knock it off. Pity don't suit you. So you're a piece of shit," I said. "You can't change what you've done. You can change shit from this point on. Say from here, things are going to be different."

"People don't change like that."

"Not if they don't try. It's like quitting smoking. Maybe I stop for two weeks and then I'm back at it. But for those two weeks, it's healthier, better. Not much, but a little. Maybe you try and for a couple months you're solid, then you slack. Better than nothing. Fix it as you go."

"Don't know if quitting being a fuckup is the same as quitting smoking."

"The withdrawals are a bitch. Now, toss me that ashtray."

"Is that the last beer?" I asked, watching Bobby drain his can.

"We got time to get more?" Bobby looked at his wrist, but without a watch, it gave him no indication of the time.

"I been thinking," I said, lighting the filter of my cigarette and causing a small fire. I crushed it in the ashtray and started over with a fresh smoke. I was definitely feeling the booze.

"Thinking can't be good," Bobby said. "It ain't our strongest suit."

"Gabe said Julie was working for some rich dude in La Quinta, right?"

"Yeah, what Chucho told him."

"And La Quinta isn't that big."

"Bigger than you think. Probably the size of Calexico. And it's got all those golf courses, weird little nooks, crannies, dead-end streets, and some gated areas and shit."

"Don't fuck up my plan."

"Sorry." Bobby belched. "That tasted like shrimp. Weird."

"How do you know so much about La Quinta?"

"Night golfing is free golfing."

"Gabe said the dude drove a Humvee. A camouflage-painted Hummer."

Bobby stood up quickly, a sway in his stance. "You're right. Let's go."

"Let me finish. I was going to say that we should drive around La Quinta and look for a camo Hummer."

"I know. I did the math. It was pluses and takeaways, not calculus."

"Still. When a guy's planning a plan, it's polite to let him plan the plan. That's all I'm saying."

"My sincerest apologies. Now stand the fuck up."

So at a quarter past hammered, we resumed our investigation. The booze had given us fresh insight and enough stupid to get us off our asses. We could have waited for daylight and sobriety, but that wasn't our modus. And it was more likely for a person's car to be parked in front of its owner's house at midnight than if we waited for the next day.

Before we headed out, we made a drunk stratagem to stay on the residential streets and not drive over twenty-five miles per hour, because that's the kind of elaborate preparations you construct when you're drunk and have a stratagem.

"Should we bring the guns?" Bobby asked.

"What guns?"

"The just-in-case guns I brought."

"Show me."

Bobby went to the closet and pulled out a long gym bag.

"When did you put that in there?"

"When you were getting beer."

Then, one at a time, Bobby pulled out four pistols, a rifle, and two shotguns. He spread them out on the bed like he was displaying them for sale. It was an impressive arsenal.

"Seven guns," I said. "For two people."

"Actually, I didn't know you were coming. These were intended for my personal use."

"Were you going to tie them all together and make a super-gun?"

"No, one at a time. If the opportunity arose. Although, let's consider the super-gun idea. I never turn my back on awesome. Seven is stupid, though. But I could definitely do something with two shotguns. And if I had a sword and some duct tape—I should be writing this down."

"Let's leave the guns," I said. "We're drunk. They're guns. I'm not loving the combo."

"What if we run into trouble?"

"If we run into trouble, we'll drive away at a safe twenty-five miles per hour, as per our stratagem. What kind of trouble can we get in? We're looking for a car."

Bobby shook his head. "It's like you've never hung out with us before. Trouble finds us, bro. We're shit magnets."

"Exactly why the guns stay here. No reason to make big trouble out of standard-sized trouble."

"Not even one of the small guns?"

"It's not really about the size, Bobby."

"Is that what Angie tells you?"

"Hilarious. Put the big bag of guns back in the closet."

"You're right. We'll be fine with just my truck gun."

"Then I'm driving. And you don't drive a truck, it's a car."

"Don't disrespect the Ranchero."

Bobby packed the guns back into the gym bag and threw them in the closet. He tossed the bedspread on top for camouflage. Not exactly the hotel safe, but our neighbors were too busy breaking bad to lower themselves to petty theft.

FIVE

I don't know if it was in spite of our advanced level of intoxication or because of it, but our search was shockingly efficient. Instead of driving around in a haphazard jumblefuck, we laid out a grid and never drove down the same street twice. Apparently, nothing focuses a drunk like a quest. Anyone who has ever yearned for rolled tacos at the end of a tequila binge knows what I'm talking about. The secret to accomplishing anything while drunk is to accept the limitations of one's not-sober state. Denying drunkenness is exactly the kind of thinking that turns finding one's car keys into the poorest man's version of a scavenger hunt.

Bobby and I took my truck because—despite Bobby's disappointment—it had no truck gun. I drove. Bobby studied a map and marked off the streets with a lavender crayon he found between the seats. We went up and down the north/south streets of La Quinta, back and forth, like tilling a field. It was all Calles and Avenidas with identical stucco and terra cotta tile houses. We kept our eyes open for a camouflage Hummer.

The first hour was boring, but we had enthusiasm on our side. The second hour was worse. Our dipping buzz and the lack of variety in the residential neighborhoods combined to test our stamina. We were losing faith in the stratagem. But the thought of being back in the soul-suck of a hotel room kept us going.

Before we switched to the east/west streets, we made a run through the looping lanes of the Palisades Golf Resort. There were at least a dozen golf courses in La Quinta. It was that kind of town. The country club houses were larger and tackier, the kind of new money monstrosities that the owner of a camo Hummer would consider classy. At least the nouveau riche, Disney-fake-European castles gave us visual variety.

"Look at these fucking houses," Bobby said. "That one's got those castle things."

"Turrets."

"I don't know if that's awesome or idiotic. I'm going to go with idiotic. Because if it's something I would build, it's probably stupid. I don't even think those rocks in front are real. Are rocks expensive? Why would you use fake rocks? Are they easier to clean? All these houses look like an eight-year-old drew them on the back of his Pee Chee folder. Like Wayne Manor or Barbie's fucking Dream House. With all the accessories. That one probably has a half-car, half-boat, half-airplane parked in the back."

"Something can't have three halves."

"Exactly. The kind of person that builds that house wouldn't know that."

I forgot about the desert wealthy. Not exactly upper class. Different than rich farmers, who still worked. A whole different subspecies in these resort towns that's all flashy and gross and big. Money can buy fake rocks, but it can't buy class.

"Turn down this street. Calle Tlaxcala. We haven't been down it."

"I'm pretty sure you pronounced that wrong."

"I'll do you one better. I'm positive I said it wrong, but how else does *tl* sound?" Bobby said. "Where'd all the desert bros come from? Look at those douchebags and baguettes."

As we turned the corner onto Calle Tlaxcala, Bobby pointed to a crowd of people spilling onto the driveway and lawn from a big, boxy structure, part Bauhaus/part World War II bunker. Loud hip-hop and bright lights emanated from the house. It had a big circular driveway with a trampoline inside the horseshoe. The trampoline: the white trash swimming pool. Couples and groups of men huddled outside, smoking, beers in their hands. I would say that someone's parents went to Aruba for the week, leaving their kid at home to make sure nothing happened to their crystal egg, but most of the men were in their twenties or thirties.

They wore the uniform of the desert bro. Think frat boy who never went to college. Jersey Shore without the water. Farmer's tans made by the sun instead of a cancer machine. Ed Hardy shirts and backward baseball caps. Oakley sunglasses, even at night. Goatees or shaped three-day growth. Essentially they all looked like middle relief pitchers on vacation. The kind of guys that thought they looked like MMA fighters, but really looked like assholes. Ending their night by picking a fight because none of the women got drunk enough to believe their bullshit or the roofies they bought were actually Pepcid. Whenever one of them laughed, it sounded cruel.

The desert bro was not defined by race. There were as many brown people at the party as white. Definitely not a race thing. It's a desert thing.

I know that I sound judgmental and mean and that I'm generalizing. But I grew up here and know the desert. Believe whatever you want, but when you come out to the desert and one of these date rapes starts yelling "faggot" in the strip joint parking lot and kidney punches you as you try to walk away, you'll remember what I said. I will, of course, graciously accept your apology.

The ladies were the female equivalent of the men, dressed to match. A lot of skin. A little wobbly on stripper heels. Navel piercings, tramp stamps, hair spray, and a few chola eyebrows. Dee Snider makeup over George Hamilton tans. And if you looked closely at their legs and arms, they always seemed to have bruises. Many of them might have been attractive under all that pancake, but it would take some serious excavating to find out.

We cruised by the partygoers. A smog of cologne, perfume, and body spray assaulted us through the open window. My eyes watered from the musky, desperate fumes.

"Holy shit," Bobby said, waving his hand in front of his face. "How bad do those fuckers smell, they got to make themselves stink like that? It's like getting pepper sprayed with eau de whorehouse."

"Dead end. Story of our night."

Calle Tlaxcala was two blocks long and ended in a cul-de-sac. Tlaxcala is the smallest state in Mexico, so it figures that the smallest street in La Quinta would be named after it. Sadly, my knowledge of Mexican geography gave me no added sense of triumph. Triumph came as I made the three-point turn and the headlights revealed camouflage.

"Well, I'll be hornswoggled," Bobby said.

We took a long look at the Hummer, the headlights blowing out the tans and browns. I'd been thinking green camouflage, but desert camo made more sense. There was no street parking, so I pulled my truck into the driveway of a house with a For Sale sign out front.

"What now?" I said. "You think the Hummer's owner is at the party? Or maybe that's his party? He could live on this street in one of the other houses. Do we wait for him to come out? Hang here?"

"Slow down, Mister Questions," Bobby said. "From the looks of that crowd, those assholes are the kind of assholes to drive this asshole of a car."

"Fair point. But how do we figure out which asshole among the gaggle?"

"I'm going to shake the car, make the alarm go off. Whoever turns it off, that's our asshole."

A simple, yet effective plan. Usually our plans were much more violent and caveman-esque in their execution. The fact that Bobby's plan didn't involve "fucking some motherfucker up" was a pleasant surprise. Though of course that part should always be implied in any of Bobby's plans.

Bobby hopped out, looking both ways in an overexaggerated manner. He couldn't have looked more conspicuously suspicious if he was twiddling his thumbs and whistling. I should have been watching him through eyeholes cut out of a newspaper. He pushed against the front fender. The body of the truck rocked back and forth. No alarm.

Bobby gave me a look. I shrugged and got out. The two of us violently shook the Hummer. Nothing.

"What the hell?" Bobby said. "What kind of asshole drives a monstrosity that most people would key on principle and doesn't alarm it?"

"You got a Plan B?"

"I wish I had my Plan Bs, I'd just . . ." Bobby drifted off, looking at the front yard of the house. He found a good-sized, real rock and threw it through the driver's side window of the Hummer. Pebbles of glass rained onto the ground, making surprisingly little sound. Still no alarm.

"Yeah, I guess we could do that," I said, looking toward the party to see if anyone saw or heard. I could feel the music from the house thumping in my chest, so I doubted it.

Bobby popped the lock and jumped in the driver's seat. I stayed on lookout duty, meaning that I stood where I was and did nothing. It was my first day as a lookout. You couldn't expect much.

"Remember this name," Bobby said. "Craig Driskell. That's the name on the registration."

"Craig Driskell. Got it."

"Nothing else in the glove box. Some pens. Papers. Under the seats? Whoa-ho!"

Shirking my lookout duties, I glanced into the Hummer. Bobby held up a snubnose pistol.

"Craig ain't playing," Bobby said.

"Better put it back."

"Yeah, I don't think I'm going to do that."

"You're going to steal a gun?"

"You say that like I'm a criminal. This fuck might have something to do with Julie's gone missing. He doesn't get to have a gun. Anyways, it'd be irresponsible to leave a handgun in a car with a busted window. You don't want a kindergartner to accidentally get his little hands on it, do you?"

"I don't think a kindergartner is going to look under the seat of a Hummer at two in the morning."

"Better safe than sorry."

"What kind of person feels the need to keep a gun in his car?"

"Driving this jerkoff-mobile is like picking a fight with civilization." Bobby smiled, and then looked at me. "Oh, I see what you did. I'm that kind of person is what you're saying. Very hilarious."

Bobby turned on the Hummer's headlights and hopped out. He put the pistol in his pants at the small of his back, covered it with his shirt, and walked toward the party. "Come on. We have to find the driver of this car. His lights are on. As good citizens, we can't let his battery die, can we?"

"The window's broke. Couldn't we reach in and turn the lights off? And I don't think anybody'd notice if we just crashed the party."

Bobby shook his head, mumbled to himself, and walked away.

Bobby and I walked through the gauntlet in the driveway and let ourselves in the front door. We entered the giant living room, the far wall made entirely of windows looking out onto the swimming pool and the darkness of the golf course beyond it.

I would be the first to admit that I knew nothing about interior decoration. I was a mattress on the floor, milk cartons and one-by-sixes bookshelf kind of guy. But even in my ignorance, I knew that living room was a marvel of bad decisions and unfortunate combinations. A display that I could only describe as Powerball chic. The product of someone that all of sudden had money and then spent that money in one Jaeger-soaked Internet shopping binge.

In the center of the room sat a matching fuchsia cheetah-print sofa, love seat, and lounge chair. The coffee table looked like an antique, beautiful and complex woodwork adorning the edges. In a different house, it would have been the room's centerpiece. Currently it was covered in beer bottles and chipped at the edges. Those were the functional elements.

The rest was an insane mishmash. A life-size sculpture of a nude woman that might have been Venus—if Venus had gotten a tit job and ass implants based on a Boris Vallejo painting of Ice-T's wife. Something that looked like a hamster maze, but I'm pretty sure was an elaborate stand-up bong. An old school, coin-op *Robotron: 2084* arcade game. A narwhal horn. An oil-on-leather painting of an Indian chief and a grizzly bear standing on a mesa looking at a distant sunrise. That "art" hung over a giant flat-screen playing a montage of gonzo porn, Russian dashcams, and street fights. There was an aquarium that only had jellyfish in it. And a Raiders flag was unevenly tacked to the wall.

Thirty more Tapout T-shirts and halter tops hovered throughout the room. Everyone was dressed so similarly, it felt like some kind of ironic costume party. Imagine a room full of off-the-clock general contractors and the girls that check your ID at the gym. The fug of aftershave and perfume was thicker indoors.

"You got any quarters?" I asked.

"You're not playing *Robotron*. We're investigating," Bobby said. "Quit making me the voice of reason. It feels all wrong."

"I was kidding." I wasn't.

Bobby tapped the shoulder of the guy nearest him.

The guy turned and gave Bobby a double take. "That your real hair? You look like Halle Berry in *X-Men*. Or Mex-men, I guess."

From the look on Bobby's face, he was doing everything in his power to not turn this guy's face inside out with his fists. "I'm looking for Craig. You know him?"

"I'm at his house, ain't I?"

"He around?"

The guy sized up Bobby and decided that he wasn't worth bothering with anymore. "Somewhere in the back."

———

Bobby and I squeezed through the makeshift dance floor that had formed in what was probably designed to be the dining room. The music's epicenter, it thumped through unseen speakers. The men fist-pumped and air-fucked by themselves while the ladies danced with each other, ignoring the attempts of the men to join their circle. When one of the bros flung his head as we passed, his heavily chemicalled hair juice landed on my arm and stung like acid.

In the kitchen, an inch of liquid pooled on the floor. Bottles and Solo cups and limes and ice covered the counter. A cat with "Pussy" drawn on its side in lipstick drank water out of the clogged sink. Bobby opened the fridge, grabbed four beers, and handed me two. We each cracked one and tapped the necks in a silent toast.

"Nice restraint not killing the Mex-men dude back there," I said.

"The things we do for our kids."

The back room—probably referred to as the rumpus room—was bigger than the living room. It had the same giant windows looking onto the golf course. I wondered how many times an errant golf ball slammed into one of the big panes.

Bobby stopped at the top of the three steps that led into the sunken room. "What the fuck is he doing here?" Bobby said.

"Who?"

I followed Bobby's eyes through the sparser crowd.

"That can't be good," I said when I saw Tomás Morales.

I had known Tomás most of my life. He was Mr. Morales's grandson and grew up across the street from me. A few years younger than me, but with no other neighbor kids to play with, we spent much of our youth together. He wasn't that kid anymore. He operated a number of criminal enterprises in Mexicali that I knew about. His presence on this side of the border was not only rare but disconcerting. The rumors about his efforts to expand and get a foothold on the US side must have been true. The question was how Driskell fit into all of it.

The bottom line was that if it was profitable, Tomás was interested. He wielded his pragmatism like a weapon, never letting a nuisance like morality get in his way.

I had once asked him what business he was in. His reply had been, "Business, period. Don't matter to me what it is. Like a good salesman can sell anything, I'm interested in profit. Right now, one of the best businesses is the business of knowing things, knowing more than other people. Information is a simple thing, but once you own a fact, it's a matter of how and when you use it. Someone said knowledge is power. And so much more."

So basically, he didn't answer my question.

While personally, Tomás had always been a loyal friend—he had helped me whenever I needed it, including the business that resulted in me securing my son—he scared the holy living shit out of me. He was brutal, amoral, and worthy of fear. There was no way that his presence in that house represented a good thing.

Tomás sat on an oversized purple couch, deep in conversation. Across from him on a matching couch sat the king of Doucheville, a guy sporting a crown of spiky hair with frosted tips and a velvet bathrobe. From the amount of leg and chest hair showing, I would've put money on him going commando underneath. He snorted a line of coke off a small mirror and passed it to one of the two underfed, bikini-clad desert princesses bookending him.

Tomás had his two favorite henchmen, Big Piwi and Little Piwi, henching behind him. The gigantic Mexicans were both over six four and three hundred pounds. Their presence carried weight, literally. Behind Bathrobe two steroid freaks tried to give the Piwis their best death stares. Big Piwi yawned, making Little Piwi yawn. I don't know what they were talking about, but if Tomás was there, they weren't trading carrot cake recipes.

Mid-sentence, Tomás's eyes found us where we'd frozen on the top step. He tilted his head slightly, not giving anything away or losing a beat in the conversation.

"My stomach just got tight," Bobby said. "If that's Driskell, the motherfucker that Julie worked for, and Tomás knows him, that's sixteen flavors of bad. Tomás don't waste no time talking to no one but bad guys or people he owns."

Bobby took a step down into the room, his eyes on Tomás. I put a hand on his shoulder when I saw the Piwis spot him. They lifted their chins in acknowledgment or possibly threat. Bobby shrugged my hand away, but stopped.

"There ain't no reason for this to get out of hand," I said. "If that's Driskell, we know where he lives. It don't look like he's running anywhere. Not without pants. And Tomás won't leave without talking to us. He hates not knowing what's going on. Let's finish these beers and wait. Better to know what the deal is, instead of jumping in blind."

"You might be scared of Tomás, but I ain't."

"I know, Bobby. You have no fear. Fear is afraid of you. You wouldn't be scared of the ground if you jumped from a plane and your parachute didn't open. 'Fuck you, ground,' that's what you'd say."

"Fuck the ground is right. I'd roll with it. People survive that shit all the time. I'm tired of your pussyfooting, with emphasis on the pussy. It's my daughter. It's my plan of attack, with emphasis on the attack."

"You go over there, get in his face, he won't tell us shit. If you're going to talk to him, be nice. We get one chance at him, and there's a lot at stake. We got to do what works, not what you want to do. On top of that, there's about a thousand pounds of hench over there."

"Yeah, but this ain't your show. This isn't about you. Not everything is about what you want."

"You're right. It's not about me. It's about Julie."

Bobby stared at me, his thinking face in full concentration mode. "You're as shitty a wartime consigliere as you are a sidekick. It's clobberin' time."

Bobby hopped down the steps and stomped over to the small group. And to think, I could have been playing *Robotron*.

"Damn it" is all I could say. And then watch whatever mayhem was about to unfold.

Tomás ignored Bobby, looking at me with a small smile as we approached. Big Piwi and Little Piwi did nothing. Bobby faced the guy in the bathrobe.

"You're Driskell, right? That's your Hummer outside?"

"This party is a private function. Were you invited?" He spoke with a fake almost-English accent, faint but affected. It sounded like my Michael Caine impression, which was awful.

"Tell me everything you know about Julie Espinosa."

"I'm sure I don't know who that is."

"Your timing is amazing, Maves," Tomás said.

"I'm not talking to you," Bobby barked and turned back to Driskell. He reached down and grabbed the lapels of Driskell's bathrobe. He pulled up on them in an effort to lift him, but all he got was bathrobe. Sure enough, no underwear. "Julie Espinosa. She worked for you, motherfucker."

The two steroid monkeys snapped out of their daze and circled around either side of the couch. The girls on the couch slinked away, making sure to bring the mirror with the lines on it with them. Big Piwi and Little Piwi took a few steps, but Tomás waved them off.

One of Driskell's goons tried to grab Bobby, but he ducked underneath his arms. Bobby gave him a hard kick to the back of the knee.

The other bodyguard reeled back to blindside Bobby from behind. Without thinking, I jumped on his back, knocking him off balance enough for him to miss. I tried to get my arm around his massive neck. Predictably, he threw me across the room.

By the time I got my bearings, Bobby had one of the bodyguards bent over, cupping the blood that ran from his nose. The other big brutus put up his hands in surrender and turned to Driskell, who adjusted his robe.

"Screw this, man. You said me and Jed were just supposed to stand behind you, look tough. I don't want none of this." He put an arm around the other guy and walked him out through the kitchen.

Big Piwi and Little Piwi shook their heads, unimpressed with Driskell's hired help.

"Why aren't your men doing anything?" Driskell said to Tomás. "I got attacked. Aren't you going to do something about this maniac?"

"He's not bothering me. Gives me a chance to see how you protect your business. I see some flaws."

Bobby stood over Driskell. "That got the blood pumping. Now you're going to tell me about Julie Espinosa."

"I already have. I don't know anyone by that name."

"I was told she started working for you, maybe a month ago."

"By whom?"

"That's not important."

"It is. Because that person is a liar. I haven't hired any new personnel in the last three months, aside from those two idiots that just left. Who is she?"

"My daughter. My sixteen-year-old daughter."

"I'm sorry I can't be more help."

Tomás stood up and waved me and Bobby over. "You and you. Let's talk." He walked out the glass door into the backyard. The Piwis followed.

Bobby looked down at Driskell. "I'm not done with you."

———————

Tomás, Bobby, and I convened in the backyard on the far side of the pool. A Piwi stood on either side of us, creating a man-wall between us and the party.

Bobby didn't waste any time.

"What the fuck are you doing here, Morales?" His body language pushed forward, chin jutting out. Big Piwi stood within arm's reach, but I doubted that he could stop Bobby in time. I put myself between Bobby and Tomás, just in case.

"We both have questions," Tomás said calmly. "I'm curious to hear what you're doing here and why you're acting like I've done something wrong."

"All you do is wrong." Bobby leaned into me, pointing at Tomás.

"Jimmy, tell Maves to calm down. I'm used to being the one that asks the questions. And I never answer any until I have my own answers. Threats don't fly. You're Jimmy's friend, Maves, but that only goes so far."

"Go fuck yourself," Bobby said.

I pushed lightly on Bobby's chest, playing peacemaker. This was turning ugly faster than I could keep up. I turned to Tomás.

"Bobby's daughter is missing. Julie. The one he was asking about inside. She's been missing five days. We were told she worked for Driskell. We came here to ask some questions. You saw how that went. Don't know who he is. Didn't know you'd be here. And while you know full well I don't have any say in what Bobby does—that I couldn't control him if I wanted to—I got his back in whatever dumbfuckery he does."

"Goddamn right," Bobby said.

"Sorry about your daughter, Maves. I'll be honest. I didn't know you had kids. Never cared. But it explains your excitement."

"I don't give two fat shits. Who the fuck is Craig Driskell?"

"He's a local businessman."

"Why am I talking to you, if you're telling me fuck-all?" Bobby said. "I'm going to go talk to him with my fists."

Bobby took two steps toward the house, but Big Piwi stepped in his path.

"That's not a good idea," Tomás said.

"I like bad ideas," Bobby said.

"Me and Driskell were having a business meeting. Because you jumped in and knuckled up, we didn't get to finish. I still need to discuss some things with Craig. I can't let your bullshit affect my business. So I'm not going to let you talk to him until after I'm done."

"You're not going to let me?" Bobby said.

"Not just me." He smiled toward Big Piwi.

"What is Driskell into?" I asked. "If you know him, I'm assuming it's illegal."

"I'm hurt, Jimmy. I have legit business connections, too," Tomás said. "But yeah, he's in the game. Fronts money for shit. Likes to play Scarface to the crowd, but keep a safe distance from the hardcore action. His cash puts him in contact with some straight-up lowlifes though."

"I can see that." Bobby fake-laughed loudly. "You keep talking. Saying things. But you ain't telling me shit."

"Do you have a photograph of your daughter?"

Bobby stared at Tomás for a moment, took the picture of Julie out of his back pocket, and handed it to him. Tomás held it at arm's length, and took a flash picture of it with his phone. He studied the photo, and then stared into space, not saying a word.

"What? What is it?" Bobby said.

"You said your daughter's name is Julie?"

"What do you know?"

Bobby didn't get an answer. When he reached for the photo, his shirt lifted and exposed Driskell's pistol. Big Piwi reacted quickly, pulling the pistol from Bobby's pants, tossing it to Tomás, and wrapping Bobby in a bear hug. He lifted him off the ground, Bobby's feet kicking wildly. Big Piwi was quicker than a man that size should be.

"Get the fuck off me," Bobby said.

"Let's all calm—" But my words were crushed by Little Piwi's squeezing arms. I guess he wasn't taking any chances. He didn't lift me off the ground, but I couldn't move. It felt like my organs were going to shoot out my mouth like toothpaste from a tube. My mouth being the best-case scenario.

Tomás held the pistol in his hand, looking toward the house, distracted.

Big Piwi might have had leverage and size, but Bobby had often been the smaller dog in the pit. He leaned forward and brought his head back fast, connecting with the center of Big Piwi's massive face. It sounded like stepping on a frog. All squish and crunch. Before Big Piwi could react, Bobby did it again. Big Piwi roared and flung Bobby to the side like a scratching cat. Bobby splashed into the swimming pool.

A few curious partygoers looked over, but the tableau of Big Piwi's bleeding face, Tomás casually holding a pistol, and Little Piwi restraining me seemed to dissuade any further investigation. I caught Driskell watching from the house.

Bobby surfaced and swam to the edge of the pool. Big Piwi reached into his jacket.

"No," Tomás said, handing his goon a handkerchief. Big Piwi gave Tomás a dejected look but dropped his arm. His jacket had opened enough for me to see his shoulder holster and an enormous pistol.

Tomás nodded toward Bobby, who had reached the edge of the pool. With one hand, Big Piwi picked up Bobby by the collar of his shirt. Before Bobby had his feet on the ground, he was kicking wildly and throwing hard punches at Big Piwi.

Little Piwi sighed loudly and threw me in the pool.

By the time I surfaced, the Piwis had Bobby on the ground, arms held to the side by Little Piwi and Big Piwi's knee in his back. He wriggled in protest, but wasn't going anywhere. I swam to the edge.

"You can get out of the water," Tomás said. "I now have all the guns."

I nodded and pulled myself up. I made eye contact with Bobby, but he looked through me at Tomás, too deep into his rage.

"Fuck you, Morales," Bobby wheezed. But with all that weight on his back, he couldn't get any decent volume.

Tomás ignored him and gave a Queen Elizabeth wave to Driskell, who continued to watch from the house. He waved back but didn't look happy about it.

"Where are you staying?" Tomás asked.

"Date Palm Motel, out by—"

"I know it." Tomás said. "That place is a shitbox. I could find you extra work if you need cash."

"Let Bobby go. We'll leave quietly. No more drama."

"What's your room number?"

"Twelve. Why? What're you going to do?"

Tomás turned to the Piwis and barked orders in rapid-fire Spanish. "Big Piwi, Tome Maves al Date Palm Motel. Indio del sur. Busque en Google para la dirección. Permanezca con él en el cuarto doce hasta que oiga de mí."

"You don't need him to take Bobby back to the motel. I can do it."

"No, you can't. We're going to talk."

The Piwis pulled Bobby to his feet. He gulped in huge lungfuls of air. Tomás took a step toward him, his face close.

"I know you're pissed, but listen to me. I got nothing against you finding your daughter. I'll give Jimmy anything I know that doesn't directly affect me. On Driskell and anything to do with your girl. I can't do it with you here though. You're too unpredictable. Big Piwi's going to bring you back to your room. Don't fight him. He's mad at you. I may not be your friend, Maves, but I'm not your enemy. Not yet."

Bobby turned to me.

I shrugged and nodded. "I told you. The kamikaze bullshit has to stop, Bobby. It's not getting us anywhere. Let me talk to Tommy. If nothing comes of it, we can always beat the shit out of the world after."

Nobody said anything. When Bobby finally spoke, his voice was a whisper. "Okay."

The Piwis waited for Tomás to give them the sign. When he nodded, they let Bobby go. There was a thirty to forty percent chance Bobby would attack again, and we all waited to see if it was going to happen. I don't even think that Bobby knew himself. After a moment, he walked toward the back gate. Big Piwi followed him out.

For a minute or so, nothing happened. I stood, dripping water. Tomás stared past me, toward the house.

"I don't know where Bobby's girl is," Tomás finally said, "but I have seen her."

"Where? When?"

Tomás pointed at the house. I turned around.

Through the enormous glass windows, I saw what Tomás was pointing at, the gigantic television on the wall in the living room.

"Oh, shit," I said, before I even knew what I was looking at. I just knew it was bad.

A banner across the bottom of the screen read "Extreme Girl Fights: Runaway Edition: Julie vs. LaShanda." Above the banner, highlights of a Mexican girl fighting bare-knuckle against a taller black girl flashed on the TV. Both the girls' faces grew increasingly bloodier, but the Mexican girl was definitely Julie. They traded wild punches. No hair-pulling or kicking, just fists to faces and body blows. A small group of men created the ring around them. It was hard to tell where they were, some kind of industrial site. The ground and structures all looked white, like they were covered in snow.

"What the fuck is this?" I said.

"It's an interesting niche market."

Julie threw an uppercut that started at her feet. It caught the black girl square on the chin. LaShanda was out before she hit the ground. None of the spectators checked to see if she was okay. The camera moved in closer to Julie, who held up her hands in triumph. She spit blood on the ground and smiled broadly through red teeth.

SIX

Julie's face star-wiped out and a new couple of girls appeared in another series of highlights. It was all quick shots. More of an ad than anything else. The girls shadowboxed in the same white industrial setting, prepping in their makeshift corners with their makeshift seconds. Lety vs. Kiki. They shouted and pointed at each other, but with little anger in their faces. One of them laughed. And then the shouting stopped and the fighting began. The bloodlust of the small, all-male crowd blurred in the handheld camera as the two teenage girls beat each other with huge flailing shots to the head. They connected with forearms as often as fists.

I grew up around violence. I'd fought and seen more fights than I could remember. However, watching those girls fight was something different, unnecessary. But the most disturbing part was that—if I was honest with myself—it was captivating, entertaining in a perverse way. I could see why people would watch it. Sometimes our depths surprise us. My stomach cramped and I finally looked away.

"This fucking world," I said. "I didn't even know that was a thing."

"You really haven't explored the Internet, have you?" Tomás said. "Bum Fights. Street Fights. Backyard Brawls. You name it. The raw fight footage market is rich and varied. This is pretty tame. The girls look more or less willing. Not like what comes out of South America or Poland."

"I don't want to know things like that. When I think I've got a gauge on how fucked up the world is, there's always something out there to raise the depravity bar."

"Supply doesn't exist without demand."

"All that means is there are sick bastards at both ends. Just because some asshole wants something doesn't mean someone has to make it for them. They're just girls." Something occurred to me. "Had you seen this before? Seen Julie?"

"No, only tonight. They've had the entertainment running on a loop. When Maves showed me that photo, I recognized her face. That smile's hard to forget, bloody teeth or not. She has star quality. I admired the fire in her eyes."

"She's sixteen, Tommy."

"Young, but not a child."

"The law would tell you different."

"The law?" Tomás laughed, unimpressed. "What law?"

"There's no such thing as a sixteen-year-old adult."

"Only on this side of the border. Put a fence up, everything changes. A few miles south, sixteen is all grown up. Why is it Americans think they make the rules? That their rules are the moral ones?"

"Christ in Hell, Tommy. That was my best friend's kid up there."

Tomás walked away, but not before saying, "Everyone is someone's kid."

I stared at the swimming pool, watching the reflection of the house lights and television violence on the water, abstracting the horribleness into something that was almost pretty.

"What happened to your face?" Tomás asked, coming back with a deck chair and sitting.

Instinctively, I touched the side of my face. The bruise still hurt. "The usual. Walked in the wrong bar. With the wrong person in it."

"You need me to talk to someone about it?"

I shook my head, wanting to get back to it. "Does Driskell make these movies? Is that his thing—what he does—why you're here?"

"I'm not going to tell you why I'm here, what my relationship to Driskell is, or why we were meeting."

"Okay, but is that movie his?"

Tomás took a few seconds before answering. "Yes and no. He's not the filmmaker. But he finances a number of productions, mostly gonzo stuff like this, some porn. He supplies the budget, the location. He doesn't find the girls or shoot the footage. He has people for that. I doubt he would have had contact with anyone in the movies, unless he took a personal interest."

"I got someone saying Julie worked for him."

"If she got paid, he was the one that paid her. But it doesn't mean they met."

"I need to know who made that movie. When they made it. If they know anything about Julie—where she's at now. Seeing her tells us what she was doing, who she was with, but still not why she's gone or if she wants to be there. That could have been filmed yesterday or months ago."

Tomás nodded. "I'll find out who made the movie, Driskell's involvement. But don't forget, if your interests and mine are opposed, mine come first."

"Right," I said, a little pissed off.

"And make sure it's clear to Maves that I'm not involved in his kid's disappearance. He's going to have to take my word on that. I can't have a fucking loco like him showing up and disrupting my business."

"I told you I can't control him, but I'll try to convince him."

"He comes after me, he's putting himself in danger. He should know that much."

"Don't threaten my friends, Tommy," I said, my voice rising.

Tomás shrugged. "It wasn't meant as a threat. It was a warning."

I sat with that for a while. I didn't want to antagonize Tomás any more than I had, but it sat wrong with me. I got back to concentrating on why I was there.

"I have to figure out how to destroy all the copies of that video," I said. "Something like that can ruin Julie's life. Is that a disc playing inside or a computer or what?"

Tomás took out his phone, pressing and sliding his finger on the screen at a rapid clip. "That's not the way the world works anymore, Jimmy."

"What do you mean?"

Tomás held up his phone. On the screen was the same image of Julie bouncing around, bloody teeth, arms up in victory.

"Are you kidding me?" I said. "Is that online?"

"Found it in a Google search for girl fights. Clips for free. Full video for sale. Already picked up by some pirate sites. It's out there, and once something is out there, it's forever. There are maybe ways to get rid of it, but it's a lot of work for little reward."

Tomás studied the screen for a moment too long, nodded, and then put his phone back in his pocket.

"I have no idea how Bobby is going to react to this," I said.

"Exactly."

I stared at Tomás for a moment. "You had Big Piwi take Bobby out of here for Bobby's sake, didn't you? You were trying to save him seeing his daughter that way."

"He would have exploded," Tomás said. "And with all these people around. He would've been humiliated."

"I thought you didn't like Bobby."

"I don't dislike him that much. I might be a sociopath, Jimmy, but I'm not a monster."

I grabbed a deck chair and sat down next to Tomás. I hated the idea of all those douchebags watching Julie and other young girls beat the shit out of each other, but what could I do? I could turn off the TV or throw a chair through the screen, but I didn't really see the benefit. I wanted to punch everyone at the party in the face. Instead, I lit a cigarette and took a deep drag.

"I thought you quit," Tomás said.

"What's the fucking point?"

I had no real reason to be at the party anymore. It was clear that Tomás wasn't going to let me talk to Driskell and I sure as shit didn't want to mingle with the edging-toward-blackout-drunk crowd. I should've gotten up and gone back to the motel. But I wasn't ready to deal with Bobby and his reaction to the fight video. He wouldn't sit on his hands. That was for sure. I was going to have to hide the guns before I pulled that Band-Aid off.

Tomás and I watched the idiot partygoers get drunker and stupider. They spilled their drinks, puked in the pool, and generally showed no regard for Driskell's home. It was like watching drunk lampreys trash a coked-up shark's house. (I've never been good at similes and metaphors.)

The best part of the show was when Driskell rushed out the front door and returned super-pissed. He waved his hands wildly and screamed in a substance-fueled rage. I couldn't hear what he was saying, but his apoplectic fit spoke volumes. His face was the color of a dog dick, veins threatening to burst. Nobody liked finding a busted window on their Hummer, but the dude had money, so the overreaction was a show for the crowd. His low-rent Tony Montana moment. I wondered if he even noticed that his gun was missing or if he was saving that for a separate tantrum.

"Does that have something to do with you and Maves?" Tomás asked.

"Most definitely. Driskell's a complete tool. This party. These shitheads. Why would you do business with that moron?"

Driskell was literally jumping up and down, stomping his feet. Everybody left the living room, their mellows sufficiently harshed.

Tomás shook his head. "In Mexico, I have latitude to run my businesses. Criminality—illegality—is different for different people. Things that are a crime for an average person—a barber or a carpenter—aren't illegal for me. The Mexican system works on a sliding scale. Crime is relative. Money is atonement."

"That's messed up. Just because you have money doesn't mean you shouldn't be accountable for the things you do."

"Am I to blame for working and benefiting within a broken system? You can't play chess on a Monopoly board. And I hate to burst your childlike bubble, but it isn't any different on this side of the border. It's only more expensive. Rather than a little mordida here and there—some strategic friendships—everyone in the US wants a piece. You can't just bribe a few cops or a politician. You have to run the money through the system, the courts. In the US, it's the lawyers that make all the profit. More than the criminals. And when the dust settles, the person with more money wins. The limits of American greed are boundless. It's good to have a network of local—white—businessmen that can act as a cushion."

"And that's where this dipshit comes in?"

Tomás nodded. "He's corrupt enough to work with, but has the appearance of legitimacy. You don't always want the guy in a business suit. Everyone takes Driskell for the wild rich guy. Which is what he is. Too clean and he'd raise suspicions. He hides in plain sight. He could've been a good front, but obviously he's too volatile, too stupid, and it's not about the money for him."

"So who the fuck is he?" I lit another cigarette.

"His file is in my laptop, but I can give you a basic rundown from memory. His father founded CaSO-Corp. For the longest time, Craig was on a fixed income—a trust fund. When his old man died, he took over the business. He liked the title of CEO, but didn't know what it stood for. It took him two years to drive CaSO-Corp into the ground. He shut down the factory, found a buyer for the name, and sold enough of the assets. He made plenty on those deals. Fucked every one of his loyal employees. But that's business.

"So he's got cash and nothing to do. Bored rich people are dangerous. It always gets weird with them. He's the worst that wealth makes. The kind of person that hasn't been hungry. Never known pain that he didn't create himself. He's got no respect for money or people or work. The only creativity he has is in his perversions. He's the kind of guy that would kill a hooker, get arrested, and not understand why he was being persecuted."

"Sounds like a piece of work," I said. "Definitely someone that could be involved in Julie's disappearance."

"Another good reason to be careful. And patient. Money is more dangerous than muscle. You could go in there, but he could sic some bad people on you."

"Worse than you?" I smiled to make sure Tomás knew I was mostly joking.

Tomás smiled back. "Doubtful. Depends on your definition. Either way, you're a tourist in this shit. I can talk to him because he's afraid to not talk to me. I can tell him to fuck off and he'll smile and take it. The moment he knows your name, you're in it. As tough as you think you are, Jimmy, this is not your side of the street."

"I don't want anything to do with him, but Bobby. Once he hears about that movie, he's going to come back here. And there ain't going to be no way to stop him."

"But that's not you. That's Maves. I know he's your friend, but I don't care about him. If you want to keep yourself and your family safe, let him go. Let him off the leash and run in the other direction."

"I can't do that."

"Yes, you can."

"Bobby would never abandon me."

"Neither would a loyal dog, but do you risk everything for a dog? You have people that depend on you. You're willing to put yourself at risk, but are you willing to risk their safety for your friendship?"

"Nothing is going to come back to my family. We're only looking for a missing girl."

Tomás shook his head, smiling. "You crack me up. The way you see the world."

"I'm not some naïve schoolgirl, for fuck's sake."

"You think because you're on some heroic mission to find a missing girl that everyone will want to help. You're all motive, no information. Without knowing who's doing what and why, you don't know who has what to protect. There are as many bad people in the world as good. It's an even split."

"Bobby backs me. I back him." I flicked my cigarette into the swimming pool. It fizzled briefly when it struck the surface.

Tomás laughed. "I don't know if I should admire your loyalty or pity your stupidity."

"Probably both."

Sitting in the dim light of the Date Palm Motel parking lot, I was stalling. I wanted to call Angie, talk to her, but it was too early/late. It was hard to believe only twenty-four hours earlier, Bobby and I had been drinking and frog gigging on a ditch bank. I lit a fresh cigarette off the one I was smoking. At this rate, I was going to need to buy another pack.

I could see the light behind the thin curtain of the motel room. I considered sleeping in my truck and dealing with everything in a few hours. Or joining the two Mexicans at the other end of the lot, who sat on their tailgate, drank beers, and laughed too loud. They looked like nice enough guys. I wanted to know what was so funny. But it was time to sack up, be a friend, and tell Bobby the truth.

When I walked into the room, Big Piwi and Bobby turned from the table, but returned to what they were doing. Big Piwi had toilet paper sticking out of both nostrils. As funny as it looked, I didn't dare laugh at the sight. They played poker, using store-bought cookies as chips. Big Piwi put an Oreo in the pot. Bobby took it out and placed it back in Big Piwi's stack.

"I keep telling you," Bobby said, exhausted, "Oreos are five. If you want to call, you need to bet ten. That's two Oreos or a Chips Ahoy."

Big Piwi folded and ate a Chips Ahoy instead.

"Good to see you boys playing nice," I said.

"My blood got hot. It does that," Bobby said. "But even I'll only slam my head into a brick wall so many times before I give up or pass out or go out to the shed and find my jack-hammer. And The Thing That Should Not Be had a big bag of cookies under the seat. Seriously, I haven't had a Nutter Butter since I was eight."

Big Piwi rose from the tiny chair, leaving its legs sharply bowed, a wonder that it hadn't collapsed under his weight. He raked all the cookies on the table into his cookie bag with his forearm and walked out the door without a word.

Bobby got up and stretched. "The whole time you were gone, I couldn't get him to shut up. Talk about a chatterbox. Then you get here and he clams up."

"Seriously?"

"Of course not. Fucker didn't say a word. Nothing. The only sound he made was when he farted. That was a major communication breakthrough. It smelled like the mole poblano from Elvia's."

"Why did I need to know that?"

"Thought you might find it interesting. It was unusual."

I walked to the closet and leaned my back against it. "Look, Bobby. We got to talk."

"Are you breaking up with me? After all these years?" Bobby smiled. Then he studied my face and his smile faded. He sat down on the edge of the bed, the weight of his legs practically giving beneath him.

"Oh, Christ. Is she dead? She's dead, isn't she?"

"What? No. Is that what my face looked like? No. Sorry. No. I don't know, but no, I didn't find that out."

Bobby let out a big breath. "Okay. What then?"

"There's a video. I saw Julie—"

"Stop. I don't want to know what kind of porn she's in. It's enough you saw it."

"No. Jesus. She's not dead and it's not porn. Let me finish, for Christ's sake."

"You suck at this shit, bro."

"You're not helping."

Bobby finally let me talk. I told him what I had seen and what I had learned from Tomás. As he listened, his face was stone. I couldn't even see him breathe. It was disconcerting. Bobby usually expressed his emotions in real time, never much mystery to how he was feeling.

"Not what I was expecting," Bobby said. "Fucked up. Did you watch it?"

"Part of it. It was like a preview. Tomás is going to find the whole thing. Send me the link or file or whatever."

"Did she look like she was forced?"

"Hard to say. Even if it was for money, she's being used."

"She won?"

"Definitely. Knocked the other girl out cold."

"Of course, she did. She's my kid."

"We should tell the cops. It could be important."

Bobby stood quickly. I flinched.

"What're they going to do? Nothing. You, me, and fucking Morales: that's the only people that need to know. And Becky. I'll tell her. Tell the cops, not only does everyone know, including the papers—cops don't keep secrets—but might spook whoever we're looking for."

"It's not really a secret. It was playing at the party. It's on the Internet. It's out there. You can't get rid of it."

"Exactly," Bobby said, "so let's not advertise. It's only important that people that know Julie and Beck and me don't know. Most people that watch it see anonymous girls and move to the next batch. Like the way you look at porn stars, like they live on another planet. Not like people. As long as we don't give reason to link Julie with that video, no one's going to do it themselves. You can't find something if you don't know to look."

"You sound calm and rational, Bobby. It's fucking with me a little. A lot."

"I don't feel calm. But, of all the things it could've been, this ain't the worst. Hell, is it even illegal? And the fact it was playing at that douchebag's house means I got a direction to head in. It's fucked up, but that video might help us find Julie."

"You're right. Finding her is the main thing."

"It is," Bobby said. "That's why I need you to step away from the closet, so I can get my guns."

I shook my head and squared my feet. "I don't think so, Bobby. We've been running ragged. I let you take your guns, you might kill someone."

"Not really your problem, Jimmy. And I don't want to be a dick and bring up old business, but you've done more killing than me. My body count is still at zero. The only thing I've ever killed is my liver."

"That's a cheap shot. Bringing up the past. What happened out in the dunes, that was different."

"The only thing was different was that it was about you, not me. I might got a rep as some insaniac, but you got more blood on your hands than me. I watched you kill a guy. Deserved it, sure, but makes you a shitty role model to be the angel on my shoulder."

"I can't let you have the guns."

Bobby looked at the ceiling, then back at me. "Go home, Jimmy. Go back to your family. To your quiet life. Quit trying to fucking save me. I was fine for the dozen years you were gone, and I didn't ask you to come out here. Never asked you to help me. This is my family, my problem. You're in my way."

"First off, fuck you. Second, that 'I didn't ask you to come here' bullshit don't fly. You call my ass anytime you need a chaos buddy on one of your drunken escapades."

"Mavescapades."

"Shut up. You know how many times in the last twenty-four hours I wanted to get in my truck and drive home, and how shitty I felt for considering it? You didn't have to ask me to come out here, you fucking asshole. And I didn't need permission. Someone has to protect you from your dumbass, fucked-up idiotness. And third, fuck you again. You almost hurt my feelings."

"I'm going to count to three. If you're still standing in front of that closet, I'm going to kick your ass. Don't want to do it. Won't be a dick about it. But one way or the other, I'm leaving with my big bag of guns."

I shifted my hands and got in a sideways stance. "Don't bother to count. I know getting all the way to three might be a challenge. I ain't moving, fucko. If the only way to keep you from getting hurt is to fight you, I'm your huckleberry."

"Nice reference."

"Thanks."

"Seriously. Move. I'm not playing."

"Neither am I."

"Okay then."

———————

The battle that followed was epic. Though there were no spectators to appreciate the fight, the display of violence was for the ages. Bobby moved for the closet door. I stood my ground. Our conversation no longer required words. It was time to talk with our fists. A flurry of punches flew, both of us standing toe-to-toe, waiting for the other to fall. So evenly matched, only a mental error would name the victor. Trading hard shots, forearms deflecting blows, dueling in the small space. The sound was deafening, the fury furious. At one point, Bobby blocked my spinning roundhouse kick and used my forward momentum to judo me against the wall. But like a jungle cat, I used the wall to push off, coming right back at him like a spider monkey.

I'm fucking with you. None of that happened. Bobby kicked my ass. With shocking ease.

I don't think I even got a punch in. What little I remember of the historic beatdown was brutally efficient. Bobby didn't hurt me any more than he had to, just enough to take me out. Like a surgeon kicking someone's ass surgically. I wish I could have seen it, but I was too busy getting knocked unconscious.

When I woke up, my face and ribs hurt like hell. I lay on the ground staring at the cottage cheese ceiling, in no hurry to go anywhere. I finally sat up feeling a little nauseous, but I kept the sick in check. Luckily I was out of cigarettes or I would have been an idiot and lit one, which most likely would have turned my intestinal rumbling into a volcano (if that's too subtle, my vomit would have been the magma).

I stood, got woozy, sat back down, took a few deep breaths, and tried again. I had a light headspin, but I wasn't going to topple. I opened the closet door, confirming what I already knew. The big bag of guns was gone.

"Fuck it," I said.

I rolled up my sleeping bag, gathered my gear, gave the motel door a hearty slam on the way out, and headed home.

SEVEN

I made it to Salton City, halfway home. I pulled over into the dirt lot of a closed fruit stand, rows of date palms behind it. Painted with a roller on the side of the yellow building, it read, DATE SHAKES-FRESHEST. The leaning structure looked just as run-down as when I was a kid. On our rare out-of-town trips, Pop and I would stop at that stand and get date shakes. It's funny how my city friends made faces when I mentioned drinking date shakes. Dates are delicious. Ice cream is delicious. Both are sweet. Ergo, sweet and delicious. Maybe it's because dates are brown and if you close your eyes, they have the texture of cockroach. But still, it's not marmite.

I dug my phone out of my pocket and tried Bobby's cell. It went to voice mail.

"Bobby, if you get this, stop what you're doing. I don't know what you're doing, but whatever it is, stop. Sit on the ground, call me, we'll go from there. Don't move, don't shoot anyone, and if you do, for the love of Edwige Fenech, don't kill them. Just don't. Call me, damn it."

Of all the places Bobby might head, the most obvious was Driskell's. According to Gabe, Julie worked for Driskell. He made the movie and was into some bad shit. Bobby would want to finish their conversation, and knowing Bobby, even if he couldn't get information from him, he would still feel the need to punish.

It was still too early to call Angie. I don't know if she would know what to do, but I sure as hell didn't. I turned my truck around and headed back north.

———————

Driving back to La Quinta, I hoped the feeling in my gut was an overreaction. As much of a complete barbarian as I paint Bobby, his violence had limits. Didn't it? He wasn't a killer. He was a brawler. Bar brawls existed to battle his boredom, but nothing had been at stake before. With his daughter's life on the line, who knew what he was capable of? And he was hauling around a big bag of guns.

The sun hadn't risen, but its orange glow illuminated the streets of La Quinta. Other than a couple overzealous joggers, an old guy in slippers and pajamas angrily walking his Shih Tzu, and a group of Mexican laborers staking the good spots in front of the U-Haul, the streets were empty. As I drove down the main road, the streetlights turned off.

Calle Tlaxcala showed no signs of life. I pulled in a couple houses down from Driskell's. I could see his Hummer at the end of the block. It was still ugly and stupid. No sign of Bobby's Ranchero.

I pulled out my fresh pack of smokes. I already wished I hadn't bought it. I wished a lot of things. I wished Bobby hadn't kicked my ass. I wished Julie hadn't gone missing. But I knew how much good wishing did. The last time I made a wish and it came true was my eighth birthday and two days out of its package, I had destroyed my GI Joe Transportable Tactical Battle Platform Playset with an M-80 and some lighter fluid. Cobra Command won that day. Wishes might come true, but that doesn't mean you can't blow them to shit.

I got out of my truck, lit a cigarette, and walked as casually as I could to the circular driveway in front of Driskell's house. Like the ashes at the bottom of a fire pit, all the remnants of the party were on display. Bottles, cans, and red Solo cups littered the small patch of grass. Someone had pulled a dick move and run a knife through part of the trampoline, leaving a huge slit. Nobody would have been doing much jumping anyway with the amount of vomit that had pooled in the tramp's lowest spot. I half-expected to find some prone bodies passed out in the yard or hedges, but apparently the battlefield had been swept for casualties.

The front door stood wide open. I let myself in, immediately stepping on a used condom. I scraped it off on the step. The house looked empty. Television voices—not live voices—came from the back. Muffled and strange, like they were broadcasting from overseas via ham radio.

The living room was a spectacular disaster. I felt for the crew of domestic workers that would undoubtedly be charged with returning the place to its original state. How do you fix a broken narwhal horn? Super Glue? The local narwhal horn repair shop, Narwhally World?

I followed the sound through the dining area and kitchen to the back room where Bobby and I had seen Tomás and Driskell talk hours earlier. The wall-mounted television played the same girl fight/gonzo porn loop. A too-young girl on her knees gave POV head to the cameraman. I would say that there was sadness in her eyes, but that would be me putting it there. There wasn't anything in her eyes, dead with acceptance. The screen had a crack in it, the sound distorted and ghostly.

I would have preferred looking at anything other than that poor girl, but my other option was the dead body in the middle of the room.

"Damn it, Bobby," I said softly.

Craig Driskell's body slouched off the edge of the couch, his bathrobe open wide to reveal his doughy, nude body underneath. I didn't see any gunshot wounds and I wasn't interested in getting any closer, but he was very dead. The skin on his torso was discolored in shades of purple, green, and yellow with bruises and still-wet blood, but it was his head that was all wrong. It looked like it had fallen in on itself, misshapen like a clay pot collapsing on a potter's wheel. And while the features of his crushed cranium could barely be described as a face, Driskell's wide-open eyes stared through the distortion.

Fists could have done that kind of damage, but it would have taken a long time. More likely a bat or a pipe or the butt of a gun. Someone had bludgeoned and stove in Driskell's head to the shape of a deflated basketball.

Dark blood speckled the couch fabric, small patches here and there. Whenever I think back, I imagine flies landing in the blood and on the wounds. I don't think there were any, but that's how I remember it. The room smelled like beef stew and feces.

Staring at the body, it didn't seem real, like a scene in a movie. I felt separated from the reality and had no idea what to do next. A dead body will do that to any normal person.

Finally, it flashed in my head—what I needed to do. I needed to get the fuck out of there.

I stuffed my hands in my pockets, trying to remember what I had touched. The front door had been open, I had walked through the house. Nothing. I hadn't touched anything. I'd take any luck I could get. But had Bobby touched anything? Then I realized, with the party the night before, it didn't matter. The place would be covered with hundreds of random fingerprints, footprints, and probably a dickprint or two.

A sound came from the living room. A footstep and a grunt.

"Goddammit! That's just gross," a male voice shouted.

Whoever was at the front door either stepped on the same condom as me, a different condom, or something equally disgusting.

I didn't wait to find out. I jumped down the three steps into the dead-man room. The thick shag made no sound on landing.

"Police! Anyone home?" the voice said. "We received a call about a disturbance. One of your neighbors reported yelling, loud noises coming from this residence. God damn, what a mess. Is anyone there? I'm coming inside."

There was only one other door in the room. I darted past Driskell's carcass, hopscotching over the blood on the carpet. Without looking back I opened the door with the heels of my hands and stepped into a long hallway. I ran to the end, the farther I got from the room with the dead body, the better.

At the end of the hall, I reached the master bedroom. Animal prints, chiffon, Roman columns. And yes, there were mirrors on the ceiling. I had to give it to the late Mr. Driskell.

He had awful taste, but he was consistent. There was also a full-size stuffed grizzly bear and a large mosaic three-dimensional penis, for the record. But the only thing I cared about was the sliding glass door that opened into the backyard.

I faintly heard the cop at the other end of the house wretch and say, "Holy shit." I was out the door, in the backyard, over the short concrete brick wall, and on the fairway of the fourteenth hole in thirty seconds flat. I leaned against the wall, completely out of breath from the half-minute of activity. I was embarrassed for myself. Without clubs or a cart, I probably stuck out like—well, like me on a golf course, but luckily it was early enough that all the golfers were still working the front nine. I made my way along the course and back to the main road without being seen.

I cautiously walked past the intersection that led down Calle Tlaxcala, just a regular neighborhood guy out for a stroll. The police car sat parked in front of Driskell's driveway. The cop fast-walked out of the house and slumped down in the driver's seat, leaving the car door open. He took some deep breaths with his head at his knees. Then he straightened, found the radio receiver, and called in.

In five minutes there would be a bajillion cops pulling fibers and canvassing neighbors. I had to get my truck off the street before they got there. Even the dumbass La Quinta cops would eventually get curious about the vehicles on the street. Especially one that had no good goddamn reason being there.

With the speed and posture of an old man, the young cop stood and walked back to the front door. He didn't look happy about it. The moment he was out of sight, I booked toward my truck. I had to get out of there quickly. On my first attempt to get my key in the driver's side door, I dropped my key ring. When I reached to pick up the keys, I accidentally kicked them under the truck. Of course. I dropped and dug around until I found them. When I rose, I realized the door was unlocked. I climbed inside, ducked down, and peeked over the dash to make sure the cop was still inside.

"Oh crap," I said.

I was facing the wrong way down a dead-end street. I couldn't imagine a fuckeder situation. To hell with it. I started my truck, threw it in reverse, and backed out of Calle Tlaxcala way too fast. At the intersection, I expected a car to turn onto the road and crash into me. But sometimes the bitch of a Fate that throws bad luck at me misses. I fishtailed onto the main road, threw the truck into drive, and headed east. Away from the death house.

I drove until I realized that I didn't know where I was driving. Five miles later, I pulled into the parking lot of a Circle K. I bought a bottle of Sauza and two packs of smokes. (At this point, who was I kidding?) I drank tequila from a paper sack and smoked three cigarettes back-to-back-to-back sitting on my tailgate.

I tried Bobby again, but he still wasn't picking up. I didn't want to leave anything incriminating on his voice mail.

"Call me back, Bobby. Goddamn it. Call me, you fucker."

Driskell was dead. And while I couldn't see Bobby entering the house guns blazing, I could picture him losing his temper and beating someone bad. If he had found out something else about Julie, something even more fucked up than the fighting, who knew what he was capable of. It wasn't like there were a whole slew of better suspects than the guy who had gone to the dead guy's house to assault him.

What had happened in that room?

And where the fuck was Bobby?

———————

Friendships start in strange ways. Single moments bond two people together. Or does it happen over time? As an adult, I have met people and known within minutes that we would be friends if we spent time together. It's a sense, an instinct. But as a kid, it had everything to do with timing and the moment. Bobby and I had gone to the same grade school, but it wasn't until sixth grade that we became friends.

Bobby would have been diagnosed with ADD, if that was a thing that the Imperial County School District recognized at the time. But that kind of language was a few years off. "Hyperactive" would have been the diagnosis and a paddle with holes drilled in it the best medicine to dissuade rambunctious behavior. Bobby wasn't much of a student, but as far back as I could remember, he excelled on the playground. Whether kickball, marbles, or a spitting contest, Bobby was the most vocal, the most outgoing, and the most unpredictably violent. He talked trash, but played fair. And rarely did a game end without a fight starting. Usually because of something Bobby said. Unlike now, he didn't win a lot of those fights. He was smaller than the other kids, and often got pounded. But like a miniature half-Mexican Cool Hand Luke, he always got up and it never stopped him from starting shit and scrapping the next day. That was Bobby's superpower. Even as a kid, he was fearless.

His reputation quickly grew. He might not have been the toughest or the best fighter, but he was unequivocally the craziest. He wasn't afraid of anyone or anything. And while I wouldn't say that he was feared, he was definitely avoided. You might beat Bobby in a fight, but you wouldn't walk away unbruised. He walked the playground as its king, even the dumbest bullies knew not to tangle with the force of nature that called itself Bobby Maves.

Back then I stayed away from Bobby. He scared me. That wasn't saying much. At that age, everything scared me. I had friends, but we were the smart kids. We were picked on, mostly threats and words. We spent recess indoors, idling away our time telling dirty jokes, playing with our pogs, and staying away from the Neanderthals who were threatened by any kid who got good grades and enjoyed reading.

So through grade school and into junior high, Bobby and I lived our separate lives, our paths occasionally crossing, aware of each other, but in separate circles.

I don't recall the exact chain of events, but at some point in sixth grade, I got on the bad side of José Ramos. It might have been that I had passed a test that he had failed or that I had made a bad joke or that he was just a dick, but I made it onto his enemies list. He was a mean little vato with a fledgling gang of underlings. At eleven, the top-button and hairnet mini-gangsters were probably adorable to grown-ups, but as a kid they terrified me. José was the youngest Ramos. And the Ramoses were a dynasty of schoolyard badasses, his five older brothers earning their reputations in fights that kids still talked about. José got the benefit of their reps, not having to earn his status. By name alone, he had become the leader of his little gang. He was a punk, but nobody wanted to mess with a Ramos.

So one day on the way to my locker, I turned a corner and José Ramos and his crew of *cholitos* were waiting for me. To this day, I take pride in the fact that I didn't piss my pants then and there. My small victories are often microscopic.

"Hey, pussy," José said.

I unconvincingly pretended that he wasn't talking to me. I looked over my shoulder, scoping out an exit strategy, but two more of his scowling cronies blocked my path. I swear that one of those sixth graders already sported a wispy mustache.

"I'm talking to you, Veeder. You're a big pussy, ain't you? Say you're a big pussy."

If you set the ball up in front of the net, I was going to spike it. It was instinct. I had no choice. Without a smile or any pleasure, the obvious joke left my mouth.

"You're a big pussy," I said.

José might have let it go, but one of his goons laughed, so José walked to me and punched me in the stomach. That was the first time that he hit me. It had all been threats to that point. Maybe a shove or a shoulder bump as we passed in the hall. But that punch was his first true act of war.

And here's where everything went tits up. It didn't hurt. The punch didn't hurt. At all. If I had been smart, I would have doubled over and feigned pain. José would have gotten satisfaction and avoided humiliation. They probably would have walked away. But for all the smarts I had in a classroom, in situations like that I was mostly moron. So José punched me and I stood there like nothing happened.

Before José could react, laughing began. Not from his friends, but that machine-gun laugh that hadn't changed in twenty years. Bobby, who had been watching from the vending machines, walked through the gang to stand next to me. Laughing the whole time and brushing past José's boys like they were a nuisance, Bobby held his side and wiped at his eyes. There were two of us and six of them, but Bobby wouldn't have cared if there were twenty of them. I was in awe. Scared shitless, but in awe.

"That was freaking hi-larious, duder," Bobby said. "I mean, the pussy line was funny, but it was kinda sitting there, you know. I could've made that comeback. But when he hit you and you didn't move—Bro, genius."

"Thanks," I said, glancing at José, whose face was red with anger. I waited for steam to come out of his ears, because if that happened in life, this was one of those times.

Bobby continued to ignore everyone but me. "You should've said something though, after he hit you. Like Stallone or Schwarzenegger or one of those action guys. You should've said like 'Next time, let a real man hit me, you know, like your sister' or 'Was that a punch or were you rubbing my stomach for luck?' Not those, something better, but that was like the choice place where you say a cool line, you know?"

"Totally," I said. But my eyes were locked on José and his boys. They were still there, still threatening. Bobby glanced over to where I was looking, laughed, and shrugged them off.

"Don't worry about those fags. Say one."

"What?"

"Make up an action-guy line." And then Bobby slowly turned to José and pointed. "And say it to him."

I swallowed. I was scared of José. I was scared of his gang. But at that moment, it was way more important to me that Bobby respected me. And I felt stronger with him there.

I gave it a moment's thought and said, "That punch was so weak, if it was hot tea it would be Earl Gay."

Bobby howled with laughter. "I don't get it, but I like it. Earl Gay. You're gay, Ramos! Classic. Another one."

I tried again. "You might want to go see the nurse, José. Because I'm pretty sure my stomach bruised your knuckles."

Bobby pointed at José. "In your face, Ramos. High five, buddy." Bobby and I high-fived. "You're Jimmy, right? I'm Bobby."

We've been best friends ever since.

For the record, Bobby and I got our asses properly kicked by José's gang. José might have hit like a girl with rickets, but his boys didn't. We fought gamely, but were outnumbered and still inexperienced. Lucky for us, we were children and kid fists were soft. Bobby and I didn't suffer anything beyond a few cuts and bruises.

Things changed that day. I had a new best friend. But more importantly, I wasn't the same scared kid. I got hurt, but I survived. Physical pain. Nothing more. I actually enjoyed moving my loose tooth around with my tongue. And getting jumped and outnumbered was nothing to be ashamed of. From then on, I had a confidence I hadn't felt before. And I had Bobby on my side. He would always have my back and I would always have his.

As the years went on, through violence and shared secrets, our trust grew river deep. Beyond a five-week period during sophomore year, nothing had ever come between us. That had been about a girl, our squabble an aberration brought on by the irresistible wiles of a fifteen-year-old siren named Ramona De La Rosa. Puppy love and hormones had pitted boy against boy. We both had failed to win her feminine affections, of course. She ended up getting knocked up by the Driver's Ed/Small Engines/Ag teacher, crushing our boy-hearts but strengthening our friendship. We chalked up the discord to the power of boobs (Ramona was blessed in that particular area). It was the last time we let anyone or anything come between us. Boobs included. Until the present.

I loved the goofy bastard. But I was becoming convinced that there was nothing I could do to help him. That Bobby was on his path and there was nothing I could do to change it. Kicking my ass to send me home was one thing. A homicide was a whole different ball game.

What have you gotten yourself into, Bobby?

Other than drinking and smoking in the Circle K parking lot, I hadn't yet devised a real plan. The drinking and smoking was going swimmingly though. But it wasn't going to get things done. Neither was driving around aimlessly. I needed information and although I was hesitant to ask a favor, I knew someone who brokered that commodity.

Tomás answered after half a ring. "Jimmy."

"Did you talk to Driskell after I left?"

He waited a few seconds before answering. "A little bit. He wasn't exactly happy with me."

"Anything out of the ordinary happen?" I asked.

Tomás didn't say anything.

"Tommy? You still there?"

"You know something I don't. What is it you know?"

"So you talked to Driskell?"

"Yes."

"And when you left his house, Driskell was fine? Nothing strange? Alive and well?"

"There it is." Skipping about four questions, Tomás asked, "How did Driskell die?"

"Should we be talking about this on the phone?"

"My line is eat-off-the-floor. And what agency would monitor your calls? You're a farmer. The Department of Agriculture doesn't tap phones. At least, I don't think they do."

"It looked like Driskell was beaten to death."

"'It looked like?' You saw this?"

"Less than a half hour ago. I was there. Not for the killing. After. When I got back to the room, I told Bobby about Julie. I tried to stop him. We fought. A knockdown, drag-out. Bobby eventually got the better of me. I figured the first place he would go would be Driskell's."

"The way you describe it, you make the fight sound close between you and Maves," Tomás said.

"It could've been."

"Was Maves armed when he left?"

"Loaded for bear. Duffel full of killing power."

"Mystery solved, Watson. Bobby was packing and looking for a fight."

"Driskell wasn't shot."

"A gun is a heavy piece of metal. More than one way to kill with it. I could tell you stories."

"You could have killed him."

Tomás laughed.

"You knew him," I said. "It's not outside the realm of possibility."

"I suppose not. I have a reputation."

"If you killed him, would you tell me?"

"Of course not," Tomás said, trying to stop laughing.

"I have to find Bobby."

"No, Jimmy, you don't. You have to go home."

"That's what Bobby told me. I'm not going to—"

"Shut up!" Tomás shouted, showing surprising emotion. "Can't you see I'm trying to help you? It was a suggestion before, now shit is real. There's a dead body in a building you were at—in a town that don't get murders. Your best friend is a suspect, most likely the killer. You need to put distance between you and the crime, between you and that maniaco Maves. When he's ready, if he hasn't been caught or left a trail of bodies on his pump-action crusade, Maves will call you. You're the only one he'd call."

"I can't abandon him," I said.

"He abandoned you when he killed Driskell. Do the smart thing. Dead men can have a way of getting the living killed."

Tomás hung up, leaving me with more questions than answers and a fresh reminder that I had no idea what I was doing.

EIGHT

It looked like every police car in Southern California had crammed into the two blocks of Calle Tlaxcala. How would the cops parked at the far end of the cul-de-sac get out? Would they wait patiently? Or run around politely asking the other cops if they could kindly move their cars? I doubted it. As soon as their shift was over, they would drive over the lawns and mailboxes and any pets in their way. That's how desert cops rolled. Protect and serve this.

I barely slowed as I drove past the intersection. I wasn't going to learn anything by joining the circus of news crews and curiosity seekers. I already knew what was in the house. And on the off chance someone had seen me or my truck, best to stay clear.

I stopped by the motel room, hoping that Bobby had headed back, but there was no sign that he had returned. I asked the manager if he had seen Bobby or his Ranchero, but he told me that he doesn't ever see nothing. Never. Nothing at all. No one. That's the way the current residents liked it, and that's the way he stayed happy and in cheese dip. I was starting to have second thoughts about staying at the Date Palm. But the price was right. I paid for another night. At the least, I could stow my gear for the afternoon and who knew, Bobby might come back. The manager put the money in his pocket instead of the cash register. I doubted that was company policy.

I headed to Becky's to see if there was any news about Julie. Or if she had heard from Bobby. I wasn't optimistic, but at the least, maybe I could help her and Russell in their efforts to find Julie, while Bobby and his big bag of guns did God knows what kind of damage to the poor bastards in his path.

I parked my truck a block away. I resisted lighting a cigarette for the short walk and was proud of myself for my full minute of self-control when I reached the house without the aid of nicotine.

My phone vibrated in my pocket. I checked the screen and answered.

"Hey, Angie," I said.

"Needed to talk to you," she said.

"Yeah. I kept almost calling, but didn't want to too early. It's been a crazy twenty-four hours. Been up all night."

"Me, too. Last night, Juan—"

A loud, shrill woman's scream came from inside Becky's house. It made me jump and almost drop the phone.

"Was that someone screaming?" Angie said.

"I got to go."

I hung up the phone and tried the front door. Locked. I put a shoulder to it, hurt my shoulder, and decided that wasn't going to work. I should have known better. Front doors are always the most solid, the hardest to kick in. I remembered the sliding glass door that led into the living room from the backyard.

I bolted around to the back of the house, jumping at each window to get a look inside, but curtains blocked my view. When I reached the sliding door, I frantically searched for something to chuck through it. I found a large potted plant, picked it up, but stopped myself the moment before I released it. I cradled the big pot and tried the door. It was open. Unnecessary destruction averted.

The woman screamed again. I started and dropped the potted plant, shattering it onto the cement in a firework of dirt, clay, and plant. So much for not breaking shit. I threw open the door, got caught in the vertical blinds for a panicked three seconds, and rushed into the house.

Another scream. I hoped I wasn't too late. I followed the scream into the kitchen.

When I turned the corner, I was greeted by Bobby and Becky having desperate, groping, animal sex. Bobby stood on his toes, his bare ass clenching and unclenching with each thrust, his pants at his ankles. Becky sat on the kitchen counter, her top awkwardly pulled down, revealing one bare breast. One hand clawed the back of Bobby's neck, deep red lines on his skin. Her other hand grasped the paper towel rack for leverage. Becky's eyes were closed tightly. She let out another violent scream. Bobby breathed heavily, a sprinter losing his wind. The smell of sex filled the room.

I pulled a large pan from the hanging rack, held it in front of me, and dropped it on the floor. It sounded like a pan explosion, the metal clang bouncing and echoing through the room. Bobby turned, surprised. Becky opened her eyes. They went wider when she spotted me.

"What the fuck is this?" I said.

"Bro, can't you see we're banging?" Bobby had never been afraid to state the obvious. "You're ruining the vibe."

Bobby slowed his hip action, but hadn't given up. I think he had every intention of finishing what he had started, just as soon as I apologized and left.

"What am I doing?" Becky pushed Bobby off her, pulled up her pants, and adjusted her top. I instinctually turned my head to give her a little privacy. A weak gesture, considering what I had witnessed.

"Becky. Wait," Bobby pleaded.

Becky punched Bobby in the arm twice. Hard shots, but he took them, not flinching. "I can't believe we—a mistake, Bobby. That's what this was."

She walked to where I stood. She looked angry and embarrassed and small. I didn't know what to do until I realized that she was waiting for me to get out of her way so she could leave the room.

"Sorry," I said and moved to the side.

Becky shook her head. "People do dumb things when they don't know what else to do." She left the room.

I turned to Bobby. "What the hell, man?"

Bobby pulled up his pants. "My balls are going to hurt all day. They're all swole up like two blowfishes."

"I'm sure you know a few ways to relieve that pressure."

Bobby laughed. "I could write a book. You think if I did, people would buy it?"

"I'm out of here," I said and headed for the front door.

Bobby caught up and grabbed my arm. I turned quickly and knocked his hand away.

"You don't get to make jokes, Bobby. Not after you beat the shit out of me." I dropped my voice down. "And not after you kill a guy."

"Whoa there, Hoss. What the fuck are you talking about?"

"Did you go out to Driskell's?"

"No. I was going there next. I kind of got distracted by . . . things."

"You didn't go there? After you left the Date Palm?"

"No. Why?"

"Because Driskell's dead. He was beat to death."

"Fucking hell."

"I went over there looking for your sorry ass."

Bobby gave me a light shove. "Wait a minute. You think I killed him? That's why you're all pissed. That's why you're mad I was getting in Becky."

"I got so many more reasons to be pissed at you."

"All of a sudden I'm some fucking murderer?"

"If you didn't go there, where've you been? Why haven't you answered my calls? I left a million messages."

Bobby pulled his phone out of his pocket and pressed a button on the side. The phone chirped. "That's my bad. I turned it off."

"How do you get from kicking my ass—fuck you very much for that, by the way—to screwing Becky in her kitchen? How does that happen?"

Bobby walked back into the kitchen. I looked at the front door, considered it, but followed him. He opened the refrigerator, pulled out two beers, and tossed me one. I set it on the counter. "I headed toward La Quinta—toward Driskell's—but I got sidetracked. I called Becky to tell her what we found, see if anything rang a bell. Figured she should know about the video and stuff. I figured Driskell could wait. I knew where he lived."

"So you came here and fucked Becky?"

"Step the fuck back, bro," Bobby said, slamming his beer on the counter, spilling some over his hand. "That judgmental shit is going to get your ass kicked twice in twelve hours. That's not the way it went down. I called Beck. She was a mess, by herself—Russell was putting up fliers—I sat in my truck—"

"It's a car," I said, and then held up my hands. "Sorry, instinct."

"I sat in my *truck* on the side of the road while we talked. She acts strong, the tough chick thing, but she's going through some heavy shit. She needed someone to listen. Russell's been great, but like us he's trying to fix things. I kept my mouth shut, let her talk. For the first time, she told me about those first years when Julie was born, when I didn't even know I had a kid. How hard it was, but how much she wanted to do it on her own. It was the longest talk we've ever had and we—it sounds stupid—but, we connected."

"It doesn't sound stupid," I said. "I thought you said you turned your phone off."

"Yeah, I lied. Didn't want to hurt your feelings. Anyway, I wasn't that far away, so I came over here. It was nice. Just the two of us. We have a kid together, but I don't really know Beck, you know. Never spent time together after high school. We talked on the couch for a long time. Calmed me down, her too. I don't think either of us knew how beat we were. I held her until she fell asleep.

"I was tired, but I couldn't sleep. I left her on the couch and tossed an afghan over her. Wanted to watch that fight on her computer. See it for myself. See Julie. See if there was anything, any clues.

"I found it online, a preview. It wasn't that hard. But the first time Julie got hit, I stopped. I couldn't do it. I tried to man up and watch it a second time, but no go. I ended up sitting on the floor in Julie's bedroom. For hours. Doing nothing. It's like when you're a kid and you want to crawl under the covers, because somehow it feels safer. You know it's not, but it is. I'm fucking scared, Jimmy, and scared ain't something I know how to do." "We'll find her," I said, knowing it was a stupid thing to say.

"Will we?"

I shifted gears. "Jump cut to the two of you in the kitchen. I still don't see how you get there."

"We were making coffee, talking. It was like a movie. She spilled some water, we both went to clean it up, our faces got close. And before I knew what was happening, we were attached at the crotch. Angry slam-fucking. She pulled my hair, scratching, screaming. She hit me in the face once. Not like a slap. Decked me."

The front door opened and closed. A voice said, "I'm home." Bobby and I looked at each other and mouthed the name "Russell" to each other.

"It reeks of fucking in here," Bobby whispered. "Smells like a . . . It smells like . . ."

"I don't think you need a simile."

"Yeah, I can't think of a good one anyway. Best I had was petting zoo, but that's more sawdusty."

While Bobby talked, he opened the broom closet next to the fridge, pulled out a mop, and poured what remained of a bottle of Pine-Sol on the floor. He pushed it around, the smell making my eyes water. I had the feeling that Bobby had been in this situation before.

Russell stopped in the doorway, wincing at the fumes. "Bobby, you don't have to do that." He gave me a nod. I'm pretty sure he had forgotten my name.

"Want to help out how I can," Bobby said. "If little things like cleaning help you guys, I'm more than happy to."

"Thanks. That's nice of you. Is Becky around?"

"In the back, I think. Haven't seen her in a while. When I'm in cleaning mode, I'm in my own world."

"I know how you feel. I'm like that when I'm baking."

"Are you sure we didn't take Home Ec together?"

Russell laughed, gave both of us a nod, and walked toward the back of the house calling Becky's name.

"You going to thank me now or later?" I asked him. "If I hadn't showed up, he would've walked in on your ass. Literally, your ass."

"He's a good dude. Now I feel like a prick."

"You think Becky's going to tell him?"

Bobby turned to me, obvious that it hadn't occurred to him that anyone would do anything but lie in the situation. "Let's get out of here. Maybe get a drink?"

"It's eight in the morning," I said.

"Breakfast?"

Bobby wasn't joking about breakfast. After some driving around, we ended up at Indio's attempt at an upscale café called Brewed Awakenings that was mostly coffee and day-olds with a side of teenage snark. Skewing their primary demographic, Bobby was the only Mexican in the joint. And while on paper the average age of the people in the place was forty, that's only because the employees were under sixteen and the patrons were over sixty.

We ordered overpriced coffees and overpriced scones and found a table in the corner. Bobby stared out the window. I stared down the shirt of the teenager at the counter as she leaned down to pick up something, caught myself, immediately felt like a pervert, and looked away. Even my eyes were failing me.

"You remember my old man?" Bobby asked.

"Sure. You talk to Rudy much? I don't even know where he's at."

"Still out by Coyote Wells, far as I know. He's sober now, but that don't make things okay or fixed. He stopped drinking. He didn't invent a time machine."

"What made you think of him?"

"Are you fucking kidding?" Bobby said with a humorless laugh. "He's all I've been thinking about."

"You're not him."

"No shit, but the father you become has everything to do with the father you had. I'm thinking that's one of the reasons I avoid my kids. I'm afraid I'll do the shit my father did to me. Made me turn out to be me. Trying to not accidentally or on purpose make a couple of fuckups."

"It's natural with what you're going through, to—"

Bobby didn't let me finish. He definitely wasn't interested in my boilerplate there-theres.

"It's like the old joke," Bobby said, "I didn't know my dad drank, until the one day he came home sober. All day, that son of a bitch was hammered. Rudy could knock them back. Fun a lot of the time, but that turned quick. As he got older, he got worse and worse. When the farm was tanking, he was too all-gone to step up. Drunk ain't a good way to save a sinking ship. My mother had to keep everything going. The house, the farm, me. And that made her old young. She was beautiful. You remember how pretty she was when we were kids?"

I nodded. "She made the best chorizo and eggs."

"No lie. Now she's an old lady. Not even sixty and she's just old. Worn down by my dad's shit and life and all the hard that comes with it. Am I different than Rudy? Am I?"

When I realized the question wasn't rhetorical, I answered. "You do your drinking. More than most. But you work. More acres than me. Never saw the booze get in the way. Until recently. With Gris and stuff. You're heading down a bad path. It ain't been good, man."

Bobby looked back to the spot he had been staring at. I followed his eyes, but there was nothing but empty street.

"I never told you, never told no one," Bobby said, "but starting when I was eleven—close to around when we met—my father would come home shit-faced, after drinking out at Portagee Joe's or by himself on some ditch bank. He would stumble into my room."

"Oh, Jesus." My jaw must have dropped, because Bobby immediately reacted to my expression.

"What? No, man. Not that. I wasn't molested. Are you kidding me? He didn't touch my butthole. Christ on a corndog."

"You said he came in your room at night drunk. I assumed."

"Let me finish, dumbass, before you jump to incestuous man-boy rape. I'm fucked up, but not that bad." Bobby talked to me like I was slow, spacing out each sentence so I understood clearly. "He would come in my room. He would wake me up. Make me get out of bed. Get dressed. I'd put my shoes on. We'd go out to the barn. And we'd box."

"Box? Like fight?"

"Yeah. I think my old man thought he was teaching me some valuable lesson. We wore boxing gloves, stupidly big on my little fists. It wasn't punishment. He needed someone to fight, but not someone who could beat his ass. Rudy ain't a big dude, but I was a fucking kid. Maybe in his drunk brain, he was toughening me up or some other bullshit. He probably wasn't punching full on, but he knocked me all over that barn. Beat me 'til I pissed myself the first time.

"I was game. I fought back. But I couldn't've hurt him. I was eleven. I could barely reach his face, so it was all shoulders and arms. After the first couple times, it became regular. Like maybe once a week, three times a month, he'd come home looking to spar. It got to where I would wait up, kind of wanting to go at it. I got used to the feel of it, getting hit, hitting. And I was learning. I might've lost at night to Rudy, but those losses translated to wins when I fought another kid.

"Then at some point—around fourteen—it changed. The whole time, he wasn't getting any bigger or stronger. He never improved, was always fucked up, and was the same little bully. On the other fist, I was getting bigger and stronger and better and I was stone fucking sober. Top of that, I was so used to getting punched, the pain didn't hurt no more.

"So one night, Rudy's all hammered, comes in my room and tells me to put on the gloves. I'm ready. I can feel it. I know one of these days, it's all going to turn. And that night, I went out to the barn. I could hear 'Highway to Hell' in my head like it was my theme song walking into a ring. I found my opening, slipped a jab, and I beat the holy hell out of him. Beat the living shit out of my own fucking father. Beat him for the three, four years he beat me. And when he hit the ground, I tore off the gloves and beat him with bare fists. Marquis of Queensberry could suck a dick. Beat him some more for all the things I couldn't think of. Drunk bastard cried and begged. It was the last time we fought—there was no way he would risk taking a beating again, defeated the purpose—so I beat him because I couldn't tomorrow.

"It was like my fucking bar mitzvah. That night I became a man. I'm not shitting you, the next morning I started shaving."

"Why didn't you ever tell me?" I asked.

"I don't know," Bobby said. "As stupid as it sounds, it was the only thing that was Rudy's and mine. Our only real father-and-son moments."

I called Angie, angry at myself that I hadn't sooner. All the drama at Becky's house had been a crazy distraction. She answered on the first ring.

"Are you okay?" Angie said, making me feel even worse for taking my time.

"It's fine. I'm fine. The screaming wasn't really screaming. I'll explain it later, but everything's okay. Sorry about that."

"I hate this shit," she said, just loud enough for me to hear.

"I know. It's not all the time," I said. "You were going to tell me something before."

"It's about Juan," she said, taking a breath before she continued. "He woke up a few times in the night. Nightmares. Shaking, scared, confused. I caught bits and pieces, but there was something. You need to come back."

"I want to, but a bad dream—"

"Juan remembers her, Jimmy. He knows that she's gone."

———————

When I got back to the table, Bobby was still on the phone with Becky. Her voice was loud enough on the other end that I caught most of it. She told Bobby that she wasn't a fucking idiot and she didn't tell Russell a thing because it never fucking happened and was he stupid and if he ever mentioned it again, she would castrate him with her crafting scissors. Bobby played it smart, apologized, and hung up.

Bobby turned to me. "Back to Becky's house, bro. We got work to do."

"Only to pick up my truck, Bobby. I have to head back, go home. It's Juan."

"What's up? Is he okay? Did he get hurt?"

"No, it's something else," I said. "He remembers Yolanda. I can't be gone while he's working this out. It's his mother."

"Damn. Yeah, I get it," Bobby said, chucking his coffee cup in the trash. "Let's go."

We left the café and walked the half block to Bobby's Ranchero. Bobby unlocked the passenger door, and then froze, staring at the key in the keyhole.

He turned to me. "I hate to ask, but can you give me a half hour? I know you got to go, but I need you to look at that fight of Julie. The whole thing. On a monitor, not a phone. I can't do it, man. I tried. I told you. It's too fucked up. It won't take long. I need you to sit at Becky's computer and watch that fight from beginning to end."

NINE

The streaming video opened with a cheap title straight out of a VHS exercise video circa 1987, but instead of some name like "The Exerfit All-Body System by Armando," they went with the considerably less imaginative "Extreme Girl Fights 18."

"There are eighteen of these? What's wrong with people?" I said to myself. I sat alone in Julie's room, but I could feel Bobby right outside the door, waiting to hear the verdict. Probably covering his ears. Definitely drinking a beer.

I had to become a member of the site "Gonzo Junction" to watch the full video. From the anatomy lesson I got on the home page, it appeared to be mostly a porn site with occasional dalliances in violence and fail compilations. The array of perversions presented as a free introduction made me feel like a Puritan. Whatever happened to the simplicity of penis-in-vagina sex? It was everything but, but especially butt. Straight sex was the poem that rhymed within a chapbook of avant-garde blank verse, pornographically speaking.

Giving these exploitative scumsacks my credit card information made me sick, but it was the only way to see the whole video. Luckily if they decided to rob me, they'd only get the eighty-five dollars or so that was left on the card before it maxed out. I wanted to sneak a quick smoke before watching, but knew that would be putting off the inevitable.

After the titles, the video opened with LaShanda hitting the open hands of a big Mexican dude. No gloves on either of their hands. She had decent form, but there wasn't much snap to her punches. Men laughed somewhere in the background. Getting a longer look at her, LaShanda looked younger than I had thought, sixteen tops. She wore a half-shirt and short shorts that showed off her dark brown skin. Her long arms were well-defined and her legs thick, the body of a sprinter. I wouldn't have tangled with her. A tale of the tape appeared on the screen as she threw jabs. *LaShanda. Aka The Black Bitch. 5'8". 128 pounds. Detroit, MI.* She looked at the camera and gave her best sneer, more theater than sincerity.

I made notes on a piece of paper, writing LaShanda and Detroit, figuring if Julie was using her real name, maybe LaShanda was too. She did her pre-fight warm-up in front of a white wall. The background gave me nothing to go on.

The screen cut to Julie, who shadowboxed, sweat already dripping furiously from her nose and the strands of hair that fell in her face. She turned to the camera and threw a few shots at it, then went back to work. She worked out alone. No seconds. She had excellent footwork and her hand speed was something to watch. Knowing the result of the bout, I could see how she overcame LaShanda's height and reach advantage. The tale of the tape came on the screen. *Julie. Aka The Desert Rat. 5'3". 117 pounds. Indio, CA.*

Jump cut to a group of men standing in a circle, a makeshift ring that the two girls would fight inside. They were between two buildings, somewhere industrial. White snow covered the ground, so light that the surface blew out, reading only as an overexposed glow. The girls faced off as they danced and peacocked. They taunted each other, barbs like "Imowna fuckin' kill you" and "You dead, bitch" and—well, actually that's all they yelled back and forth.

When the talk was over, the fight began. No Michael Buffer. No referee. No ringing bell. No explanation of the rules, if there were any. No pomp at all. It just started when LaShanda threw the first punch, catching Julie on the side of the head, the abruptness as jarring as the immediacy of the violence.

I've attended a number of violence-centric events calling themselves sport or entertainment or competition. I've been ringside at boxing matches and MMA cage matches and even pro wrestling. I've seen karate, capoeira, and a number of other displays of martial artistry, demonstrations that ranged from brutal to beautiful. Hell, I've been to bullfights, cockfights, dogfights, and even a rabbit fight (which still haunts my dreams). But two teenage girls whaling on each other beat them all for pure discomfort.

Watching the video had the same effect on me as getting in a fight. My skin quivered and my heart raced as the added adrenaline coursed through my body. I found myself making fists so tight that my fingernails left moons in my palms. I got a taste of it when I watched the preview at the party, but seeing the whole thing, I learned something I didn't like about myself. I found the video compelling. I know I'm talking about my friend's daughter fighting another underage girl. But there was something so raw and real and violent and wrong that made it hard to look away. The same human drive that made it impossible not to rubberneck a car wreck for blood and bodies. We can't control the primitive inside us.

When the two girls got in a clinch, pulling at each other's shirts, wiping streaks of blood on each other, the cameraman was forced to do a complete 360 to stay on the action. That's when I saw it—or rather, him. I backed the video up, waited with the mouse over Pause, and clicked at the spot.

"Bobby, get your ass in here. I found something," I yelled, turning toward the door.

But Bobby was already in the room. He stood in the doorway, watching over my shoulder. I don't know for how long, but long enough. He wept. Silently. His entire face contorted in complete heartache. His shoulders and stomach shook with each breath. Hunched over, holding his side, his body looked close to collapse. He wiped his face with his hand, tears and snot smearing his cheeks. He let his body slide down the doorframe and sat on the floor, broken.

I stood to approach him, but Bobby held up a hand and shook his head.

"It's okay, man," I said.

"No" was all he got out.

And I watched the most fearless man I knew finally confront true fear. For the first time I think Bobby recognized that this wasn't an adventure—a Mavescapade—but there was something real about everything that was happening.

Rubbing at his eyes, he rose silently and left the room. I didn't follow. Water ran in the bathroom and Bobby blew his nose. I heard Becky's voice. The two of them spoke softly to each other, a mother and father living through a nightmare. I couldn't make out most of what they said.

I only heard Bobby. "I'm sorry, Beck. For everything. I'll get her back."

When he walked back into the room, his eyes were blood-shot, his face red, and he looked a little shaky. He took a breath, pointed at the monitor, and said, "What have you got?"

I couldn't think of a way to console him, to be his friend. All I could think to do was get back to work. All I had to say was "Take a look."

I pointed at the monitor. On the screen, Julie and LaShanda were a grotesque paused blur, nothing but streaking color. The crowd behind them appeared in sharper focus. And there he was. Behind some screaming guys in the front row, Chucho watched the action with a stupid smile on his face.

"That rat fuck," Bobby said. "Somebody's lying to someone."

"Chucho told Gabe that Julie worked for Driskell. Maybe that was bullshit."

"Driskell did look surprised. With those two big guards, if he knew her, he would've been more overconfident, said 'I knew her, so what?'"

"Gabe could've lied too. Sent us on the wrong track. Chucho is his boy. He'd want to protect him, yeah?"

"We don't know where Chucho is, but I bet Gabe does."

"Looks like we're headed back to Thermal."

———

Bobby and I were silent for the drive back to Gabe's house. Not that we could have talked with the deafening pre-confrontation Grand Funk Railroad on the stereo. We stared out the front windshield, lost in thought and anticipation. Bobby was most likely bouncing concern for his daughter against the punishment he was about to dole out.

I couldn't stop thinking about Juan. I knew I needed to get home. Angie could only do so much. Their relationship was different. It wasn't fair to either of them for me to be gone.

But seeing Bobby crushed by that video, it was hard to take off in the middle. We finally had a decent clue. I decided to chase down this lead, but no matter what, to be home to tuck Juan in at the end of the day. A shitty compromise. But when you're in the shit, that's the kind of compromise you get.

Sleep-deprived, I had lost track of time. It was somewhere between late morning and early afternoon, the sun bright and hot. We rolled to a stop in front of Gabe's house. The neighborhood showed no signs of life, its residents working, looking for work, or on the couch giving poor people a bad name.

Gabe's motorcycle sat in the driveway next to the LeBaron.

"How you want to do this?" I asked Bobby.

"Gabe might've told us the truth, but we need to be sure. Need to find that Chucho. Hell, he might even know where Julie is. Gabe's scared of me. Let's make him terrified." Bobby reached under his seat, pulling out a pistol.

"Do you really need that?" I said.

Bobby didn't bother to answer. "Front door. We go in hard. Show him we're not fucking around. He's got answers. I know it. Those answers, they're our property. We don't leave without them."

Bobby rooted around deeper under the seat, found what he was looking for, and handed me a pistol. I would describe the caliber or brand or whatever else gun stuff I was supposed to know, but I grew up with shotguns and rifles. And while I had fired handguns, I knew shit-all about them. It was a revolver. I knew enough to know that. It had a short barrel and nice weight. I looked down the barrel. I opened the cylinder. It was loaded. I didn't know what else to look for, so I nodded.

"When was the last time you fired a gun?" Bobby asked.

"Few months ago. Rattlesnake in Juan's sandbox. Before that—" I stopped, remembering the time before that. When I had shot a man in the Algodones Dunes. A man who threatened me and my family. I didn't feel guilty, but I can't say it made me feel good.

"That going to be enough firepower for you?" Bobby asked.

"It's more than enough, but I'm not bringing it." I handed the pistol back to Bobby.

"You sure?"

"I wouldn't know what to do with it. I'm not going to shoot anyone. And the idea of waving it at that kid—I can't do it."

"Don't underestimate the effectiveness of waving a gun around, Jimmy. It gets the quick answers. And we don't have time to fuck around." Bobby returned the pistol he had handed me under his seat. "You want to wait in the truck?"

"It's a car," I said. "No. I'm coming in with you, but I don't need a gun to have your back."

Bobby nodded and jumped out of the Ranchero. I followed his lead, staying low like we had seen actors playing SWAT team members do in movies. We ran along the sidewalk, onto the dirt lawn, and to the front door. I was out of breath from the less-than-one-block of physical exertion.

"Are you kidding me? That's pathetic, man," Bobby whispered, shaking his head.

"Quitting made it worse. I shouldn't've quit."

"That is definitely not the moral."

I gulped in air. "Hold up, I got to take a puke."

I bent over a dead potted plant, but nothing came up. I tried to coax it by miming vomiting, but no bounty. I rose and gave Bobby a look of attempted grit and determination. I doubt I pulled it off.

"Sorry. I'm good," I said. "I'm ready."

Bobby shook his head and muttered something. All I heard were the swear words. He tried the doorknob, but it was locked. He shrugged. He knocked. We waited.

Angel answered the door, his drawing pad under his arm. Bobby reached in and pulled him toward us, getting one hand over his mouth. The drawing pad fell to the ground. I dropped to a knee and put a finger to my lips.

"Is Gabe here? Nod your head if he is," I whispered.

Angel nodded.

"Where in the house? In the bedroom?"

Angel shook his head.

"Living room?"

Angel shook his head.

"For crying out loud. Are you going to name all the rooms?" Bobby said, and then leaned into Angel's ear. "If I take my hand away, you promise not to yell? I hate to threaten a kid, but that's a threat."

Angel nodded.

Bobby slowly peeled his hand from Angel's mouth. Angel didn't look particularly scared.

"Where is he?" I asked.

"Garage," Angel said. "Working on a bike. What did he do?"

Bobby turned Angel toward him so that they were face-to-face. "Stay here. Sit on the ground. Don't go inside. You got me?"

Angel nodded and sat down on the step. I picked up his drawing pad and handed it to him. He pulled the pencil from behind his ear and started drawing.

Bobby and I tore into the house. We barreled through the entryway, turned at the small dining area, and rushed into the kitchen. Gabe's mother looked up from her cooking. A simmering pot on the stove filled the air with an aroma both oniony and sweet, a sauce or a stew that was going to be delicious and spicy. We stormed past her and charged through the garage door. Gabe's mother's Spanish curses attacked our backs.

In the garage, Gabe crouched on his knees working on a bike, wrench in greasy hand. It looked like an old Indian motorcycle, maybe from the late forties or fifties. It was only half-built, but it was a gorgeous piece of machinery. I don't ride, but I have always had admiration for good design. Our entrance wasn't exactly movie-ready, more of a stumble. Bobby pulled his pistol. Gabe knew better than to make any sudden moves.

"Remember us?" Bobby said.

"Oh, shit," Gabe said. The statement completely unnecessary. It was implied by the context of the situation.

I closed the door to the kitchen, muting Gabe's mother's cries.

Bobby pointed his pistol at Gabe's head as he walked closer. I stayed by the door, letting Bobby take the lead. At ten feet away, he stopped. His hand shook a little, but that only made the threat more real.

Gabe started to stand. "Easy, fucko. You're good there," Bobby said.

Gabe froze in an uncomfortable squat.

"You weren't exactly honest with us last night, were you? Didn't tell us everything."

"I don't know where Julie is. Seriously, Julie's Dad, I ain't lying."

"Why didn't you tell me about the fights? The videos? Your buddy Chucho?"

Gabe looked confused. "What fights? I don't know what you're talking about."

"You lied to me," Bobby yelled.

"Are you kidding for real? You kicked my ass, then you kicked it again. I'm gonna give you a fucking reason to do it three times? And then you let Julie's mom have a crack at my ass? I told you what I know. Truth."

"What about Julie and Chucho?"

"What about them? Wait, you think—"

"Where's Chucho? We got questions for him. He's the one we need to talk to."

"Chucho and Julie don't barely know each other. What did you hear?"

"You said Julie had a black eye? How long ago?"

"Month or so. A little before I stopped seeing her."

I had a question that had been buzzing in my head. "Chucho told you that Julie worked for Driskell?"

"Who is Driskell? I feel like I'm walking in on a movie in the middle. I don't know what the fuck is going on."

"Driskell's the rich dude in La Quinta. He said he hadn't met Julie. Ever," I said.

"Maybe he's lying."

"Or maybe you're lying. Or maybe Chucho lied to you."

Gabe didn't answer. Not out of defiance. He was thinking.

"Driskell's dead," Bobby said.

"No shit?" Gabe said. "I mean, since I didn't know the dude—"

"Someone beat him to death."

"That's fucked up." Gabe's eyes got a little bigger. "Wait, man. Did you guys kill him?"

Bobby didn't bother to set Gabe's mind at ease. "Where is Chucho?"

And then all hell broke loose.

The kitchen door swung open behind me, hitting me in the back and knocking me forward. Like a domino, I fell into Bobby. His pistol fired. When I righted myself, I saw blood spraying from the side of Gabe's head.

"Fuck, fuck, fuck," Gabe screamed, grabbing at the side of his head. I exhaled, relieved he was alive. The bullet had taken off a chunk of his ear. A lot of blood, probably hurt like hell, but not major.

Bobby looked as surprised as Gabe. "Oh, shit. It was an accid—"

Gabe threw the wrench at Bobby, who twisted in time to get hit in the shoulder instead of the neck.

"Don't kill me, don't kill me," Gabe yelled.

"We're not going to—" I said, but was interrupted by motion behind me.

I turned toward the kitchen door and got a face full of burning, Gabe's mother throwing the contents of the simmering pot in my face. Both the heat and the spice burned my skin, just below scalding. My eyes were on fire, stinging and wet. I pushed her back in the kitchen and slammed the door, trying to wipe my face with my shirt.

Gabe had found the garage door opener, the door creaking open slowly, morning light blinding in the relative darkness. I blinked out the jalapeño and onion, trying to get a gauge of the action.

"Don't kill me," Gabe pleaded.

Blood ran in lines down Gabe's jaw and neck. He and Bobby would be thanking God every day that he hadn't jerked the other way, a half-inch from a bullet in the brain. Why was his gun even loaded?

"Don't fucking move," Bobby yelled.

But Gabe wasn't taking orders. He scrambled to his feet and Indiana Jonesed under the rising garage door as the words were out of Bobby's mouth.

Bobby ran after him, ducking under the door. I took off after them.

Gabe headed toward his bike in a sprint, but looking over his shoulder at Bobby, he changed his mind. He juked right, fooling Bobby and causing him to trip over his own feet. It was a highlight reel move. The kid must have been a running back in high school. He headed into the house right past the drawing Angel, who barely looked up. Bobby got through the front door before me.

"Might got a weapon in there," Bobby shouted over his shoulder. "Watch it."

"He's just scared, man," I said. "A guy with a gun just threatened him. Shot him. What the fuck happened?"

When we reached the living room, Gabe sprawled prone on the floor. It looked like he had slid on the carpet trying to navigate the turn into the hallway. He scampered to his feet, but Bobby tackled him, just as he stood. He fell back hard, the bloody side of his head slapping against the carpet and leaving a Rorschach. Bobby climbed up his body until he lay across the kid's back. He held the pistol to the side of his head, pushing it hard enough to make Gabe's neck flex.

"What the fuck are you doing?" I yelled.

"Cut. It. The. Fuck. Out," Bobby said to Gabe, his mouth close enough to touch his good ear.

"Let's turn this down a notch, Bobby," I said. "Looking at the sitch, I'm thinking that we're the bad guys here."

Bobby turned to me, and then back to Gabe and the gun to his head.

"Okay," Bobby said, "I can see that."

"We're not going to hurt you, Gabe." I tried my most calming tone. "Well, not any more than we have. Honestly, that was an accident. Maybe you don't know nothing, but Chucho does. We need to find him to find Julie. Tell us where Chucho lives. We'll leave you alone."

Gabe's mother rushed in the room, Bobby's Plan Bs held high over her head. She was quickly becoming my arch-nemesis. I grabbed both of the steel pipes just as she was about to swing them down on Bobby's head. She froze, the arc of the pipes stopping abruptly. She looked at me, registered what happened, and let go of the pipes.

I stood there for a moment with the pipes held out in the air. Then the nice lady punched me in the stomach. The cigarettes, the running, and the uppercut did math in my guts. I puked on Gabe's mother's head, threw the pipes to the side, and grabbed her. She was strong, but I got my arms around her thick body. I felt bad about vomiting on her, but also because in my effort to subdue her I was grabbing her tit pretty hard. What can I say? It gave me the best leverage. I held her as best I could without hurting her, but that didn't stop her from screaming *mancha de sangre asesinato* at me. Bloody murder, to you and me.

"Por favor. Somos no aquí dolerlo. Queremos hablar. Sólo hable," I said, trying to explain that we only wanted to talk to Gabe. Which was admittedly unconvincing, considering that he was bleeding all over the living room.

Gabe's mother stopped screaming, the silence abrupt and jarring. It was like she had decided all at once that it did no good. But that's not really how screaming works.

"That's right," I said. "Let's all just calm down and—"

Then I saw why she had shut up.

Miguel, Gabe and Angel's five-year-old brother, stood in the hallway, his teary eyes wide and frightened. Angel walked in from the front door, more curious than anything else. The two of them stared at the two strange men assaulting their family.

"Quit hurting him. You're hurting him," Miguel yelled at Bobby.

Gabe held out a hand, trying to calm the boy. "I'm okay. I just fell."

Miguel wiped some snot from his nose with the length of his arm.

"You're right," Bobby said, looking up at me. "We're definitely the bad guys."

"Why is it everything we do turns into such a clusterfuck?"

"Bad luck? Probably stupidity. I get excited," Bobby said. "It really kind of snowballed."

"Definitely ain't bad luck if it happens on the regular. The gun didn't help."

"Don't blame the gun. It's the only innocent here."

"Except for the children."

"Right. And the old lady. And maybe even Gabe. Everyone but us, if you think about it."

"Let's salvage this."

Bobby got off Gabe. "Your brothers are here. They're scared. That's on us. I'm going to take a look at your ear, stop the bleeding. Do you want to call the cops? An ambulance?"

"Out here, they'd arrest me for getting shot," Gabe said. "How bad is it?"

"The bleeding is slowing. Need to get some pressure on it. It looks worse than it is."

"I can't believe you shot me."

"You ain't going to believe me," Bobby said, "but I feel like shit about that. I'll be civil from now on. But you need to know, you're going to tell me how to find that fuck, Chucho. You got to have an idea where he is."

Gabe turned to Miguel. "I'm okay, Miguelito. See, we're friends. Angel, take Miguel back to your room. Show him some of your drawings, okay?"

Angel nodded, took Miguel's hand, and they disappeared down the hall.

I let go of Gabe's mother. "Towels? You have towels? Toallas?" I went into the kitchen and started looking through the cabinets. She pushed me to the side and pulled some towels out of a drawer.

When we got back to the living room, Gabe was sitting up. His mother pressed a towel against his ear.

"Tell me what you know about Chucho and Julie and I'll tell you where he stays."

TEN

When we told Gabe about the fight video and Chucho's appearance in the crowd, he had no trouble believing that Chucho was capable of some kind of involvement. But the timing concerned him. He and Julie had still been dating when she got the shiner. That Chucho and Julie were involved in something together behind his back really sat wrong with Gabe.

I got the sense that his feelings for Julie were stronger than he let on. And that his friendship with Chucho was struggling. Bobby and I had no evidence to suggest that anything was happening between them beyond the fights, but that doesn't mean he didn't infer it.

"Chucho and me, we've known each other since forever, like little kids," Gabe said. "He's a dumbfuck troublemaker, but it don't make it easier to give him up. But if Julie's in trouble and he can help, I guess I got to. And if he's still got her mixed up in that fighting shit, fuck him.

"I talked to him this morning. He wanted to know what I told you. Never mentioned Julie. I was fixing that bike in the garage for her, you know. Now I don't know why I am. Chucho said he was heading out to the desert tonight, that shit was too heavy, something like that. He'll be at the shop until then."

Chucho didn't really have a home proper. He crashed in a room in the back of a garage in an industrial section of southern Indio. As far as Gabe knew, if he wasn't with Los Hermanos, that's where he would be.

So that's where we went.

It was afternoon, but Sanchez Motorcycle Service & Repair was closed up tight. Razor wire over chain link surrounded the expansive property, which consisted of a wide parking area with two dozen motorcycles in it and the main building, which had four garage bays and a door leading into an office. Only one window, the office, but it was so covered in product stickers, I doubted that anyone could see in or out. A coil of thick chain held the rolling gate onto the property closed, a big lock keeping us out. On top of that, a pit bull and a Rottweiler roamed the property.

We had swapped out Bobby's Ranchero for my truck in an effort for some anonymity. Also, Bobby didn't allow smoking in his sweet ride. We assessed the security of the garage. The only movement: the two maneaters that looked like they could swallow a hand whole.

"You think he's in there?" I asked.

But Bobby didn't need to answer. Right as I said it, Chucho walked out the office door and lit a cigarette. His face was bandaged from our last encounter, heavy tape over the bridge of his nose. Bobby and I ducked down. But Chucho didn't look in our direction. He carried a big sack and poured some dog food into two bowls. It took the dogs about three seconds to scarf it down and bark for more.

Chucho scratched behind their ears. He flicked his smoke into the lot and went back inside.

"At least the dogs aren't hungry," Bobby said.

"Yeah, they'll just maul us, chew us, and spit us out. Great."

"You're a pessimist."

"We ring the bell, see if he wants to talk? Or would that be too easy?" I asked.

"Last time, he picked a fight. I knocked him unconscious. Once he sees us, what do you think he's going to do? Invite us in for high tea?"

"We wait for him to leave?"

"Yeah, fuck that."

"It's the middle of the day, Bobby. There's razor wire and dogs and who knows what the fuck else. We don't know if he's alone. We know nothing. I got bolt-cutters, so the gate's no problem, but I forgot my anti-dog repellent. And did we not learn nothing from our last front door attack? Which was less than an hour ago, by the way?"

"Apparently not."

"We did it your way at Gabe's. We can't do this stupid."

"You act like you've never broken into nothing before. Remember when we broke into Chad Garewal's shed because we thought there was a stack of *Playboy*s in there?"

"We were thirteen. We got caught. And it was *Penthouse*s."

"No, *Hustler*s."

"That's right. Oh, shit. I wasn't ready for *Hustler*. Scared my dick. Ruined me on vaginas for the whole year. Too anatomical."

"But if I remember good, we scaled a fence, climbed onto a roof, and all sorts of other *Spider-Man, Mission Impossible* shit.

We're grown men now. I think we can get in there with stealth and agility."

"I ain't been able to do a pull-up in at least ten years. And my agility broke up with me and took the vinyl years ago."

"Drive around back. See the complete layout."

I found the alley that ran behind the buildings. Brown grass poked through cracks in the asphalt. Two Dumpsters sat next to the fence. I let the truck creep past the back of the garage. There was no back gate, so at the least Chucho wasn't going anywhere except out the front.

The chain-link fence ran against the back of the building, less than a three-foot gap between the two. The dogs could get back there, and it looked like they did often. The ground was saturated with dogshit.

"See," Bobby said, "this is where our ninja training finally pays off. We park up against the fence, climb onto the cab or jump on those Dumpsters, toss a blanket over the razor, up and over and onto the roof. You see how they almost touch? Bing, bang, boom."

"Bing, bang, boom is right. You know how much noise that'll make? That's all chain link and corrugated tin. It's clangy. We'd need a distraction."

"I got an idea."

"Is it a Molotov cocktail?"

Bobby stared at me but didn't answer.

"You are not making a Molotov cocktail," I said.

Bobby and I watched a mangy orange tabby dart under one of the Dumpsters.

Bobby laughed. "I have an idea that's so crazy it just might work."

"You've been waiting your whole life to say that."

"I'm surprised it's taken me this long."

It took twenty minutes and about a pint of blood to catch that alley cat.

Bobby and I sat in my truck. We were back in our stakeout position, parked a half block up from the front of the garage. We kept our eyes on the gate. Chucho hadn't reappeared. He was still inside.

I held the cat in my lap, petting it lightly. My arms were covered with scratches and bites, but the little monster had finally calmed down. It was difficult to tell if the sound it made was purring or Satan trying to speak through its fangy maw.

"So getting the cat was easy. The rest of the plan should go like clockwork," Bobby said, feeling the three bloody lines from the cat's claws on his cheek. "Little fucker almost took out my eye."

"I'm going to name him Evil," I said. "Evil Van Der Scratchy."

"He's a bastard, but scrappy as hell. Got to respect that."

As if on cue, Evil bit my finger.

"Okay, that's it. I can't hold Evil any longer. Between the toxoplasmosis and the rabies, I'm thinking it's time to make our move."

"Waiting for the dogs to go to the back together. They've been making regular rounds, but one at a time. Eventually they'll go together."

Fifteen minutes later, we watched the dogs disappear around the side of the garage. Evil and I got out of the car to put the plan in motion.

"You're going to have to run, smoker," Bobby said.

"I can do it."

Bobby got out and grabbed my bolt-cutters from behind the seat. We walked toward the gate, me holding Evil. He had had it with being held. He was a feral animal, after all. Evil bucked and squirmed and scratched and bit.

"I should've thrown the evil bastard in a gunnysack." I got a better grip on his scruff and held him away from my body with one hand. He twisted and clawed at air.

Bobby cut the padlock on the gate and unwrapped the chain as quietly as he could. After what felt like forever, he rolled the gate open a few feet and whistled. The dogs came running from around the garage. I set the cat on the ground and Bobby and I ran like madmen back to the truck.

We hopped into my truck, watching the opening in the gate. The cat plopped down onto the ground, not threatened at all, wriggling as if it wanted its tummy rubbed.

"The dogs saw Evil. Why aren't they chasing the cat?" I said. "Dogs chase cats. For the millionth time, I've put my faith in the accuracy of cartoons and been disappointed by the outcome."

"Maybe they're pets, for show. Not vicious, just look the part."

"Wait." I pointed to the gate. "Check it out."

One of the dogs poked its head through the opening in the gate. The cat hissed and took off down the street. The pit bull didn't chase, but instead walked out onto the sidewalk, testing its freedom. The Rottweiler followed. And without looking back, they headed down the street away from the garage at the most leisurely pace. Off on a new doggy adventure.

"They didn't care about the cat. They just wanted out," I said.

Bobby drew two pistols from his belt and handed one to me. For Gabe, a gun didn't make sense. But for a punk like Chucho, I didn't argue. I took the pistol and nodded.

"Gate, check. Dogs, check. Let's give our regards to Chucho," Bobby said.

"And let's hope it's just him in there."

Bobby and I hopped out, guns in hand, and took off in a sprint for the gate. Once on the property, we hit the perimeter and moved along the fence toward the office door, the only visible entrance to the building. All the garage doors were shut.

We put our backs against the wall next to the door, both breathing heavily. I felt a little light-headed from the run. I really had to take better care of myself. I felt like a sixty-year-old man's grandfather. Bobby reached for the knob and gave it a try. He looked at me and shook his head.

That's when the dogs came back.

Apparently their incredible journey was a short one, their wanderlust limited to a jaunt around the block. The pit bull spotted us first as it sauntered back onto the property. It barked and the Rottweiler followed suit. Their lips curled up at the side, saliva dripping from their long teeth.

"Oh, fuck," I said. Because there's nothing else that anyone has ever said in that situation.

The dogs ran at us, feet skidding on the asphalt. Bobby fired two quick shots at the doorknob. It disappeared, leaving a hole in its place. He kicked open the door and rushed inside the office. I was right behind him, but dogs are fucking fast. I felt teeth latch onto my ankle like a bear trap. I fell inside the door, my leg still outside in the dog's mouth.

I dropped my pistol and watched it slide under the couch against the wall.

"Get it off me!" I screamed. The dog jerked my leg back and forth, trying to tear it off.

Bobby pointed the pistol at the dog.

"Shoot it," I said. "Shoot the fucking thing."

Bobby shook his head and jammed his pistol in his belt.

"What the fuck are you doing?" I screamed.

"I can't."

"Yes, you can. Sure you can. Shoot the dog."

Bobby leaned down and punched the dog hard between the eyes. It whimpered and loosened its grip on my ankle long enough for me to scramble inside and kick the door closed. The dogs scratched and barked and threw their bodies at the door.

Bobby wheeled, waved his gun around the office. Nobody there.

"I can't believe you wanted me to shoot a dog," he said.

"The fucking thing was eating my leg," I said. I took off my shirt and wrapped it around the wound. There was a lot of blood and it was going numb.

"You shoot a dog, that's like a one-way ticket to Hell. It's just wrong. I couldn't do it," Bobby said.

Chucho et al (if there was an et al) had to have heard the gunshots and the dogs and the racket we had made. We had to move quickly. Without a knob, the door to the yard wouldn't stay shut. Bobby slid a desk in front of it. I got up and helped. I couldn't put all my weight on the leg, but I could walk. At least, short distances.

A big window looked out into the garage area from the office, but it was pitch-black. There were two doors, one into that garage, the other led farther into the building. A loud metal bang came from the garage, followed by a barrage of swearing in Spanish.

Bobby threw open the door and disappeared into the darkness of the garage. I hopped after him, but the pain kicked in and my leg gave underneath me. I leaned against the doorjamb and felt along the wall for a light switch.

A gun fired, the flash bright but not revealing anything. The bullet pinged off at least two metallic things.

"We just want to talk," Bobby yelled.

"Stay the fuck away," a voice yelled back.

Another shot fired. I caught sight of the light switches in the brief flash. I counted three to myself, and then jumped up and hit all the switches. The garage lit up in the brightness of the fluorescents. Bobby hunched behind a large rolling tool cabinet. It was old and heavy and the thick steel looked like it could withstand a howitzer. I scanned the rest of the garage but couldn't see anyone else.

"Where is he?" I said.

Bobby pointed toward the far corner and a row of metal shelving that held various parts and tools. Chucho was cornered, but he would be able to see out through the openings better than we would be able to see in.

"Chucho, we didn't come here to do anything but talk," Bobby yelled.

"Fuck you, whoever fuck you are. You shoot the door, Goyo's dogs, and then tell me you're here to talk? I ain't stupid."

"We didn't shoot the dogs. Listen. You can hear them barking."

"I ain't going to let you do me like Craig."

Chucho fired again. It ricocheted off the top of the tool cabinet and knocked a can of motor oil off a shelf.

"Fuck this," Bobby said. Staying low behind the rolling steel cabinet, Bobby pushed it, crab-walking, toward Chucho's position. As he got closer, Bobby put his back to the cabinet and pushed it as fast as he could. The cabinet crashed into the shelves. The shelves tilted but didn't fall. Parts fell down. From Chucho's yelps, it sounded like some of them hit him.

"What the fuck?" Chucho said.

Bobby crashed the cabinet against the shelves again. That was the one. The shelving fell inward, all the heavy parts and tools falling with the shelves onto Chucho. Bobby quickly jumped on top of the shelving, gun pointing into the mess.

"Don't," Bobby said.

"Okay, okay," Chucho said.

I hopped closer, using the wall and anything else to keep my balance.

Bobby reached into the pile of parts and came up with a small pistol. He shoved it into his waistband. "Keep your hands away from your body. Don't fucking move. You don't know how much I want to shoot you." Bobby lifted the metal shelving up at the edge.

Chucho avoided any sudden moves and slid out from underneath the shelving. He lay on the greasy floor, breathing heavily. He looked like he had a few fresh cuts and bruises.

"Can you stand up?" Bobby asked.

Chucho nodded and stood slowly. Hopping on one leg, I patted him down and checked his pant legs for any weapons. I found a lettuce knife in his boot and pocketed it. I sat on a stool over by a workbench and gave my leg a rest.

"Don't kill me," Chucho said.

"I'm not here to kill you, you asshole. I didn't shoot at you once. You were the one doing the shooting," Bobby said.

"You broke in, had guns," Chucho countered.

"If I wanted to kill you, don't you think I could've by now?"

Chucho was about to answer, but the door to the office slammed open. We all jumped and turned at the noise.

Julie walked toward Bobby and Chucho from the office. She wore a pair of cutoff jeans and a T-shirt that said "Bitch" in glitter across the front. More importantly, she held a revolver pointed directly at Bobby. She did not look scared, her hand held frighteningly still considering the weight of the gun. Instinctively, Bobby had his pistol up and pointed at his daughter.

"No, no, no," Chucho and I said in unison, the two of us immediately becoming distant bystanders in what I hoped wasn't an unfolding tragedy.

"Julie. Thank God," Bobby said, his gun hand falling to his side. "Holy shit is it good to see you."

"What are you doing here?" Julie asked, her gun hand still steady and straight and aimed at Bobby.

"You can put the gun down."

"What are you doing here?"

"I've been looking for you. Oh, Christ, I thought you might be dead or hurt or I don't know what. You won't believe the shit we've been through. I'm here to save you."

"What was all the shooting?" Julie asked. Then she saw Chucho. "Did you hurt him?" It almost looked like she was smiling.

"Put the gun down, sweetie. I know it's been scary, but you're safe now. Your mother and I have been freaking out.

We didn't know where you were. If you were okay. What happened?"

Julie didn't respond. She stared back at Bobby. The expression on her face, some sick combination of anger and amusement, made my stomach queasy.

"It doesn't matter," Bobby said. "I don't care what happened. I'm taking you home, sweetie. All this is over."

"Why would you care?" Julie said. There were tears in her eyes, but she wasn't crying.

"I'm your father. Of course I care."

Julie laughed. And then she shot Bobby.

PART TWO

ELEVEN

Jail cells aren't the most conducive environment for sound sleep. Take my experienced word for it. A veteran of over-nights in the hoosegow, I'd been brought in for more than my fair share of drunken brawls (thinking I was impressing a girl I wanted to have sex with) and been thrown in paddy wagons at more than one protest march (thinking I was impressing a hippie girl I wanted to have sex with).

Many people's biggest fear of jail is that you have to keep one eye open for the possibility that your cellmate's crush has graduated to the physical stage of the relationship, but that's more a prison thing. In county jail, it's far more likely that your fellow incarcerates have developed a grudge against society and need to actualize that aggression on something soft and punchable. Still not a best-case scenario, but at least the scars are visible.

And even if you get the cell to yourself, the sounds of the men that surround you are more than enough to keep you awake. The dark rainbow of human experience voiced through the cries of the detained. Past the almost-pleasant snoring and farting lie the grim sounds of crying, vomiting, and helpless murmuring. Beyond those auditory tragicomedies, all that remain are the grotesque, abstract sounds that are definitely violent, though amorphous.

Not a place for some shut-eye, when the only bedtime story you might hear is a deep baritone threatening you. And instead of sheep, you'll be counting the mistakes that put you behind bars. And the only stuffed animal you'll be hugging is . . . You get the picture.

———————

I'd been awake over forty hours. I figured that my body would eventually shut down. No such luck.

Hours after the cops brought me to the holding cell at Indio Police Department headquarters, I lay wide-awake, dog tired, and staring at the ceiling. The room had no bars, only a locked door with a small, wire-reinforced window. The only furnishings were a slab bolted to the wall that acted as both bed and bench, and a stainless steel sink and toilet with no seat. I had no idea of the time. It was still quiet outside the door, so I assumed that it was before midnight. Police stations get louder once the late-night drunk rush kicks in.

I stretched my arms and legs, the screaming pain in my bandaged calf reminding me that a dog had gnawed some of the meat off my drumstick. According to the paramedic, the dog had chomped down hard, but not enough to warrant a hospital visit. I asked her about rabies shots. She said that was for strays. I attempted to bribe her to tell the cops I needed to go to the hospital, but the fourteen dollars I had failed to impress her.

I shifted to a sitting position. My face itched like hell and I felt a few blisters that had formed from Gabe's mom's sauce.

There was no mirror, but I imagined that I looked like Two-Face, except the blisters covered my entire face. One-Face.

I got up and walked to the door. My leg throbbed but held my weight with only a slight limp.

"Hey! Anyone out there?" I shouted.

A middle-aged Mexican man's round face filled the small window. His voice was muffled through the glass. "What?" he asked.

"When do I get my phone calls? I need to talk to my family."

"Not my job."

"Any news about my friend? His name is Bobby Maves. Robert Maves. They took him to the hospital when I got brought in. He was shot."

"Not my job."

"Yeah, but you can find out, right? Ask someone?"

"That's not my job."

"You're just going to say that, no matter what I say, aren't you?"

"Not if you ask me something that is my job."

"What's your job?"

"I'm a security officer. I guard."

"And?"

"That's it."

"And you're guarding right now?"

"Doing a good job of it, too. You're in your cell. Another successful day. I might get a gold star on my report card."

"And you won't do anything that isn't guarding?"

"Not my job."

"I fucking hate mediocrity."

The guard looked at me. He might have been thinking of something to say. He might have been considering giving me a blanket party. He might have been working out a plot point for his *Gor* fan-fiction novella for all I knew. Whatever thoughts had passed through his fat brain, he had thought better of it and walked his fat legs back to wherever he stationed his fat ass.

Damn screws. They never gave a con a break.

Not surprisingly, the local PD didn't take kindly to two maniac vigilantes breaking and entering and getting shot in the middle of their town, even if it was in the service of said maniacs looking for a missing teenage girl. They hadn't officially charged me with anything yet, and hopefully wouldn't. Maybe trespassing, but without Chucho, they didn't really have any other story besides Bobby's and mine. And it was Bobby who got shot and me who got dog-chawed. That's not to say that we hadn't committed a few criminal violations. Was accessory to punching a dog in the face a crime? I tried shifting my thoughts to something that made me happy, but thinking about my family only made me feel useless.

What the fuck was I doing here?

I had tried to help my best friend. Tried to save a lost girl. Tried. Then it all went to shit. Noble, schmoble. It didn't matter why I did the thing, only the result. It's like I was constantly driving recklessly on the road to Hell (fueled by good intentions, of course). But staying in the fast lane the whole time, the only way to take the off-ramp was to cut everyone else off.

When Julie shot Bobby, everyone in the room felt the immediate wrongness of the act, the Greek tragedy of it, the shock and inevitability rolled together. For the briefest of moments, the world froze. And despite the other shots that had been fired, the single gunshot from Julie's gun was the one that lingered in the air. Nobody moved. Not me. Not Julie. Not Chucho. Not even Bobby. The movie froze to a still photograph. A bloody version of Cartier-Bresson's decisive moment.

Then Bobby fell, blood blossoming onto the front of his shirt. His pistol plunked to the floor, hand reaching to stop the flow of blood escaping from his left shoulder. But it was his eyes that told the story. Bobby never took them off Julie. Sad eyes that didn't understand.

Freed of Bobby's weight, Chucho scrambled from underneath him. He picked up Bobby's gun and briefly pointed it at Bobby. I don't even think he knew I was there. He decided against it and hobbled to Julie. Still pointing her gun at Bobby, Julie looked like the child that she was. Small and alone and surprised by her own capability. She snapped out of it and let out a small laugh. Chucho pulled her toward the office door. Once she turned, she never looked back at what she had done. Then they were gone.

I grabbed a fistful of dirty rags from the ground, ran to Bobby, and pressed the wadded-up mess against his shoulder. It quickly became saturated with blood. I reached my hand around his back to feel for an exit wound. There wasn't any, but I didn't know if that was bad or good. At least it was one less hole to plug up.

"She shot me," Bobby said.

Chucho's motorcycle revved to life outside, disappearing quickly.

"My girl shot me."

"We'll get you to a hospital. Just hold on. You're going to be okay." I dug around my pocket for my phone while trying to maintain pressure on Bobby's wound.

"I don't want Julie to feel bad. About shooting me. I don't want her to be sad about shooting her old man."

"Doesn't really matter right now, but okay."

"Kids do stupid shit."

"I'm sure she didn't mean to. She was scared."

"No, she meant to. That's not the thing."

Bobby's eyes went a little glassy.

"We'll talk about this later." I shook him. "Stay with me, Bobby. Try to stay awake."

Noises came from the office.

"See. Someone's here already. You're going to be okay."

"You didn't call no one," Bobby said, his voice slurring.

He was right. EMTs or an ambulance would've had to already be parked out front. It wasn't the paramedics. It wasn't firemen. Hell, I would have settled for a Reiki Master or intuitive healer at that moment.

It wasn't even a someone. It was those fucking dogs again.

"Of course," I said.

The two dogs stood in the office doorway, drooling and staring and working on their horror movie personae. Luckily Chucho had only grabbed Bobby's pistol and had forgotten about his own. I rolled Bobby over. He grunted in pain. I grabbed Chucho's pistol from his waistband and pointed it at the dogs.

"You fuckers even think about it and I'll plug you both. I swear to God."

I fired a shot just to the left of them. The dogs jumped and yelped, frightened by the sound. They didn't exactly run away, but they retreated, doing their best to maintain their dog dignity.

I finally dug out my phone and called 911. I gave the too-calm lady our location and told her that my friend had been shot, but kept the details vague. She instructed me to be patient and apply pressure to the wound.

Patience. Pressure. I would have repeated it as a mantra, if Bobby and I didn't have a few things to discuss before he passed out and the ambulance arrived.

After all, we had to get our story straight.

The cops came with the ambulance. After the paramedic lady patched my leg, I went with the cops. Bobby went with the ambulance. They were cool enough to tell me that it looked like he was going to be okay, that the bullet wound appeared to come from a small caliber, and that it hit high enough to dig into the meat of his upper pec muscle. They weren't cool enough to let me go.

The EMT handed me off to a very patient, or possibly bored, detective who took my statement. I told mostly the truth, although I didn't mention the guns we had brought. Mine was still under the couch in the office and Chucho's was at the bottom of a big drum of used motor oil, a needle in the haystack of the very messy garage.

The gist of my statement was that Bobby's innocent teenage daughter had gone missing. We had reason to believe that she was at the garage with her boyfriend, Chucho. The gate had been unlocked and open. Thinking that the garage was open for business, Bobby had gone into the office. I had waited outside. The dogs attacked me. Someone shot Bobby, he didn't see who.

To his credit and damn him, the detective had some good questions.

"You say the gate was unlocked. Looks to me like it was cut with bolt-cutters."

"It was like that when we got there."

"It also looks like the office doorknob was shot off. Any idea why that is?"

"Yeah, I don't know. I'm thinking someone broke into the garage before us, robbing the place or something. We maybe walked in on them. Probably who shot Bobby."

"Why did you go onto the property if those two big-ass dogs were in there?"

"Obviously I wouldn't've. I didn't know they were there. They must've been around back. I'm stupid, but not that stupid."

"And you didn't see nobody? You were outside and you didn't see no one?"

"No, sir."

"How many shots were fired?"

"I don't remember. At least one."

"Closer to one or five?"

"I seriously couldn't tell you. There were dogs mauling me."

"Uh-huh."

"Should I have a lawyer here? Am I in trouble?"

"Do you have something to hide?"

"No. It's more of a specific, should-I-call-a-lawyer-right-now kind of question, not so much a general, you-have-the-right-to-an-attorney kind of question."

"I'm trying to determine the events leading up to your buddy getting shot. Who did it and why that person ran. Especially since it was you doing the trespassing. Tends to suggest there was something more going on. Maybe even something to do with the missing girl."

"I get that. I'm just saying that I was the guy outside who got attacked by dogs. That was my role in the whole thing."

"Yeah, I'm hearing you. Can't say I believe it, but I'm pretty sure you didn't shoot your buddy."

The detective wrote some notes in his little book. He stared me in the eyes, one of those psych-out/lie-detector looks that cops throw at you. That look they think makes it seem like they're reading your mind, but mostly just looks like they're pinching mud.

I knew my statement was a house of cards on a windy day, but I wasn't going to be the one to tell the police that Julie shot Bobby. Although they might look harder for a teenage shooter than a teenage runaway. Punishing could be easier than saving.

The detective didn't press me any more than that. He repeated variations of a few questions mostly for clarity, and let it go at that.

That had been hours earlier. And other than my brief chin-wag with the guard, I stared at the walls and ceiling. I considered taking another stab at sleep, but my heart rate still raced from the action and I was antsy to get out of there.

The door to the holding cell opened. My fat Mexican friend filled the lower half of the door frame. Short and thick, he must have stood on his toes when he talked through the window.

"Veeder," he shouted.

"Why are you yelling? I'm three feet away."

"Your lawyer's here."

"Is he now?" I said, not knowing that I had a lawyer. I hadn't even made a phone call. A red-faced Mexican man I'd never met walked into the cell and thrust out his hand to shake. His suit was nice, but not flashy. His smile was artificial, but cordial. And his handshake was firm, but not finger-crushing. I liked him immediately, even though I knew that his likability was entirely manufactured.

He turned to the guard and dismissed him like a waiter who lingered at the table too long. "You can go, officer. I need to speak to my client alone, as is my privilege and right."

The guard nodded and left, head down like a disciplined puppy. I liked my lawyer even more.

"I am Hector Costales." I only heard his accent in the pronunciation of his name, newscaster-style. "I should have you out inside of an hour. I don't predict that charges will be filed. At least not until the investigation is complete. As you are a property owner, have a child, and are white, they won't see you as a flight risk. They consider you a witness more than a threat and know where you'll be if they need you."

I nodded. "Thank you."

Hector Costales continued to smile. "You're not curious who sent me? I would have thought that would be the first thing you would ask."

"It's not really a mystery, Mr. Costales."

"Hector."

"I don't have a lot of friends with lawyers on call. Or money. Or that give three shits about my well-being. Thank Tomás when you talk to him. Tell him I'll pay him back."

Hector nodded. "My client is not out of pocket. I am on a kind of retainer."

"The real question is how did he know I was here?"

"As you know my client, you already know the answer. If something happens in the desert, my client knows about it. It's his bailiwick." I'm going to sound racist, but there was something odd to me about a Mexican using the word *bailiwick*. It's the second whitest word I could think of after *insurance*.

"Any news about Bobby? Maves? Robert Maves? The guy I was with," I asked.

He checked his watch. It was a nice watch. "As of forty-five minutes ago, his condition was stable. He is at JFK Memorial here in Indio. I can take you there as soon as you are released. However, as he was brought in for a gunshot wound, the police might not let you in right away. They'll want to question him first."

"Yeah. I talked to them already."

"And told them nothing, I hope. That's what I advise you to do."

"Nothing but the truth. I didn't see anything."

Hector Costales winked. "Your timing is surprisingly good. The Riverside County Sheriff's Department had to pull some Indio PD personnel for a murder investigation in La Quinta. Understaffed, they're not going to want to deal with whatever scrape you and your friend Maves got in. A mystery not worth solving. The rare upside to racism and classism.

A dead millionaire in La Quinta eclipses a Mexican farmer shot in Indio any day of the week."

"God Bless America," I said, trying to read his face and figure out if Tomás had told him anything about my presence at Driskell's house. But Hector Costales might as well have been wearing clown makeup, with the frozen smile he had on his face. I wondered if he was crying on the inside.

———————

True to his word, I walked out of the Indio Police Department fifty minutes later with the sun setting in the west. It took another half hour to find the impound lot where my truck had been brought. It ended up being right next door to the station.

I thanked the good fortune that we had swapped Bobby's Ranchero for my truck. Who knew what kind of arsenal he had in that thing? Nunchakus in the glove box? A rocket launcher behind the seat? For all I knew, the whole thing was a fucking Transformer. Which would explain the bright orange and red paint job and racing stripe.

When the guy at the impound lot tried to brush me off and tell me to come back the next day, I went ballistic, throwing swear words around like I was the Johnny Appleseed of foulmouthery. Of course, that didn't help. But money talks. The fourteen dollars that hadn't impressed the paramedic was enough to keep the impound lot open an extra fifteen minutes. Fourteen dollars to one person could be a different fourteen dollars to another. There was a lesson in there somewhere, but I obviously wasn't good at learning from my mistakes or successes. I just plodded forward like the stupid fucking monkey that I am.

Driving to the hospital, I felt a sense of relief. Even though our quest had been an abject failure, we had found Julie and established that she was unhurt. We had also established that she was armed and dangerous. Sometimes you don't win the war. You don't even win any of the battles. All you have left to celebrate is the victory of getting home alive.

When Angie picked up, she didn't sound happy. "I thought you were coming home."

"I am," I said. "It went to shit here. Bobby got shot. I've been sitting in a jail cell for the last few hours. Just got out."

"Is he going to be okay?"

"Got shot in the shoulder. He's at the hospital. I'm heading there now. And then home. I should be back in three hours or so. Hopefully in time to tuck Juan in, maybe talk to him a little. If not, at least I'll be there in the morning when he wakes up."

"He didn't talk to me for most of the day. Really kept to himself, which isn't like him."

"I'm sorry I'm not there to help."

"You will be. See you soon. And Jimmy," Angie said, "I'm glad you didn't get shot."

The nightshift at JFK Memorial Hospital in Indio, California, defined chaos. In all its noise and turmoil, the waiting room bordered on self-parody, almost too over the top to be believed. It was like an angrier version of the DMV, but with dying and bleeding people yelling in Spanish and kicking vending machines. Okay, it was exactly like the DMV.

When I tried to cut in line to "ask just one question," the eighty-five-year-old man at the front of the line showed me the hilt of a hunting knife in his belt. As politely and quietly as I could, I made my way to the back and stood impatiently behind a woman who I was pretty sure was made out of tuberculosis. She coughed freely and wetly onto the head wound of the bleeder in front of her. With each violent jerk, her wig shifted on her head like a fried egg in oil.

After an immune-system-testing forty-five minute wait, I was told that I was in the wrong line talking to the wrong person at the wrong desk in the wrong part of the hospital. Through a mask of pure apathy, I was told that Mr. Maves was on the second floor in the Detention Unit and I needed to talk to the desk up there. I didn't know if she literally meant I needed to talk to the desk, but that's what she said. I thought about finding the old man who wouldn't let me ask my one question, so that I could kick him in the shin. But considering the efficiency of the hospital, he had probably already died. I let that thought comfort me.

As I stared at the wall directory, trying to make head or tail out of the maze, my newly appointed lawyer, Hector Costales, appeared, grabbed my arm, and walked me down the hall. He stepped quickly, forcing me to keep pace on my hobbled leg.

He handed me a suit jacket that he had gripped in his hand. "Put this on."

I did. It fit.

He handed me a comb.

I hadn't showered in a while so the greasiness made my hair stay in place. Poor man's mousse.

Hector Costales slammed on the brakes. Three steps later, I stopped and turned back to him. He looked me up and down and winced.

"It'll have to do. Try to keep the gimp hidden," he said.

He reached into his briefcase and handed me a legal pad and pen. An unintelligible scrawl covered the lines and margins.

"Stare at this like it's the most important thing in the world. Like you're studying for a test. Act like you're writing, but don't write. Those notes are important. Don't look up unless it's to make sure you don't trip."

And then he was moving again, not waiting for a reply.

DETENTION. Painted on the wall in thick, government letters so that there was no misunderstanding. It showed you how messed up Indio could be. JFK was a small hospital, yet there was an entire floor devoted to patients under police detention. Beneath the DETENTION sign was a hallway with a metal detector and, in front of that, a desk with a cop sitting at it.

Hector Costales picked up the only item on the desk, a clipboard. Using the pen tied to it, he wrote on it and handed it to the cop. No words spoken. The cop read the clipboard, gave us both a look, and nodded. He handed us each small plastic bowls. Following Hector Costales's lead, I emptied the contents of my pockets into the bowl.

Once we were through the metal detector, another cop took over. He conferred with the desk cop and then escorted us down the hall. When we reached the door to number 113, we stopped and the cop unlocked the door. The whole thing was done as efficiently and impersonally as possible.

The room looked like a standard hospital room, except there were locks on the cabinets and bars over the windows. There was no television either. Bobby lay on his back in bed, an IV running into his arm and his left shoulder patched up thick with gauze. He turned when we entered, a goofy smile on his face.

"Hey, buddy," Bobby said, slurry as a ten-beer night. "Can you check and see if this hotel has a pool? The mean waitress won't talk to me no more after I asked her for a handie."

"Maybe we should come back," I said.

"Why'd you bring Luis Guzmán with you?" Bobby pointed at Hector Costales. "I loved you in *Pluto Nash*."

"We'll come back later," I said.

Bobby's distinctive laugh filled the room. "I'm fucking with you, Jimmy. The painkillers are good, but this ain't my first demolition derby. My body has built up a tolerance to most forms of not-sober."

"Ain't really a time for jokes," I said. "I thought you might die. All that fucking blood. Cops and ambulances and doctors later, and everything is still double-fucked. I spent the day in a jail cell when I need to be home. You spent the day in a hospital—the detention area, I might add. Which is essentially hospital jail. Not very funny."

"Yeah, you're right," Bobby said. His voice shook a little. "I just can't cry no more. Spent the last hour, thinking and bawling. Like watching the end of *Rudy* or *Old Yeller* over and over. I couldn't stop."

"It's okay to cry."

Bobby shook his head. "You think I don't know that? Shit, man, when have you ever known a drunk that don't get weepy? You take me for one of them dumbasses thinks crying ain't manly? Crying ain't weak. Crying means you care. Means shit matters. What's manly about not giving a shit? Or caring what other people think? I'll make a fucker cry that thinks crying is stupid, see how he likes it to cry."

Bobby stopped, shut his eyes tight, and then opened them wide. "Okay, maybe the painkillers are a little stronger than I thought. My brain took a back road there." Bobby nodded toward Hector Costales. "You going to tell me who the Mayan is?"

"He's our lawyer."

"No," Hector Costales corrected me. "I am Mr. Veeder's attorney."

"What about Bobby?" I said.

"What about him?"

"I'm sure that Tomás meant for you to represent both of us."

"I am sure that he did not, as he told me specifically that I was not to represent Mr. Maves. 'That estupido Bob Maves is on his own.' His words."

"Why does Morales hate me?" Bobby asked.

"He thinks you're trouble," I said. "I don't know where he got that idea."

"He's a fucking super-villain."

"You did attack him the other night."

"He's always had a problem with me."

"When we were kids, you used to fuck with him a lot, call him Tommy Teto and *Where's Waldo*. Could still be mad about that."

"You forgot Mexinerd. In my defense, he was a ten-year-old that wore giant cataracts glasses and carried a briefcase around. Also, I was a dick back then."

"Even crime lords have feelings."

I noticed Hector Costales's eyelids drop a little on my use of the phrase *crime lords*. Lawyers preferred discretion. I didn't.

"If you're not here for Bobby," I said to Hector Costales, "then why are you here?"

"I am here because you wanted to be here. This was the best way to make that happen. Even family can't see him in detention. Only his lawyer. The men outside believe you are my associate. Not a lie, but not the truth."

"But you're not going to help Bobby?"

"No."

"Tomás said you're here to do what I want?"

"Please do not try to play the genie in a bottle game, wishing for three more wishes. I have strict instructions."

"He must have some serious shit on you."

"You have no idea." For the first time, his smile wilted.

"Can you grab me some coffee then? Is that within the parameters of your purview or whatever you call it? Bobby and I need to talk."

"Cream or sugar?" Hector Morales asked, his smile returning.

"Black."

"Can you ask him to bring in some doughnuts or bear claws or something?" Bobby asked.

"And a bear claw," I said.

TWELVE

"Okay, now that he's gone, what's your plan to bust me out?" Bobby said. "Climbing through the air ducts is a classic. I've always wanted to do that."

"My plan for busting you out is to wait for a few days until both the police and the doctors release you. Not as fast, but foolproof."

"You're no fun," Bobby said. "What are you going to do now?"

"Go home. All I want to do is hold my son. Be with Angie. Get back to being a boring farmer."

"I meant about Julie."

I parked a cheek on the corner of the bed. After the last few days, even standing felt like a chore. I rubbed my eyes with my fingers.

"What is there to do? I know she ain't home, but I thought we were done."

"We still need to find her," Bobby said.

"We found her, Bobby. We found her and she shot you. Not on accident, either. She thought about it and she shot you. I get that she's still not in a good situation, but she's not tied up in the back of a van. She might be into a bad thing, but she wants to be there. She had a choice back at the garage."

Bobby tried to sit up, but abandoned the idea. "Just 'cause she don't want to be saved don't mean she don't need to be. She's running with a dude that gladiators her out for pit fighting. He's got her turned around. Making bad decisions is part of a teenager's job description. Don't mean you let them do any old shit. If you looked out the window and Juan was building a bike ramp to jump over the Ash Canal, would you let him or stop him before he killed himself?"

"He doesn't know how to ride a bike yet."

"You know what I mean. When a kid's doing something stupid, it don't matter if they want to do that thing. What matters is it's stupid. So as a parent, you forbid the shit out of that shit. I'm forbidding Julie from doing what she's doing. She just don't know she's being forbidded."

"You find her, what do you do? Drag her back?"

"If we have to. She's sixteen. Shooting me is the last bad decision I want her to make. If I don't find her soon, she's going to make an even bigger mistake. She ain't safe. I know it. You know it."

"We don't know where she is. How would we find her?"

"Not we, brother. You. I know it's a big ask, but you have to look while I'm in here."

I pushed myself off the bed. For the briefest of moments, I considered walking out the door. It would have been easier than saying no, which is exactly what I wanted to say. At that moment, not only did I not know how to help, I didn't want to.

"I'm putting you on the spot," Bobby said. "But I need your help, bro."

"You'll be out of here in no time."

"Even then, I can't do it alone. My shoulder's going to slow me down. Muscles is all tore inside. You got to get on this. Before the trail goes cold."

"What trail? There is no trail."

Bobby looked away for a moment. "When have I ever asked for anything, Jimmy?"

I felt my face get hot. I let out a dry laugh. "Are you fucking kidding me? You call me at four in the morning all the damn time. Two nights ago I got my tooth knocked out. Which I'm sure you'll be happy to hear I passed this morning. Saw the gold crown just as I flushed. Not enough time to grab it before it went on its undersea adventure. When do you ask for anything? Every time you get drunk and half the times in between. And now you're asking for everything. I've kicked down my last door for you."

"I've helped you with plenty of shit. Big shit."

"Maybe I ain't as good a friend as you. Maybe I got limits that you don't have. I can only jump off so many cliffs before I hit the one that's too high."

Bobby turned to face me. "She's my daughter, bro."

"She is. But this trip hasn't barely been about her. This whole adventure's had less to do with Julie and more to do with your guilt. Or just something to do. Like a fucking quest. You're worried that if something happens to her, you'll blame yourself, won't be able to handle it. I know she's your daughter and maybe you care, but you don't barely know her. It's why you're not upset about getting shot. You think you had it coming."

Bobby looked like he was about to get out of the hospital bed and throw down. "Pretty harsh."

"You're putting me in a fucked position, Bobby. I have to be home. For my son. You're asking me to fail you or fail my family. Can't you see that?"

"Your family will be there. My daughter is missing."

"She's only missing to you, Bobby. Julie knows exactly where she is."

Bobby took some deep breaths. I waited for a response, but it didn't come.

"I'm going to go," I said and took a couple steps toward the door.

Bobby nodded. "Can you do one thing for me?"

"Bobby."

"Can you ask Becky to bring Julie's journals by? I want to keep reading them, try to understand."

"Yeah, I can do that. I'll stop by her place before I head out."

"It might not look it, Jimmy. But I'm trying."

The look on Bobby's face broke my fucking heart. Saying no is hard for me to do. Saying no to a friend even harder. Saying no to Bobby crushed me.

Hector Costales returned with my cup of coffee. No bear claw. "That's our time. My guess is that, as the victim, Mr. Maves will be transferred to the general area of the hospital by tomorrow. You will be able to visit more then."

"Feel better, Bobby," I said and left the room.

———•———

Hector Costales and I walked out of the hospital together. I reached to shake hands, but he held up a finger, pulled out his phone, and dialed a number. I shrugged and took a step toward the parking lot. Hector Costales grabbed my bicep and shook his head.

He spoke into the phone. "He's here next to me." He listened for a few seconds and held out the phone.

"Tomás?" I asked him.

Hector Costales nodded. I took the phone.

"Hey, Tommy," I said.

"Making sure everything's running smooth, that Hector is doing his job to your satisfaction and all that shit."

"He's been great. I'm not in jail and I just saw Bobby."

"Good. Because if he hadn't, I would've had to bust his kneecaps."

I looked at Hector Costales, who had taken a few steps away to give me some privacy. "Seriously, Tommy. He's doing a good job."

Tomás laughed. "I was kidding. Killing lawyers is too much of a pain in the ass. You have to wait until dark and stake them in their coffins."

I looked around to see if anyone was in earshot. "It's different when you joke about maiming people than when other people do. You know, for obvious reasons."

"I think it makes it funnier. What is it they say? It's funny because it's true."

"Tell me how much everything costs. I'll pay you back when I can."

"Not necessary."

"I'm not going to be in debt to you."

"No debt. We're good. Even. You heading home now?"

"Yeah. Home."

"You and Maves are done running your own detective agency without driving each other crazy? You're back to being on the farm? Because that's where you should be."

The tone of Tomás's voice was sterner than just advice. There was something dark underneath. But there was usually an unconscious element of threat behind his words.

"This isn't the first time you've pressed me to stay out of this. You know I don't like to be told what to do."

"I'm just saying that home is the safest place for you."

"Then it's a good thing that's where I'm going."

"Yes, it is." Tomás hung up.

I walked to Hector Costales and gave the phone back to him.

"Everything okay?" Hector Costales asked.

"Nothing is okay."

I wanted to help Bobby. I cared, but I cared about a lot of shit that I couldn't fix. If it was my job to stamp out the world's injustices, we'd all be screwed. This was a question without a correct answer. A problem with no solution. And all the attempts to fix it would probably make it worse.

Bobby was different than me. He believed that if you were in the right, if your motives were noble and good, everything would work out. He forgot about the ten or so John Wayne movies where the Duke's character died at the end. Not a big percentage considering all his roles, but they're out there. It's a possibility.

I knew what I owed Bobby. And that debt could never be fully paid. I knew what he had sacrificed, what he had helped me do. Bobby was the friend who helped you bury the body without thinking twice, without any other option crossing his mind. And in the case of our past, that body-burying scenario was not purely theoretical.

Bobby's loyalty knew no limits. And as shitty as it made me feel about myself, I was starting to really see the margins of my own allegiance. It was one thing to disagree with Bobby's methods or be exhausted by his drunken shenanigans, but he had specifically asked for my help.

There were practical concerns, of course. I didn't know where Julie was and wouldn't have a clue where to start looking. I didn't know anything about Chucho or his gang—how dangerous they were. There was a good chance they were involved in Driskell's death, considering they were bad dudes and associates. They were definitely armed. With Bobby's pistol, for one.

Even if I agreed that Julie's future should not be jeopardized by the idiocy of her youth and the bad decisions that were inevitable in teenagerdom, she was mid-rebellion, not a hostage, not lost. Shooting your own father was one of the hallmark clues of a total disinterest in being rescued.

In short, the situation was fucked. And I wasn't the guy to unfuck it.

I didn't believe that it wasn't important. I believed that it was impossible.

I wanted to go home, lock the doors, and cut off the rest of the damaged world. I wanted to play with Juan, tell him stories, watch him grow and change and learn. I wanted him to know that I would always be there, that I would never abandon him. That I would always come back. I wanted to wake up to Angie, look at her when she thought she looked her worst, but she looked her best, puffy face and sleepy eyes and all. Hell, I wanted to get out in the fields. Get my hands dirty in the right way, in the honest way. Shovel shit, not deal with shit. Pet a dog, not get mauled by one.

I needed to abandon my friend. It was the smart thing to do. For myself and for my family. But historically, when I had the choice between being stupid and being an asshole, nine times out of ten I chose stupid.

I stopped by Becky's place on the way out of town. I could have called, but that felt too impersonal. I hadn't discussed it with Bobby, but I felt like she had a right to know what had happened. It wasn't going to be easy, but she was Julie's mother, and she deserved to know the truth more than I did.

Russell walked me into the living room and called for Becky. She came into the room, gave me a quick hug, and sat with Russell on the couch. Russell's hand unconsciously and rhythmically rubbed her back. I sat down in the big chair in the corner.

"There's no good way to tell this, so sorry if I jump around. And this has to be between us. Nobody else can know any of this. You'll know why in a second."

Becky and Russell looked at each other. They both nodded to me.

"Bobby and I found Julie."

"Where is she?" Becky sat up halfway out of her seat. "What happened? If you found her, why isn't she here?"

"Let him finish, Beck," Russell said.

"The gist is this. We found her. She didn't want to go with us. Worse than that, she shot Bobby."

"She what? With a gun?" Becky said. "She doesn't know how to shoot a gun."

"She learned. It happened right in front of me."

"Is Bob okay?" Russell asked.

"He will be. Hit him in the shoulder. He's over at JFK in the police detention area, but you should be able to see him by tomorrow. Speaking of, if you go, he asked me if you could bring Julie's journals."

Becky rocked slightly in her seat. She breathed heavily and audibly through her nose.

"I think you need to tell the whole story," Russell said. "It's like reading the last page of a book. It doesn't make any sense if you haven't read everything before."

So I told them. I figured if anyone should know what was going on, it was them. I laid out the whole tale, beginning to end. Everything Bobby and I had done and everything we had found out.

"Holy shit," Becky said under her breath. "While we were putting up posters, you were running around like two crazies?"

"That's kind of our thing."

"Shouldn't we report all this to the police?" Russell asked me, but looked at Becky.

"Do we really want to tell them that Julie shot Bobby?" I asked. "And Bobby and me would be in a ton of shit, because that's not the story we've been rolling with. From the moment he got shot, still bleeding on the ground, Bobby was adamant about protecting Julie. Don't know how it would help them find her either."

"Makes sense," Russell said. "Though what do I know? This is all new to me."

"Hey, me too," I said. "The only thing I'm more used to is getting into trouble and making shit up as I go."

"What happens now?" Russell asked.

"For me?" I said, "I'm going home. If I knew where she was, had a clue, it might be different. But I got to get back to my life. I might talk to some friends in the police. Not report it, just chat. People I trust. See if they have a take."

"That little fucking bitch," Becky shouted. She hit the armrest of the couch three times in rapid succession.

Russell and I didn't say a word. The air became harder to breathe. Becky seethed, one streak of eyeliner running down her cheek. I couldn't think of anything to say, which only made me feel like more of a dick. I hoped that she'd hit me, just to feel useful.

Becky stood up decisively. "I'm going to put a pot of coffee on." She walked out of the room, leaving me and Russell to stare at each other. Russell was the one to finally break the silence.

"It's the shock of it, is all. She'll calm down," Russell said. "And don't think Beck doesn't appreciate everything you've done, or at least tried to do. She does. I can't imagine dealing with that level of violence. This business is so far outside my bailiwick."

That statement confirmed my previous assertion, the word *bailiwick* sounding perfectly natural coming out of Russell's mouth.

Loud banging and broken dishes erupted from the kitchen. The cacophony was followed by a volley of impressive swearing.

"I'm going to help Beck with the coffee," Russell said, standing up quickly and heading into the kitchen.

I considered sneaking out while their backs were turned, but I reached for the newspaper on the coffee table and settled in. Of course, the front page of the *Desert Sun* was all about Driskell's murder and upcoming funeral. Big news. Millionaire murders don't happen every day in La Quinta. I read the article and when I got to the end and the accompanying obituary, I read them both again.

After the storm passed in the kitchen, I drank two cups of coffee with Becky and Russell, sitting mostly in silence. After a half hour, I tucked the newspaper into my armpit and said my good-byes. The desert night was cool and humid, a cold sweat forming and coating my skin like a film.

I stood next to my truck and lit a cigarette. I took another look at the newspaper.

"Fuck," I yelled too loud.

I couldn't be positive—I would have to check a few things out—but after reading the paper, I was pretty sure I knew where Julie was.

I didn't know what I was going to do with that information, but I knew it wasn't over. And I wasn't done.

When I walked in the front door, Angie stood up from the couch and crossed her arms. That was her scolding pose. I knew that from past idiocies. Angie wasn't a nag, in fact she hated when I put her in the position to be the grown-up. Her posture must have been instinct, because she quickly relaxed, her arms falling to her sides.

"Juan's asleep," she said.

I closed the door as quietly as I could, walked to her, and kissed her.

"You should poke your head in his room," she said. "Make sure he knows you're home. I'm sure that'll help him to sleep through the night."

I nodded. "It's good to be home."

I held out my arms to the side. Angie walked in close and let me wrap them around her. We stood in the middle of the living room and held each other for a while, her squeeze getting tighter and tighter.

"What happened to your face? You look like the Toxic Avenger."

"The doctor said it would heal in a week. It's a funny story," I said.

"But it's always more of a laughing-at-you than laughing-with-you kind of funny."

"I tried to keep it under control, Angie. Really."

"But."

"But Bobby. Fucking Indio. The whole thing. It got away from me. Almost from the start, it got away from me."

"Is this a break or are you done?"

"We found Julie," I said.

Angie looked up at me, not letting go but loosening her grip. "That's great news. It wasn't a complete disaster. Where was she?"

"We found her but she didn't want to go. She was the one who shot Bobby."

Angie pushed off me. "Get the fuck out of here."

"She shot him and took off again. Left him on the ground bleeding. Saddest thing I ever saw. Stupid and sad."

"And you were there? You saw that?" Angie said.

I nodded.

She took my hand and headed toward the hall in the direction of our bedroom. "Check in on your son and then let's go to bed."

"That sounds perfect."

She took a few more steps, stopped, and looked me in the eyes. "Bobby's sixteen-year-old daughter shot him."

I didn't know if she was asking me a question or saying it out loud, so I didn't say anything.

"That's seriously fucked up," she said.

———◆———

I opened the door to Juan's room as quietly as I could, but old houses don't do quiet. The door creaked and moaned and generally gave the impression that it was in some kind of pain from the few inches it had moved. A bit overdramatic for a door.

Juan blinked open two very sleepy eyes and stared up at me. I gave him a smile. It took him a second to register that it was me.

"Pop?" he asked sleepily.

"It's me," I said, walking into the room. I sat on the bed next to him, leaned down, and gave him a kiss on the head.

"You came back," he said, sounding a little surprised.

"That's right."

"Are you going away again?"

"I don't think so, but if I ever do, I'll always come back."

"People don't always come back," he said.

"I do." I kicked my shoes off and stretched out on the bed next to him. He hugged up against my chest. I wanted to enjoy being with my son, but exhaustion caught up with me and in less than a minute I was out.

I woke up the next morning alone in Juan's bed. The sun was up and if animated bluebirds had flown in the window to dress me, I wouldn't have been surprised. I hadn't slept that well since the time I ate some suspect "chicken" in Mexicali and then accidentally took an Ambien thinking it was Imodium. A great night's sleep, but I had to throw away the sheets the next morning.

Angie appeared in the doorway, holding two cups of coffee. "This is as close as I get to breakfast in bed."

She sat on the edge of the bed and handed me one of the mugs. I took a sip, burning my mouth and spitting it back in the cup.

"It's hot," I said.

"It's coffee, Jimmy."

"Thanks."

"It's just coffee."

"No, I mean for everything. For being cool. I know it's hard sometimes having two children."

Angie climbed in the small bed next to me. I set the mug on the nightstand and sat up with my back against the headboard.

"I'm looking at this whole mess," I said. "I'm looking at Julie. She might've been raised by Becky, but she turned into the teenage-girl version of Bobby. Whether example or genes, who knows? But she's him. Or parts of him."

"And you're thinking about the example you're setting for Juan?"

"It's hard. I want him to see that I'm a loyal friend. That I help the people I love. But it's also my job to protect him, to be his father. If I run off with Bobby doing a bunch of half-assed dangerous moronics, get myself killed, what then? This father stuff is still so new to me, scares the shit out of me some days, but if nothing was going on, none of this Julie shit, I know the place to be is here. I know what I'm supposed to do is take care of this family."

"Life ain't one thing at a time, babe. There's always something else going on."

"Bobby wants me to keep looking for Julie. He still wants to save her. And I think I might know where she is."

"When you go away again, make sure that Juan understands."

"Are you telling me to do it? To help Bobby? I don't even know if I want to."

"I'm not telling you to do anything. I'm telling you that you already know what you're going to do. You might want to debate the pros and cons, make it feel like you've given it due diligence, but you know what you're going to do."

"How do you know—?"

"Because I know you. And even if I don't agree with some of the shit you do, none of it surprises me. I know who I'm with." Angie kissed my cheek. "I hate to point you toward danger, but I know you well enough to know that you don't want to set the example of abandoning your best friend when things got bad. Even if it's the right thing to do."

"I don't know. It could be dangerous."

"Do you need me to give you permission for something you'd do with or without my permission?"

"Yeah. I do."

I drank some coffee, keeping my eyes on Angie the whole time.

"Remember this," she said. "I'm not the supportive-no-matter-what kind of girlfriend. I have limits. This relationship is solid. It can survive a lot. But it's not unbreakable." Angie took a deep breath. "You have my permission."

"Thanks."

"I didn't sign a permission slip to go to Disneyland. This is serious shit."

"Now I got to figure out what to do."

"Start by getting your lazy ass out of bed, spending some time with your son—you really need to figure out a way to talk to him about Yolanda—and then decide if you're going to save a teenage girl against her will."

"Right. A normal Thursday."

"It's Sunday."

"Getting the day right doesn't make the joke any funnier."

"No, a better joke would."

"Did you find the girl that was lost?"

Juan lay on the ground, breathing hard. We had played a game we invented called "Super Soccer." We found all the toy balls in the house and set them in a big pile. I was the goalie. The goal was two chairs set up at a random distance. Juan would kick, head-butt, and throw the balls at the goal. (Hands were allowed in "Super Soccer." We're

Americans, after all. We believe in freedom.) I would try to stop them by deflecting them or catching them. The game moved very fast and it was hard to keep score, but it was fun as hell. Although at times, I got the sense that Juan was directing the balls at me rather than trying to score a goal.

Through gulps of air, Juan asked again. "Did you help Uncle Bobbiola find her?"

"Kind of. Not really. You were right. She's a good hider."

"Are you going to go again? To look more?" He looked up, his wrinkled brow telegraphing his concern.

I thought about it for a moment and answered. "I might. But you have to know that if I do, I'll come back. I'll always come back."

"Why can't you just stay here?"

"Uncle Bobbiola is my best friend and he needs my help. That's what you do for friends. Even if you're not sure you can help, you try."

"But if you can't help, how do you help?"

"When did you become a Zen Master?" I laughed. "You don't know until you try. Trying is the important thing."

"Always try to do your best. That's what you tell me."

"Because that's all you can do. You can't do better than your best." I said, "Your mom said you were having some scary dreams. Do you want to talk about them?"

"No."

"I think we should."

"Super Soccer!" Juan screamed, changing the subject.

I let him, not sure how to broach the subject anyway. "What's the score?" I asked.

"Forty-hundred to zero. I'm winning."

As Juan wrangled all the balls in the room into a fresh pile, I had no idea what he remembered or thought he remembered from his past. But I couldn't help but be reminded that he wouldn't be here—that I wouldn't have a son—if Bobby hadn't helped me and risked his neck for no reason other than friendship.

It was time that I stopped acting like I had a choice. I knew what I had to do.

———

During Juan's nap I got on the computer. I dug up my user-name and password to get back on the gonzo girl fight website, pretty sure I was unleashing a virtual version of the bird flu on my poor old computer. I clicked on one of the thumbnails that wasn't Julie's fight. I couldn't watch that one again.

It played out pretty much the same as Julie's fight: warm-up against a nondescript wall, then cut to the fight in the industrial, factory setting. Everything bleached white. I let it run while I reread the article and obituary in the *Desert Sun* about Driskell.

The obit elaborated on what Tomás had told me. Driskell was the heir to the founder of CaSO-Corp, but had run the business into the ground. It was the spelling of CaSO that had caught my eye the night before, at Becky's place. When Tomás had talked about it, it sounded like a generic name. But seeing that small *A*, my liberal arts school "Chemistry for Poets" class came back to me. CaSO was calcium sulfate, also known as gypsum or Sheetrock or plaster of Paris.

I looked back at the fight video, two girls swinging wildly, connecting infrequently. In the crowd of men, I caught sight of some Los Hermanos jackets. But it was the ground that confirmed it. The same powder was on the ground. Powder I had thought was snow. But I was way off. It was plaster.

The girls were fighting at the abandoned CaSO-Corp gypsum factory. I watched two more of the videos. Shot at the same place. The same buildings. And the same factory towers. I eventually even caught a glimpse of the CaSO-Corp logo on one of the towers to confirm. All the fights were shot in the same place. And I knew exactly where that was.

They were in Plaster City.

THIRTEEN

Plaster City sat twenty miles west of El Centro on Evan Hewes Highway, the old road that had been at one time the only east/west passage through the mountains to San Diego. After the freeway was built, it got little use, nothing but desert between El Centro and Ocotillo. A few map dots, but even the largest town, Ocotillo, wasn't much more than a gas station, garage, diner, and scattered trailers filled with antisocial desert outcasts who avoided "the big city" of El Centro. Plaster City sat smack-dab between blink and you-missed-it.

That whole stretch of desolation, the Yuha Desert, was chaparral, tamarisk, and diffused ugly. Nearer the border, it got more interesting, but only in the awfullest ways. There was a designated area dedicated to a specific kind of thorn. A thorn! The Crucifixion thorn, on the off chance you wanted to make your Easter more authentic. There was a geoglyph that might have been cool from a plane or a helicopter, but from the ground it looked like someone got crazy on their ATV, leaving circular tire tracks on the dusty hardpack. Someone once told me it was a horse. But that person did a lot of mushrooms, so it was hard to really take his word as gospel.

The best thing out that way was the Mount Signal Café. They made great pancakes and their own root beer from scratch. Unfortunately, the Mount Signal Café closed twenty years ago. But you could make a strong argument that dicking around in the husk of an abandoned restaurant was still the most fun to be had in that part of the desert.

Google street maps gave me a pretty clear picture of Plaster City, at least in terms of the structures. It also confirmed that it was indeed the site of the fight videos, easy enough to compare the factory towers. I hadn't been out that way in a while, but it didn't look like much had changed from the way I remembered it. And it still creeped me out.

When I was a kid, Pop preferred the old road. So on our shopping trips to San Diego, we would pass by (never stop at) Plaster City. If the sun hit it right, it glowed on the horizon, a blinding white against the world of dull brown. I had always been afraid of it, ghostly and unreal, the cold starkness in the extreme heat of the desert. It didn't help that Pop always made the same joke. "It looks like Hell really did freeze over."

The images and maps foretold the biggest obstacle. There was only one road—the old highway—that ran through Plaster City. No other way in or out. Surrounded by barren, flat desert.

I had been in a similar situation two years before, but that had been different. This time I was trying to save someone who didn't know they were being saved and didn't want to be saved.

It got worse. There really wasn't an inconspicuous way to get a good look at the surrounding buildings of Plaster City without raising the inhabitants' suspicions. There were plenty of people who used the old road, but there was absolutely no reason to stop in Plaster City. Not even to take pictures. It was ugly as shit. There was no gas station and the old company store wouldn't still be open after the factory closed. If I stopped, eyes would be on me immediately.

I decided to go out there and see what I could assess in the fifteen seconds it took to drive from one end of town to the other.

The factory came into view a couple miles ahead. The gypsum factory made up the entire south side of the town, the highway splitting the town in half. Its tall towers loomed in the distance. As I drove closer, I saw the few buildings on the north side of the highway. There were a few freestanding structures with boarded-up windows that may have once been offices, but it was the old truck yard with a number of loading bays that confirmed my suspicions. The truck yard had been converted to a shantytown of sorts. Some mobile homes, a few fifth wheels, but also some converted truck trailers and makeshift structures made from pallets and corrugated tin. There was even the wall of a double-wide propped up against the side of the loading dock like a massive lean-to.

The funny thing is that I wouldn't have been able to see anything if I had stopped, but driving past, I was able to see through the privacy slats that ran through the chain link. It was like watching an old zoetrope, images flashing in animated glimpses.

The dozen motorcycles peppered here and there within the fenced-in area were the most revealing things I saw. I only caught sight of a few people, but couldn't determine whether they were men or women.

Two men on motorcycles passed me coming the other way, one of them giving me a quick glance, and turned into

Plaster City toward the gate to the compound. I couldn't see in the rearview whatever procedure they used to enter, but I had gotten a look at their patches. Los Hermanos. The same patch as in the fight videos. The same one Chucho wore. This was his gang's clubhouse.

Beyond the makeshift town, there didn't appear to be any other residents. It was the perfect hideout and the most likely place to lay low. It was a low-rent fortress.

If Chucho and Julie thought they were on the run, they would embrace the sanctuary of the people they trusted. Chucho would go to his bros, his gang. And out here in the middle of the desert, nobody cared what you did. It's why people moved out this way, to be left alone. You could do anything in this stretch of desert. No one to bother, no one to complain, and no one to get nosy about whatever business or pleasure was going on.

I had no real proof, only a hunch, but it made sense that Julie and Chucho would be here. Now what the hell was I going to do about it?

"I think I know where she's at."

"Where?" Bobby shouted on the other end of the phone.

"Plaster City. That's where those fights were."

"Oh, man. I should've recognized it. But I'm guessing there's something stopping us from just driving in and picking her up."

"A whole bunch of somethings. It's where Chucho's gang makes camp. Why I think they're there."

"So you're back in the band? You're going to help get her?"

"I got conditions."

"What am I going to do? Say no?" Bobby said, his annoyance obvious. "What are they?"

"I run the show. Even when you get out of there. No more cowboying bullshit. Unless I say that's what we do. I got a kid to think about and every time shit goes catawampus, I risk everything. No bitching about my decisions. You don't like how I do it, say the word. I go home with a clear conscience."

"Is that it?"

"And I'm home every night. No matter what. No Mavescapade bullshit."

"How do I know how long shit's going to take or where we're going to be?"

"Those are my terms."

Bobby was silent for a moment. "Okay. We do it your way. No interference from me."

"Good," I said. "We'll find her, Bobby. We'll find her and bring her back."

"Damn right we will."

———————

"Holtville Police Department. How can I direct your call?"

Ceja sounded bored on the other end of the phone, probably anticipating another call about someone locking their keys in their car or a missing 4-H lamb. The best he could hope for was breaking up a bar fight, but bar fights before noon only happened on the weekends.

"Hey, Ceja. It's Jimmy Veeder."

"Jimmy. Hey. Sorry again for getting a little agitated at Pinky's. There must've been something in that tequila. I never get that out of control."

"Yes, you do. Every time. And you apologize with the same excuse every time. There is 'something' in the tequila, Ceja. It's called tequila."

"I said I'm sorry. You don't got to be mean."

"I need a favor. You hear about Bobby?"

"A little, not much. Indio called down here to ask me about him. Heard he got shot while looking for his girl. Don't know more than that."

"You want to help?"

"If I can."

"With Bobby in the hospital, I'm asking around, doing some looking for his daughter. I think she's involved with this Mexican gang. I want to confirm some stuff, but I need more information, maybe some files."

"Sorry, Jimmy. I'm not your guy for that."

"This is Bobby we're talking about. Wasn't it Bobby who introduced you to your wife?"

"He didn't really introduce us. I mean, he took me to the titty bar where she worked, where we met. So kinda maybe."

"Bobby's done more than that for you."

"It's not like that, Jimmy. I'd help if I could, but I'm a Holtville cop. There's three of us. We don't investigate things. We don't barely got files. We drive around, give tickets, roust illegals and hobos in the park. We're like the town security guards. Mall cops do more police work."

"But you can put in a request or something?"

"They'd ignore it. If I start to nose in on an investigation up in Indio—I'm not even in the same county—they're going to wonder why, but mostly they're not going to care a lick. You need someone up there, or at least in the Imperial Sheriff's Department, or maybe Federal. Do you know any G-Men or Homeland Security? Bobby's a good guy. But you're asking the ball boy to hit a home run. Ain't going to happen."

"All right, man. Thanks."

I didn't know a G-Man, but I did know someone in the Imperial County Sheriff's Department.

———•———

And that's how I ended up driving to Indio with Griselda Villarreal, Deputy Sheriff and Bobby's ex-girlfriend. I hadn't seen her since before they broke up a couple months earlier. She looked the same. I wondered if she aged at all. She could still pass for sixteen and I'm pretty sure she was older than me. It wasn't just her height—she was only a scoonch above five feet—it was the softness of her features. But I never let that fool me, she was a badass. I had seen it first-hand on more than one occasion. She had to be. Not only was she a female cop in the Imperial Valley, but she dated Bobby Maves.

While I possessed a natural distrust for the police, I trusted Gris implicitly. So I told her everything. Even information that I definitely shouldn't have told a law enforcement officer, considering the number of crimes that had been committed so far. I even told her about Julie shooting Bobby, a secret that I had divulged to a few more people than was probably wise. But if I was asking for her help, I was going to be on the level. This was my show now and the only way I could do it was my way. She agreed to meet with me, but wouldn't agree to help until she talked to Bobby face-to-face.

I had gotten word from Bobby that he had been moved from the detention ward to the non-locked-door recovery area. The owner of the garage refused to press any charges, most likely due to a call from Hector Costales. And while the police threw some threats at Bobby, they had no real interest in pursuing a few misdemeanor charges. Bobby had been shot. They figured that was punishment enough.

So Griselda and I drove to Indio, the Salton Sea on our right and the desert all around us. The second time inside of the week that I had gotten the chance to ride in the front of a police car. I would've asked her to run the siren and the light, if I hadn't've gotten that out of my system tooling around in Ceja's cruiser.

"Thanks, Gris," I said, breaking up a long silence. "I know I'm putting you in a weird position telling you more than the other cops, but you're family. You have every right to report me or arrest me or walk away, but please don't."

"The police aren't your enemy."

"Not most of the time. But they are when you do a bunch of illegal shit," I said. "Even if you got a good reason. And when a father's daughter shoots him, best to handle in-house. Doesn't seem like there's an upside to getting outsiders involved."

"But you can't handle it. Even if you find Julie, extract her from whatever bad situation she's in, what happens then?"

"Jump off that bridge when I get to it. I can always bring the cops in later, after I've fucked everything up myself."

Griselda shook her head and let out a small laugh.

"Here's the crazy thing," I said. "When I'm around Bobby, I'm the sanity, the voice of reason. God help us, I'm the brains of the operation. But then I get around real people like you, I can actually see how berserk we both are."

"Once a troublemaker always a troublemaker," she said. "I'm glad you called. Instead of kicking down more doors, punching the closest face, and getting your ass shot or stabbed or whatever."

"Yeah, that strategy hasn't been working the best," I said. "When was the last time you saw Bobby? Have you seen him since . . . ?"

Griselda didn't say anything for a while. I stared out the windshield, feeling like a jerk for asking. It had been meant as small talk, but the talk had grown big fast. She spoke without looking at me.

"He broke up with me, you know."

Even though I was the only other one in the car, it took me a second to realize that Griselda was talking to me. It was the way she had said it, distant, almost a question.

"What?" I said.

"I don't know what he told you, but it was Bobby who ended it."

"He didn't tell me that. He didn't tell me anything. I couldn't get him to talk about it, always changed the subject or made some joke."

"There's a side of Bobby people don't see. You might be one of the few that does, but I don't know. I saw a part of him that he didn't show to many. Not just a vulnerability, but something more reflective."

"I catch it in fits and starts, but usually I get the Bobby Show."

"The Mavescapades."

"He loves a good portmanteau, that guy. After you two broke up, that's all I got, until this with Julie. Now he's off the chain. Like a sad Tasmanian devil or a depressed Hulk. His emotions changing every second and him catching up to them five minutes later."

"I hate that he's hurting. That he's alone with this. I still care about him."

"I got no right to ask, so feel free to tell me to shut the fuck up and mind my own business, but why did he break it off?"

She shook her head. "Some bullshit about not being good enough for me. About holding me back. And if I wasn't going to do anything about it, he had to. We'd been together more than two years. He woke up and decided that he was ruining my life, that I was letting him. He was even sober when he explained it. But I stopped listening after a while. It all sounded like excuses. Like an attempt to use logic to explain the illogical. Maybe he believed it. Maybe he was scared of the commitment. The only thing I know was that no matter what I said, he had an answer. His mind was made up."

"Yeah. When Bobby commits to a thing, he's like a pit bull with a rib eye. Try to take it away."

"It got to that point where trying wasn't going to change a thing. He wore me down and it wasn't worth the fight. It was just done. And that was it."

"If he wanted to get back together, try again, would you?"

"He really hurt me," Griselda said. "I want to help how I can with Julie. Past that—I can't answer your question, because I don't know."

We pulled into the hospital parking lot with that in the air. I couldn't imagine how Griselda felt—what she was thinking—seeing Bobby for the first time since they broke up. And I couldn't imagine how Bobby was going to react.

I probably should have called him to tell him I was bringing her.

———

"What's she doing here?" Bobby said, "I told you we weren't involving her. We were keeping her out of it."

Griselda stood behind me at the door to Bobby's room. He currently shared it with an empty bed, which gave us some privacy. Bobby didn't have as many tubes in him as before, but his shoulder was mummy-wrapped and it looked like he couldn't move his left arm if he tried.

"We were keeping her out of it," I said, "but as soon as I took over this blunderfuck, that gave me the authority to ask whoever I wanted for help."

"I don't want her involved."

"I'm standing right here, Bobby," Griselda said. "Don't talk about me in the third person while I'm in the same room."

"But you literally are the third person," he said loudly.

"You should've come to me right away. Even if we aren't together, I still care," Griselda shouted back.

"Guys?" I said.

"I knew if I asked for your help that you'd put your job, yourself at risk. That's the reason we broke up."

"Guys?" I said again, trying to be heard over their rising volume.

"We didn't break up. You broke us up. I didn't have a say."

I put my fingers in my mouth and whistled loud enough to wake a coma patient three doors down. Griselda and Bobby turned to me, hands going to their ears. It was speech time.

"I'm helping you, Bobby, but damn it, I don't want to. If you don't like how I do this, zero is the exact amount of fucks I give. Hell, I haven't even got to the point where I know what I'm doing.

"Putting rules and shit on how I find Julie limits my effectiveness. I get to ask whoever I want for help. And since the only people I know are a ragtag bunch of misfits, which works in the movies, I'm going to reach out broad. One of those misfits is Griselda. She not only cares, but she's smart and tough and a fucking cop. If that hurts your precious widdo feewings, suck it up, cowboy.

"Right now, I'm going to go out to the waiting room and read two-year-old *Golf Digest*s while you two do your best impersonations of grown-ups and reach some sort of fucking accord. I'm not asking you to get back together—although you're idiots if you don't. What I am asking is that you work it out so that you can be in the same room together. So that we can work together.

"I don't want to see either of your fucking faces until the treaty is signed."

I didn't wait for a response. I turned and walked out, feeling good about my speech, particularly the "ragtag bunch of misfits" line. I always wanted to say that. Although I wished that it wasn't true.

While I tore a recipe out of a *Good Housekeeping* magazine (five-ingredient brownies made in a coffee mug in the microwave!), Becky and Russell walked into the waiting room. They saw me and came over. I folded the page and put it in my shirt pocket. I gave Becky a brief hug and shook Russell's hand. He held a stack of Julie's journals in the other one.

"If I haven't already said it," Becky said, "thanks again for your help. And I'm sorry about last night. I lost it."

"Completely understandable," I said. "And I ain't done. With Bobby laid up, I'm going to keep looking for Julie."

Becky turned to Russell and then back to me. "As much as I want her home, she obviously doesn't want to be there. Even if you find her, what then?"

"I honestly don't know."

I didn't tell her that I thought Julie was in Plaster City. It was still conjecture and I didn't want to get her hopes up or open the door to any rash actions. Instead, I said, "I'm getting more people to help. We'll be meeting soon. Coming up with some sort of plan. Both of you are welcome to be there."

"Definitely," Russell said. "Not sure how I can help, but if I can I will."

"Why are you out here and not in the room with Bobby?" Becky asked.

"Bobby's with a friend. A Sheriff's Deputy for Imperial County. Unofficial visit. She's helping."

"Griselda?" Becky asked.

"Yeah. I didn't know if you knew her."

"We've never met. Bobby's talked about her. I thought they broke up."

"They did."

Twenty minutes later, Griselda walked down the hall toward us. I introduced her to Becky and Russell. Griselda told Becky that she was sorry to hear about her daughter and would do everything she could to help. Becky thanked her. They were both way too formal, the real story in their eyes. Becky and Griselda sized each other up, which was funny as they were both physically similar. Bobby definitely had a type.

"Well, we should be getting on our way," Griselda said.

"Thanks again," Becky said.

They awkwardly shook hands, and Becky and Russell walked down the hall toward Bobby's room. I started toward the exit, but Griselda stopped me with a light smack to the arm.

"Did you really catch Bobby and her boning on her kitchen counter?"

I wish I could have seen my face, because whatever my reaction looked like, it was funny enough to bust up Griselda. And she wasn't an easy laugh.

"He told you about that?"

"Bobby decided that if we were going to work through things that he had to come completely clean."

"He's all-or-nothing."

"I actually asked him not to tell me everything, but once he got rolling . . . I'm not sure what he sees in her, but with all those emotions confusing him, I can see how it could happen."

I didn't have the heart or stupidity to point out how similar she and Becky were physically, so I shifted the conversation. "So are you two going out again? I mean, did you . . . ?"

"Slow down, tiger."

"But you'll help?"

Gris nodded. "Yeah. I'll help."

"Now comes the hard part, figuring out how to get into Plaster City. We have to know for sure if Julie's there."

"Someone has to see her. Actually see her there. Without eyes on Julie, there's no probable cause. I can't do anything on hunches and guesses."

"There's got to be some way to get in there," I said.

"Plaster City doesn't have any residents beyond the gang that's there. And it doesn't sound like we'd be able to turn someone inside the gang. What we could use is someone who lives out there with their ear to the ground. Only freaks and weirdos skew that far out of town, but that's a tight-knit group. And for all their paranoia and crazy, they're a curious bunch. Not much gets by them. We need a desert rat."

I laughed at the idea that popped into my head. I stopped laughing when I realized I was going to go through with it.

"What?" Griselda asked.

"I know someone out there. In that part of the desert. Outside Coyote Wells. You thought Bobby was pissed for bringing you here, he's going to lose his shit when he finds out I asked his father for help."

"I didn't even know his father was alive. He never talks about him."

"Yeah, there's a reason for that."

It's a strange feeling to get lost in the desert. The forest makes sense, all those trees blocking the view. But in the desert, it was the redundancy of the landscape that got me all turned around. Technically, I guess I wasn't lost. There had really only been the one dirt road. I could make my way back, but that didn't mean I knew where I was.

Relief hit me when the buildings came into view. There were a bunch of them, all part of one collective grouping. A compound that consisted of a double-wide trailer, a large hay barn, corrals and pens that held a number of different animals, and about a dozen small sheds that made me think that shed-building might be Rudy's hobby.

I pulled onto the long gravel driveway that led up to the double-wide and parked my truck under a big jujube tree. A wooden deck had been built in front of the trailer with a tattered blue tarp duct-taped to posts for shade. The uneven deck dipped dramatically at one corner. The man sitting on one of the deck chairs didn't seem to mind.

Rudy Maves put a hand over his drinking glass and waited for the dust that my truck kicked up to settle. When it did, he took a long drink and wiped his forehead with a handkerchief. His eyes never left me as I climbed out of the truck and walked toward him.

Rudy looked like he had aged fifty years in the roughly fifteen since I'd last seen him. Floating somewhere around sixty years old, the drinking and the desert sun had darkened and cracked his white face a deep tan. The darker skin made him look much more like Bobby. And, of course, he had the same bone-white pompadour that Bobby had, only higher with enough pomp to act as a visor, shading his eyes. More than one *National Enquirer* Elvis sighting could probably be chalked up to Rudy Maves.

I looked for some way to get up onto the deck. There didn't appear to be any stairs and it was about four feet off the ground.

"Ain't no steps. You got to want it," Rudy said in lieu of a greeting. "Wood porch is an easy build. A box, really. Steps takes talent. Going to fetch a pool ladder when I can find one used."

I put my back against the deck and lifted myself to a sitting position on its edge.

"Careful, son. It's been a long while since two people's been up on here."

"I trust your craftsmanship."

"After I told you I couldn't build steps? You ain't so bright, are you? I ain't never built nothing that didn't eventually collapse." Rudy squinted at me for a moment. "I know you."

"I called, but the phone just rang."

"Yeah. About an hour ago. I couldn't think of anyone I wanted to talk to."

"I'm a friend of your son's. You might remember me. Jim Veeder."

"Sure. You two was joined at the hip, always getting Bob in all kinds of trouble."

I couldn't help but let a laugh slip out at that.

Rudy gave me a disappointed look, but continued. "Big Jack's boy. I remember your old man better than you. Morales was his bar. Rough place in my day. Don't think I ever left that place without a wound of some kind. Tough son of a bitch, your old man. One time, he knocked me unconscious, out cold, one punch, because I said that Lee Marvin was a bad actor."

"Sounds like Pop."

"Funny thing was, I was thinking about Lee Van Cleef when I said it. Just too drunk to get my facts right. Never faulted him for it, but just the same I didn't argue screen talent with him no more. How is Big Jack?"

"He died. About two years ago."

"Sorry to hear it. Barroom legends never get their due. There should be a museum. I'll include him in my prayers tonight. You want an Arnold Palmer?"

"Sure. Thanks." He didn't offer me a seat, so I stood with my hands in my pockets.

"Minerva!" he yelled over his shoulder. "Arnoldo Palmero, por favor."

Rudy turned back to me. "You want ice?"

I shrugged.

"Con hielo," he shouted. "If there's spit in it, you can have mine." Rudy smiled and I saw even more of Bobby in his face.

"Looks like you got some animals out here. Where does the water come from?"

"Artesian well. I like the company of animals, they . . ." Rudy stopped abruptly. "That's right."

"What?" I asked.

"Minerva left three weeks back. You ain't never getting that drink."

"I'll be okay."

"They all leave, son," Rudy said. "But you didn't come out here to chat about my love life or my bestiary. And even though I'm a desert outlier, don't worry, those two things are yet to intersect. What kind of trouble have you gotten my boy into?"

"It's not Bobby. It's your granddaughter. She's gone missing."

"Which granddaughter?"

"Julie. The older of the two."

"How long ago she go missing?"

"About a week ago."

"Why are you here and not Bobby?"

"He got shot in the shoulder while looking for her."

"Who shot him?"

"Julie. Your granddaughter."

Rudy set his drink down. It toppled over and rolled the length of the deck and off the end. Both of us watched, making no effort to grab it. I didn't see it land, but I imagined a huge pile of glasses on the ground below.

I said, "I think she's out in Plaster City, but I can't prove it. Until I know for sure, the cops can't do a thing. It's private property mostly. The owner is dead so it's in a kind of ownership limbo perfect for squatting. The gang that pitches camp there is the crowd Julie runs with. She's mixed up in some bad shit."

Rudy stood up and cuffed me on the back of the head. It didn't occur to me to defend myself. "No cussing, son. Foul language degrades both the speaker and the listener. I don't allow no harsh language here. When you're on my deck, you show respect."

"Swearing is out, but hitting people is okay?" I felt the back of my head for a bump.

"More people need to get hit."

Erring on the side of diplomacy, I ignored the assault. "Julie got mixed up with a bad crowd. Thinks she's grown up. We want to get her away from those people, but there's a good chance she won't want to go."

"You talking about them Mexican bikers, yeah? Los Hermanos. I know them by sight. Seen them. They been out in Plaster for some time. No one out here gives too much of a holler. Mostly live-and-let-live types out this way. Far enough from civilization, they can whoop it up all they like and they ain't going to bother no one."

"You know anything about the fights they hold out there?"

"Fights? Like dogs?"

"No. People."

"Boxing matches?"

"Of a kind. Girls. Teenage girls beating the living sh— heck out of each other. Julie's one of their fighters."

Rudy wiped his face with his handkerchief. "That's where the world is headed, son. No respect for human decency. Children fighting? Julie can't be more than twelve or thirteen."

"Julie is sixteen."

Rudy nodded, but his expression showed conflicting emotion. Hard to describe, like he was questioning all the decisions in his life in a brief moment. He turned to look at the expanse of barren desert that was our view.

"It's a business," I said. "People pay money to watch these girls—mostly runaways—fight. Live and on the Internet."

"The world has lost its shame. How could someone . . . ?"

"I can't answer that without swearing."

Rudy continued to nod, taking it all in.

"Do you mind if I smoke?" I asked.

"On another day I would lecture you on poisoning your body, but not today. You can smoke, so long as you let me have a couple drags."

"I could give you your own."

He shook his head. "Don't want a whole one."

I lit a smoke, took a drag, and handed the cigarette to Rudy. He took a deep inhale, closed his eyes, took another one, and handed the cigarette back.

"You came out this way thinking I could help, I suppose. What do you think I can do?" Rudy asked.

"I just need to know whatever you know about Plaster City. I grew up down here, but I know nothing about this part of the desert. Is there any way in? Anything."

"I don't know Plaster much more than what you can see from the road, but I can ask the other outcasts. Nothing that'll raise no alarms. See who knows what. We're not a meddlesome bunch out here in the Yuha, but we see things."

"Bobby's at JFK in Indio, if you want to visit."

"I don't like to leave my place."

"He should be out soon. I might be able to convince him to come here."

"Why don't we kill that chicken right before we eat it and not no sooner? I'll call you if I hear things."

FOURTEEN

People wanted to help. That was the thing about the Imperial Valley. Whenever I had asked for a hand doing anything, I never got a "no." I always got an "I'll put the stove on simmer and be there in ten minutes."

Buck Buck Buckley and his brother Snout were downright excited. Snout's enthusiastic shout of "Avengers Assemble" had bolstered my confidence, making me feel like maybe we were starters and not the scrubs off the bench. Optimism had a way of skewing realistic views.

That enthusiasm only lasted up until I played the first girl fight video for the crowd. I didn't show the one with Julie. That would have been too much. In the one I screened, the girls looked like they were barely thirteen. The same group of shouting men, maybe forty or fifty of them, played their part as ringside spectators.

Sitting around the table with beers in front of them and staring at my computer screen, my crackerjack team went from hearty introductions and how-have-you-beens to open mouths and murmured swearing. Griselda had already seen the videos, but it's not the kind of thing that one got inured to. Angie watched for the first time, mouth closed tight, anger in her eyes. Even Buck Buck and Snout appeared affected. And those two idiots were in their comfort zone when it came to illegalities and violence.

"They're girls," Snout said, confused. "Pretty little girls."

"It's like watching someone dissect a kitten," Buck Buck said. "We get to hurt the people that made this, right?"

But it was Russell who looked the worst for it, the furthest out of his element. He added a new dynamic to our team, some actual brains. Russell had told the crowd that Becky wanted to be there, but had to work. Just because your daughter is missing, don't mean the bills stop coming. He told me in confidence that Becky was worried about her inability to curb her anger. She felt awful about beating up Gabe and admitted to feeling a lot of anger toward Julie. She was concerned, wanted to help, but was afraid she would make things worse.

Russell had also offered to bake some brownies for the meeting, but I declined the offer. He brought rugelach instead.

Bobby was supposed to be released in the next day or two, but I didn't think it prudent to wait. We had to get moving. If Julie was in Plaster City, she wouldn't stay there forever. With his injury, Bobby should be in the dugout anyway, even if he wanted to be on the field. By setting the plan in motion without him, I avoided that argument.

Not that we had a plan.

When I decided that they'd had enough, I shut the video down. Everyone looked at me, pissed off. Not sure if the anger was from the content of the video or directed at me for showing it to them. Probably both.

"Sorry about that," I said, "but everyone needs to know what we're dealing with. The real problem we're facing isn't in these videos, it's here."

I turned and pointed to the map of Plaster City and the Yuha Desert that I had tacked to the wall. I had searched the house for a retractable pointer, but after twenty minutes, I decided it wasn't in the cards. The map included the surrounding terrain, but considering that was all roadless, open desert for miles in every direction, it didn't really add any information. The Algodones Dunes were on the east side of the Valley, classic sand dunes. The Yuha Desert to the west was flat, visible-for-miles desert. Dry, alkaline dirt that created a giant cloud from walking, let alone driving. You couldn't sneak up on a blind sloth in the Yuha.

"So here's where we're at. I got shit-all for evidence, but I'm pretty sure that Julie is in Plaster City. That's where they have the fights and that's where her boyfriend's biker gang lives. They call themselves Los Hermanos or Los Hos. Griselda can tell you more about them."

Griselda tipped an invisible hat, one of the rare times I saw her out of uniform. "Not much to tell. They're not in the gang books here or in Riverside, which means they're more wannabes than anything else. A cop I know who keeps track of tagging in the county said he'd seen some tags, but that's the length of law enforcement's awareness of their criminal enterprises."

"So what are we scared of?" Buck Buck said. "A bunch of tough-guy posers."

"Just because they're not affiliated," Griselda said, "doesn't make them not dangerous. And they're business savvy enough to make and distribute these videos. A good fighter never underestimates his opponent."

"Thanks, Gris," I said. "We have to catch sight of Julie. Then I can contact the Sheriff's Department like a good citizen and they will have reason to investigate, to get a warrant, all that cop shit."

Griselda nodded.

"But unless we have eyes on her, I can't ask Gris to go in guns out. Too many repercussions if I'm guessing wrong. So what we got to do is find a way to get a look around inside. You know, easy stuff, taking a peek inside a Mexican biker gang's compound. Without raising their hackles or making them suspicious. We don't want to spook them or Julie. Because once she's on the run, we've lost her."

I pointed to the highway, the one road leading into Plaster City.

"So nothing fancy. No confrontation. A two-part plan. We concentrate on finding out if she's in there. After that, we figure out how to get her out. Hopefully with the help of the law, but—close your ears, Gris—if not, any way we can. I'm taking any and all ideas."

"How many bad guys we talking about?" Buck Buck asked.

"Don't matter to me," Snout said, cracking his knuckles.

"One more reason to get a look around. That's one big area where they live. There's a bunch of structures. I didn't get a good look. Could be fifty in there, but probably more like twenty or thirty. That's the gang and their old ladies, if they got any. If there're any teenage girls there, we got to treat them like innocents. Could be prisoners, there by free will, but most likely some bastard marriage of the two."

"Let's storm the castle," Snout said. "I'm all about making a battering ram for the front of the van. We charge in there, fuck things up, save the day."

"Not really a plan, more of a sketch. And have you been listening? I already ixnayed the direct attack."

"He gets excited," Buck Buck said, apologetically. He gave Snout a slap to the arm.

"What?" Snout said.

"Here's what we should do." I said. "We all have different ideas, different brains, different backgrounds. We each take a half hour, think about the situation, come back with our plans, and brainstorm it out. See what this brain trust can come up with."

I stood up and stretched my back. "No idea is too stupid for this crowd. I'm going to check on Juan. See how Mr. Morales is holding up taking care of him."

"What about Tomás?" Angie asked. "Can you ask him to help?"

"I'm not convinced he's uninvolved," I said.

"You're still in contact with Tomás Morales?" Griselda said, shocked. "His name's come up a whole lot in the last few weeks. Some big push for control north of the border is the word. Seriously, any major crime, there's implications that he's involved. That kind of exposure is strange. Especially for him. The guy is slick. No criminal record. All associations. Used to keep it low-key, now if it's in the Imperial Valley, illegal, and organized, he's got his thumb in the tamale pie."

"I know him, Gris, but that's all," I said. "It's not in my plans to ask him for any favors."

"If he's involved and you tip him off to what we're doing out at Plaster City, you're putting us all in danger," Griselda said.

"I'm putting everyone in danger no matter how you slice it."

Morales Bar was doing a good business. It was a weekday night, but Mr. Morales had brought in a three-piece band as entertainment. With only a vilhuela, guitarron, and a trumpet, the three men were great and shockingly loud in the Quonset hut bar. One of them had given Juan a small concertina to play along. He had his old man's rhythm so he couldn't keep time, but he danced and played with abandon. The band's volume drowned out whatever musical mangling he did. The Linda McCartney to their Wings, as it were. The Mexican farm workers nearest the band tossed him quarters.

Juan spotted me and waved with one hand, letting the concertina Slinky to the floor. I waved back. He picked up the end and got back to business. I watched him play. I could have watched him all night. I never would have thought that the best part of my day would be seeing my son laugh and play and smile. Mostly because I never would have thought that I'd have a son.

I walked to the bar, Mr. Morales meeting me with a wet bottle of beer. I took a drink.

"How's the babysitting? Juan looks like he's having a blast."

"I had him barbacking, but he's useless carrying kegs."

"It'll probably be another hour. Is that okay?"

"He's got about forty drunk uncles keeping an eye on him. Take your time."

"You talk to Tomás at all?"

Mr. Morales looked down the bar at the customers waiting for more beer. They didn't shout or attempt to make eye contact. They knew better.

"No. He's a criminal."

"Come on, you know a lot of criminals." I turned and waved my hand toward the bar crowd. "From what my Pop told me, you're a bit of one yourself."

"Ain't no criminals in here. Maybe a few thieves, plenty of brawlers, but no bad guys. We all do illegal things. Who doesn't? But what Tomás does, those things are wrong, unforgivable. And he does them not for need, but something else."

"Power," I said.

"Okay," I said, "let's see what we all came up with."

Snout raised his hand. I pointed to him and he stood and held a piece of paper like a kid giving a book report. "You said no idea was too stupid. So remember that. We wait until the next time they have the fights, okay. We dress Griselda up in a school girl's uniform and—"

Griselda interrupted. "I'm going to stop you right there, Captain Pervert."

"You look young, right? You probably get carded. And I bet you kick some major ass, being a cop and all. Do you know martial arts? I could teach you some hopkido I learned in a book."

Griselda opened her mouth to respond, but I cut in. "First off, we're not putting Gris in a position where she has to punch a child in the face. A serious flaw in the plan. But more importantly, Gris can't actively participate until we know that Julie is there. She could get in a fuck-ton of trouble if anyone knew she was involved with whatever we end up doing."

"We don't know when the next fights are anyway," Griselda said, still giving Snout the hairy eyeball.

"Buck Buck," I said, "What do you have? Before Gris kicks your brother's ass."

"Crop dusters. Do some flyovers and see what we can see. Pirate Jenkins owes me a favor and he's got an old biplane."

"Please tell me they call him Pirate because he has a parrot."

"He might. I don't know. He's got one eye and one leg though. But don't worry, he don't let that stop him."

"Yeah, only lazy pilots have depth perception," I said. "Don't you think that maybe the people on the ground would notice a low flying plane? They're not exactly quiet."

"I didn't think of that. I just wanted to do a Red Baron."

Russell cleared his throat. "That actually segues nicely to my idea."

Other than the hellos at the beginning of the meeting, it was the first time I could remember hearing Russell speak.

"Thank you, Russell," I said. "It'll be good to hear an idea that isn't completely insane."

"You said no judging," Snout said. "It's hard going first."

Russell didn't bother to stand. "It seems to me that if you want to get inside a fenced-in area, you can't do it directly. You need some form of subterfuge," Russell said. "You need to hit a ball over the fence and ask the neighbor to go into his backyard to retrieve it. Perceived innocence should allow us to walk in."

Buck Buck said, "Having a pickup baseball game out in the middle of the desert is going to be a little suspicious."

"That was a metaphor. Have you heard of Plaster Blaster?"

"Um. I'm all about doing whatever it takes," Snout said, "but I don't see how making a plaster cast of my dong is going to help."

After the laughter waned, Russell explained. "I don't know if it still happens, but in late fall, early winter, a bunch of people—scientists, engineers, hobbyists—go out to that part of the desert and fire model rockets. It's in a dry wash close enough to Plaster City to give it its name. And they're not launching your grandfather's rockets. Big ones."

Buck Buck got excited. "Why didn't I think of that? I been out there once to watch. YouTube it, man. Dork nerds—no offense, Russell—get way into it. Someone made a full-size X-wing one time. It was badass. Blew up in three seconds, but that makes it awesomer, because they did all that work knowing that's what was going to happen. It's not like it was going to reach the moon. They just wanted to see that rad bastard fly."

"I hope whoever was in the cockpit ejected in time," Snout said.

"There wasn't anyone in the cockpit, dumbass," Buck Buck said.

"Then who was flying it?"

"If that isn't until fall, how does that help us now?" I said, interrupting them. I knew Buck Buck and Snout well enough to know that if I didn't nip that debate in the bud, they would eventually come to blows. In the Buckley family, whoever won the fistfight won the wordfight.

"Plaster Blaster might be in fall," Russell said, "but this gang wouldn't know that. People test rockets out there all the time. Good visibility, low wind, even terrain. They've probably seen some. I was out there a month ago with some students from my class."

"So the idea is, we go out, shoot off some rockets, and see if we can't get one to land inside the biker's fence in Plaster City," I said.

Buck Buck took over my train of thought. "The rocket lands in biker country, we knock on the door, a couple nerdly nerds looking for their man-toy rocket ship. No reason to think we're up to no good. They don't want no trouble. Either they let us get it or they tell us to fuck off."

"Stupid, but plausible," I said. "Our kind of plan."

"I have the perfect disguise," Buck Buck said.

"Let me guess. A pocket protector and tape-repaired glasses?" I said.

"And a bowtie," he said.

I turned to Russell. "Can you really aim those things that well? How close would we have to be?"

"Let me e-mail some people in the rocket community. It's doable. It's all math."

Tucking in Juan, I could hear Griselda and Angie talking in the other room. It made me nervous when those two got together. Egotist that I am, I always assumed they were talking about me. There would have been some relief if I'd heard laughter. At least as the butt of the joke, I was entertaining. But all I heard were whispered voices and silence. That made me itchy.

Juan looked tuckered out from his debut music gig over at Morales. He looked up at me through tired eyes, as I pulled the sheet to his chin.

"What happened to my mom?" Juan asked.

"Angie? She's in the other room."

"Not her."

That had been a dodge, a reflexive stalling tactic, and I felt a flush of shame for having come out with it. I knew he wasn't talking about Angie.

So this was it. I had hoped that Juan would have been a little older when we finally had this talk. And even though I knew the topic would arise, I still had no clue the best way to handle it. I decided to go with honesty.

"Your mother died."

Juan didn't react, kept the same serious expression. He might have been young, but when you live on a farm, you gain a better understanding of mortality at a young age. Death is such a fundamental part of raising animals and farm living that it's seen as the natural thing that it is. And Juan was about the same age as I was when I found out my mother was dead and not just absent. But as she had died in childbirth, I didn't have any memories to contend with.

"She loved you very much," I said, not actually knowing if that was true. One truth, one lie. At least it was balanced.

"She's in heaven?"

"That's right." I counted that as half a lie. Just because I didn't believe in heaven didn't make it not true.

"I think of her. I see her. But now when I try, I can't see her good no more."

"What she looks like? Her face?" I asked.

"She had dark hair."

"That's right. Long dark hair. She was very pretty."

Juan closed his eyes really tight, making his face into a little fist. "I can't see her."

"Maybe when you go to sleep, she'll be in your dreams."

Juan nodded, keeping his eyes closed but allowing the muscles in his face to relax.

I leaned down and kissed Juan's forehead. "Good night, son."

"Good night, Pop."

I didn't get up right away. Sitting with my son, I didn't want to leave. I didn't ever want to leave. While I still wasn't sure if I'd totally gotten the hang of this whole fatherhood thing, I knew, sitting there in the dark, that I cared about Juan more than anybody or anything I'd ever cared about. Including myself. I loved my father. I loved Angie. But with Juan, there was more to it. I didn't just love him, I needed to protect him, to teach him, to be there for him no matter what. At that moment, I felt closer to knowing what it meant to be a father. Far away still, but closer.

Angie and Griselda clammed up when I grabbed a beer and joined them in the dining room. I'm pretty sure it was an act and they did it to fuck with me.

"Are you talking about my tiny penis again?" I said.

"Guilty," Angie said. "It's just so small."

"Angie did refer to it as 'adequate' and 'functional,' if that's any consolation," Griselda said.

"I'll take what I can get," I said.

We drank in silence for a minute, my presence changing the dynamic of the room. Eventually, Griselda stood up.

"I'm going to take off. I'm picking up Bobby before my shift starts."

"Bobby's getting released tomorrow? He didn't call me."

"He called me."

I smiled and nodded. "That's good. I'm glad. Be sure to debrief him."

"Okay," she said, walking to the door.

I cleared my throat. "I said, be sure to debrief him."

She gave me a smirk, but said nothing.

"Seriously?" I said. "You're going to ignore that setup? No punch line? That's like not returning a high five. You can't leave me hanging."

She exhaled dramatically. "Okay."

"Be sure to debrief him," I repeated.

"I will give him all the pertinent information," Griselda deadpanned. "And then I will remove his underwear. Or briefs. Thusly, debriefing him in two very different ways."

"You ruined it, Gris. You ruined it."

Angie and I went straight to bed, but I couldn't sleep. I should've gotten up, but chose instead to stare at the shapes the exterior bug light made on the wall. I couldn't remember the difference between a rhombus and a trapezoid, but the light made one of those.

I knew better than to let my brain spin all my worries and personal criticisms in my head, but somehow I couldn't escape the sucking whirlpool of my thoughts. I should have found a crossword or grabbed a book. Usually a chapter or two did the trick, shaking the Etch-a-Sketch, but that would have required getting out of bed and I was too tired to move. Too tired to sleep. And too tired to defend myself from myself.

"You're awake, aren't you?" Angie said.

"Yeah."

"You thinking about Julie and Bobby and this whole fuck-ing mess?"

"What else would I be thinking about?"

Angie rolled over and propped herself onto an elbow. "You want me to tell you everything's going to be okay?"

"Yeah, lie to me," I said. "You were pretty quiet at the meeting. And when I say 'pretty quiet,' I mean you didn't say a word. I'm doing the right thing, right?"

"I've been keeping my mouth shut. Mostly because I'm outside of all this. I hope Bobby gets his girl out of this mess, but I don't feel like I can contribute."

"What do you think of the plan? The rockets. Pretty crazy, huh?"

"I can't believe the smart guy is the one that came up with the stupid idea. But as idiotic as it is," Angie said, "it was the least dangerous idea on the table. I'll take stupid over dangerous any day."

"Although I'll admit that I'm a little tired of stupid."

Angie sat up, adjusting some pillows behind her so that she could lean against the headboard. "Here's the thing. We started raising Juan together at the same time we started dating. Practically the same day. You had no choice. I understand. But I did, and I chose to be here. The weird thing is that it always feels like you're the one with one foot out the door. Afraid to completely commit to this life."

"I love Juan. And you. I'm not going anywhere."

"But you are. You do. I know this, with Julie, it's different. But you always run when Bobby calls. This is real, Jimmy. What we're doing here, in this house. It's real life stuff. Juan needs you."

"I know, Angie. I didn't realize me leaving would bring those memories back. We talked about Yolanda a little. I think it went okay. Who the hell knows?"

"We'll figure it out, but we can only do that with you here. Here and engaged, not running around all over the place with Bobby, acting like an asshole."

"I'm not always acting like an asshole."

"I can't tell you to not be Bobby's friend. I know how deep that runs. And how important that friendship is in your life. But you have to be a father first. I ain't saying that for me."

"I know you're right, but I've got to finish this thing."

"I get that," Angie said. "But after you finish it, it has to really be finished. No more fucking about."

———•———

It was good to see Bobby on his feet. He looked a thousand times healthier, despite his arm in a sling. There's something about a hospital bed that makes people look sicker than they are. Even the people in the waiting room that are supposedly well look like shit compared to how they looked moments before they walked into the hospital. Maybe it's the lighting.

I dropped onto the lounge chair in his living room. Bobby ducked into the kitchen and came back with a couple beers. I took one.

"You sure that's okay with whatever medication you're taking?"

"It better be. I've been knocking them back all morning. Gris is at work. I got bored. I don't know if daytime TV has always been this bad, but fucking hell."

"So are Gris and you . . . ?"

Bobby shrugged off the question and took a pull of his beer. "We're not nothing until this whole mess is figured. I'm not hiding shit from her, but I'm still me."

"Make it work, dummy. Not just 'cause you two work, but you're a lunatic when you're single and heartbroke."

"I'm a lunatic all the time."

"Gris gave you the rundown so far? Where we're at, what we're doing?"

"You know I want in, right?"

"Not with a broken wing, brother. Not until you heal up."

"One hand tied behind my back." But Bobby smiled weakly. It was obvious he wasn't happy about acting in a supporting role, but he wasn't about to let his pride affect Julie's safety.

"Russell said he'd call me later today. Pretty sure the rocket would work, just figuring out some maths and sciences."

Bobby nodded, a little distracted. "I been reading Julie's diary, her journals or whatever. Would never've done it if she were here, like trespassing, reading secrets. But seeing as how she shot me, I figured, fair play.

"The move from Twentynine Palms to Indio was hard on her. She's a kid. She don't understand that Becky had to move for work and to get away from this asshole jarhead up there. I got the whole story on that from Beck. Julie don't see that Beck's trying to make a better place for her, because she had to leave her friends and her life.

"So she gets to Indio and you can tell the way she writes that there's this point that she wants to do shit to hurt Beck. There's a scary, teenage revenginess all over the journal."

"Revenge on Becky and you," I said.

"Not me. Just Becky. I don't come up, not once in all the journals. I'm only an influence on her in not being one. Only impact I have is being not there. Thing is, if I were around, would it have been any better? Damned if you do, you know?

"She mentions a few fights she got in. Not the videoed ones, but regular two-girls-behind-the-gym catfights. Here's the fucked part. You can tell she loved it. Or I could, because I know that feeling. I'd read it to you, but it's awful. She talks about how it feels to get hit, how she likes the pain. But more, she talks about landing that punch that does damage, where she can see the other girl's eyes go glassy. And the next punch that she lands as the girl is falling to the ground."

"Damn," I said.

"That's heavy shit," Bobby agreed. "It's one thing to enjoy the scrap, but to want to hurt someone bad? What kind of pain do you have inside that makes that feel good? I like a melee, but I don't want to hurt no one. This girl—my girl—is all about hurting."

"Does it mention anything about Gabe and Chucho and Driskell and all that stuff?"

"They stop before all that. This is all a girl who thinks she's a woman. And part of being a woman to her is taking care of herself, not relying on anybody else, and fucking up people that get in her way. Julie might be in pain, but in these journals, she never sounds weak. In fact, she sounds fucking dangerous."

My phone rang, playing "The Gonk" loudly. I answered quickly.

"Hey, Russell. You talk to your friends?"

I listened and then hung up.

"So?" Bobby said.

"He can do it. He can land a rocket inside the compound. He'll have everything he needs the day after tomorrow. We're good to go."

FIFTEEN

It's not on newer maps, but every old map of the Imperial Valley has a dot between Seeley and Plaster City marked "Dixieland." Maybe it was a town, but no one seems to know. I vaguely remember a diner there. Probably called the Dixieland Diner. But I could have manufactured that in my head. Whatever Dixieland was, it ain't no more. A dot on an outdated map with no evidence of anything ever having been there. No concrete foundations, no burnt-out chimney, no weathered fence. Scrub and chaparral its current and permanent residents.

The remnants of a dirt road ran through the spot. Deep-rutted and unmaintained, the road was still popular with off-roaders and dirt-bikers for getting deeper into the wasteland. That rocky path led to Pumice Creek Wash, a flat expanse of nothingness. The far west end of that dry wash was less than a half mile from the eastern border of Plaster City.

Before getting the gear together, I did my due diligence and made a call to Gabe to see if he had heard from Chucho. There was a chance Chucho and Julie were somewhere else, after all, and we might be able to avoid going through with the rocket plan. Gabe told me that he had tried Chucho a few times, but no answer. Even a few mutual friends hadn't heard from him. I thanked him, telling Gabe that if we found Chucho and Julie in Plaster City, I'd let him know.

We rode in Snout's van, which unfortunately was painted identically to B.A.'s van from *The A-Team*. Something more inconspicuous would have probably been better, but it was the only van we had access to. And before you ask, yes, the horn played the opening bars of the theme song.

Buck Buck and Snout rode up front, while Russell and I bounced around in the back. Gris was with Bobby in Seeley. It hadn't been easy to get Bobby to hang back, but beyond his injury, he was too recognizable, both Chucho and Julie knew him. And with his hair, Mr. Magoo could spot him from a couple hundred yards.

We drove past two Border Patrol SUVs headed the other way. Usually they stayed south of the highway, as the stretch of desert between the border and the highway was the high traffic zone for illegal immigration. I was relieved that we weren't stopped. Owning a van in the Imperial Valley was practically probable cause.

We had it all planned out. Russell would land a rocket inside the bikers' compound. Buck Buck and I would go to retrieve the rocket. If we spotted Julie, we would call Griselda. It could end right there, if we got lucky. But I leaned somewhere between realist and fatalist. The most we could hope for would be to get a better idea of how many people were in the compound. Maybe some other clue. And to not get our asses kicked.

"Is this going to be close enough?" I asked Russell.

"They're really designed to go straight up," Russell said. "Technically, you're not supposed to aim a rocket more than twenty degrees from vertical. Dangerous. I might have to dip it under to cover the half mile. My fellow enthusiasts would frown on that. I can't hit a bull's eye, but close. Half mile is 2,640 feet. I can do it with a three-stage."

"We're going to shoot rockets. How cool is that?" Snout said, doing a little dance in his seat and giving Buck Buck a punch in the arm.

"Snout really likes explosions and explosion-related paraphernalia," Buck Buck said.

"Maybe we'll come out some other time, under different circumstances," I said. "I'd love to show Juan."

Russell nodded, but he had switched gears, concentrating on sorting through wires or whatever he was doing. This wasn't his normal day. It wasn't leisure. The weight of what was happening was written all over his face.

"This is going to work," I said, giving him a pat on the shoulder. His nod was unconvincing.

It worried me that we were putting a bunch of our eggs in this basket. If Julie wasn't there, we could be inviting trouble from a group best avoided. Julie and Chucho could have taken off to Yuma or Mexico or San Diego or pretty much anywhere on the damn globe. But if they had, what could we do? This was the thing in front of us, something we could do. And even if it led to nothing, it was better than doing nothing.

When people are scared or in danger, instinct tells them to run to friends, to a safe place, to people they trust. The only other place that Julie might have headed was Twentynine Palms to be with her old friends. But they were from her old, normal teenage life. Now she's a bad girl on the run, and if Chucho had a say in the matter, this is where he'd go.

Snout stopped the van at the edge of the wash. He hopped out, singing "Rocket Man." And when I say singing,

I mean shouting the chorus at full volume. The back doors of the van opened. We slid out and took a look at Plaster City in the distance, a mirage of white structures. Russell looked through the scope of his high-tech laser range finder. I used my low-tech finger to point.

"You see that fenced-in area on the right? That's where we need the rocket to land. Anywhere inside there."

"Bigger area than I thought. That's good." He looked at his range finder. "This is saying 1,900 feet."

Here's where country living had its advantages. City folk have no idea what the length of a mile is. Not by eye, at least. They measure in blocks or minutes. In the country, particularly country as flat as the Imperial Valley, everything is measured in miles and half miles. Three hundred twenty acres is half a square mile. So for instance, the acreage near my house is a half mile by a half mile. Or in simpler terms, it's a half mile from my house to the stop sign on McCabe Road. I could count off that distance in paces and be right within twenty feet.

"Sorry, Russ," Buck Buck said, "that doohickey ain't right. It's short."

"This is one of the best range finders on the market."

"How many feet did you say a half mile was?"

"Exactly 2,640 feet," Russell answered.

"It's wrong. I got one not quite as good as that one, and on hot days and far distances, the laser goes wonky. From the heat waves. There ain't nothing between us and that building there, but I trust my eye."

Russell nodded. "I haven't used this much, but it would make sense that the heat from the ground might refract the light. We have to be right, though. How far would you say it is?"

"Under a half mile, but not by much. Closer to 2,400 feet. Snout?" Buck Buck said.

"Definitely not over a half. Yeah, looks about right. Jimmy?" Snout said.

"I would've said somewhere between 2,400 and 2,500. It sounds crazy, but I got to go with Buck Buck over science on this one rare occasion," I said.

"I trust the consensus," Russell said. "I've got two identical rockets. If I don't get the first one right, I should be able to make the adjustment on the second one, so long as it gets close."

We let Russell do his thing and set up the rocket. So simple, he didn't even need our help. A stand and the propulsion mechanism—that was it. According to Russell, it was all about getting the angle and the engine load right. Which came down to his calculations. I would've helped, but math.

Snout, Buck Buck, and I sat in the shade of the van, giving Russell space to work. He paced a rut and made notes with the nub of a pencil on a scrap of paper. He talked to himself about Newtons and thrust and pounds, constantly looking back to Plaster City and his target. He even licked his finger and felt the air, but I'm pretty sure he did that for show since the air was as dead as Paul Lynde, peace be upon him.

The rocket was a thing of beauty. Three feet tall and bright orange with long fins. You could see the separate stages and where they would break apart. The tip of its nose looked sharp enough to draw blood. It was sleek and if you told me that it could make it to the moon, I wouldn't've called you a liar.

"The idea," Russell said, "is that it hits altitude above the target area, the nose opens, and it drifts down on its chute inside the fence, onto a roof or something. There's no wind, so we're lucky there. Let's try it and see what happens."

"Can I press the launch button?" Snout asked, forehead knotted with worry that he might be refused.

When Russell said, "Yes," I thought Snout was going to shit from happiness. It had happened before when Buck Buck got him a bouncy castle for his thirtieth birthday. Snout did another little dance, this time singing "Major Tom" at full volume.

Snout demanded a countdown. No one argued. A rocket launch without a countdown was sacrilege, bad luck. And there was no reason to spit in Fate's face.

At "Blastoff," Snout triggered the rocket. The engines burned, shooting fire and smoke, the rocket motionless for a moment. Then, strangely slow, the rocket rose above the smoke. But it didn't go slow for long, something clicked and that mother shrunk into the distance at superspeed. We whooped and hollered and high-fived. Except Russell, who had his scope on the rocket, watching its ascent.

"Come on, come on, come on," Russell repeated like a mantra.

Remembering why we were there, we stopped our antics and watched Russell expectantly.

"Second stage. Come on."

I squinted into the distance. I could see the trail of smoke, but I couldn't make out the rocket as it got near the sun.

"Third stage. We've got the distance. Open, open, open."

Snout grabbed my arm and squeezed like my date at a horror movie.

"Chute's away. Appears to be over target. Falling, falling."

Russell dropped the scope, letting it hang from his chest. He turned to us.

"Yeah?" I asked.

"It's inside the compound. It worked. Looks like maybe on top of a structure. Hard to tell, but definitely within the perimeter."

"Great job, Russell." I shook his hand. Buck Buck and Snout gave him hearty backslaps that pushed him forward into me.

"I'll admit," Russell said. "Most of my earlier confidence was bravado. I'm a little shocked that it worked on the first attempt."

There had been so many defeats over the last few days, this small victory was unbelievably important. I wanted to celebrate, but I would have to wait. The rocket was just the beginning of the plan.

———◆———

Buck Buck and I had drawn the short straws by the process of elimination. Bobby was hurt. Julie would recognize Russell right away and infiltrating a biker gang compound wasn't his charge. Snout was out, mostly because Snout was Snout. I knew it was risky to go myself, as both Chucho and Julie had seen my face, but it hadn't been for very long and I was the only one in the group who knew what Chucho looked like.

Buck Buck studied the photo of Julie as we walked.

"She might look different, so really look at the eyes," I said.

Buck Buck hadn't been joking about the disguises. When he pulled out his duffel bag of white button-up shirts, pocket protectors, and tape-repaired glasses, I laughed hard enough to choke on spit.

Buck Buck looked hurt, but stuck by his guns. "Look, Jimmy. When you got a bad lie to tell, you're best to keep it strange. I might not be the smartest guy, but to me, this is what a grown man who plays with toy rockets looks like. In my brain, this is what I see. My guess is them bikers ain't no smarter than me. Means this is what they think a rocket nerd looks like, too. To you, we look ridiculous. But to them, we look how we're supposed to."

I felt bad for laughing. The ironclad logic of his argument threw me. I started to think that Buck Buck played dumber than he was. And the disguise, especially the thick-framed glasses, would go a long way to hiding my appearance. In costume, people saw the costume first and had to work their way to the person underneath.

Armed with nothing but a row of ballpoints in our front pockets and high-water pants, Buck Buck and I hiked the half mile over the flat desert wash to Plaster City. Buck Buck kicked at the dirt, watching the clouds of dust fall straight to the ground, nowhere to go in the windless air.

"Look," Buck Buck said, "I know you're used to sidekicking for Bobby and not me. And I'm used to Snout being my sidekick. But I'm sure we can work it out. Batman usually's got Robin, but I'm sure he teamed up with Aqualad or Speedy and they still beat the bad guy."

"Am I Aqualad in that scenario? I don't sidekick for Bobby," I said. "I can't believe people can't see this. He's my sidekick. Which means you're Aqualad. I'm Batman."

"I'm really more of a leading man."

"Okay, how 'bout this? You're still Batman. I'll be Superman. They teamed up all the time. Snout and Bobby are the sidekicks."

"I can work with that. But I want to be Green Arrow instead." Buck Buck scooped up some dirt without losing a step. "It's kind of crazy this was all underwater once." He let the dirt sift through his fingers and held up his hand, showing me a few tiny seashells.

"When I was a kid, we'd dig up all kinds of shells. There's like oyster-sized ones around here somewhere. Pop knew the good spots. I really need to take Juan out here."

"Shells are like bones, right? Which makes this like a graveyard kind of."

"Considering how old everything is, no matter where you step on the planet, you're probably walking on something's remains."

"Creepy."

He rubbed his hands together, letting the shells and dirt fall to the stark white ground. The sign that we had reached our destination. We were at the edge of Plaster City.

Where we had entered, a half dozen double-wides sat out in the open. With no outside additions like a deck or porch, they looked like they had been used as office structures, part of the factory grounds. Some of the windows were boarded. The ones that weren't were broken.

I poked my head in the open window of the first building. It smelled like a dog's breath. The inside was gutted, no interior walls, like an empty truck trailer. Birdshit, animal bones, and thick dust lined the ground. Cobwebs fell like hammocks from the ceiling. I could only imagine the size of the spiders that made them. The desert doesn't fuck around when it comes to spiders.

Buck Buck peeked over my shoulder. "Why would you make a dumbass tent town when all these need is a good hosing off?"

"Putting up a fence like that's harder than getting a bunch of shitty campers. And if you're up to no good, you want a good fence."

"Suppose," Buck Buck said. "I've been thinking about our plan."

"Yeah?"

"Were we drunk when we came up with it?"

"No. I wasn't, at least."

"It's just that it's one of the weirder, dumber things we've tried. It's weird that this is the best we could come up with sober."

"You're bringing it up now?"

"I'm not saying it's not a good idea. Or it won't work. I'm saying it's dumb. That's all. Constructive criticism."

Looking toward the fence, I wondered if there were eyes on us. From where we stood, the van was in full view. I could vaguely make out Russell and Snout setting up another rocket. A good lie is in the details. Anyone paying attention could have watched us shoot off the rocket, walk the distance, and stand where we were. We weren't hiding. But would they even bother with a lookout way out here?

The white hardpack turned into white pavement, transitioning from desert to civilization. Still no activity or movement from the fenced-in area. Buck Buck and I stopped next to an empty propane tank across the street from the gate. I heard music and men's voices. I didn't know there was such a thing as Mexican Death Metal, but if I could give the music a genre, that's what it was. Death Mexal. Growling Spanish lyrics accompanied by grinding guitar, rapid-fire drums, and—I swear—a hint of tuba.

"We knock?" Buck Buck asked.

I shrugged. "How else?"

"Screw it. Do it."

I held up a palm. I wanted to rehearse. I added a spitty lisp to really sell the sitcom-nerd stereotype. "Hello, there. I apologize profusely for the inconvenience, but my scale-model rocket landed inside of your vicinity somewhere. I would request you retrieve it yourself, but I fear that one of the engines did not ignite. It might explode and I'd hate to put a noncombatant, as it were, at risk."

"Is that really what you're going to say?"

But I never got my chance to deliver what I'm sure would have been a Razzie-worthy performance.

We took one step onto the road when the sound of squealing tires sent us ducking back behind the propane tank. Buck Buck and I watched a sun-faded burgundy Chrysler LeBaron with a primer door and its hood held down with bungee cord race down the road, skid to face the gate, and crash right through it, sending the big square of chain link straight up into the air.

"That's one way to do it," Buck Buck said.

"I know that car. That's Gabe, Julie's old boyfriend. I talked to him this morning and—Oh, shit. I might have told him I thought Julie and Chucho were out here. He's either coming to fuck Chucho up, save Julie, or both."

"He's pissed, that's for sure. What do we do? Scrap the plan?"

"The kid's a better distraction than our dumbass plan. Let's take a closer look. See if we can spot Julie."

Buck Buck and I ran across the street and peeked through an area of the fence near the gate that had been damaged by Gabe's battering-ramming. It gave a decent view of the grounds and the various structures through a pair of Dumpsters that smelled like cabbage farts. For some idiotic reason, they had created a picnic area with a few rusted and battered patio sets with torn umbrellas right near the Dumpsters.

There were ten trailers or motor homes parked in a haphazard fashion within the lot, as well as a couple of big tents. Nearer the loading dock were some storage containers and a truck trailer. It looked like someone had planned a little community, abandoned it, and the current residents were squatting. Either that or someone had watched *The Road Warrior* one too many times. Motorcycles sat parked in front of most of the structures. I counted sixteen.

Mexican bikers appeared from all different directions, surrounding the LeBaron as Gabe got out. Only four of the bikers were armed. Two pistols and two shotguns. The rest of the men stood around, curious, more startled than ready to fight. The only one I recognized was Cold Sore. That thing still hadn't healed.

Gabe had skidded to a halt in the center of the lot. He left the engine running and got out of the car. He didn't look intimidated or scared by the leatherclad army around him. He examined everyone's face, and then shouted, "Julie!"

The bikers looked at each other but didn't make a move on Gabe. A couple of them made jokes in Spanish that I couldn't make out, forcing a smile or a laugh.

"That's got to be most of them. Least the ones at home," I whispered to Buck Buck. "A car crashing onto your land brings everyone out."

"I count nineteen. Only a couple pieces, but that don't mean they ain't packing deeper."

Gabe continued shouting. "Julie. I know you're here. I just want to talk."

"You see any girls?" I asked Buck Buck.

"No chicks at all. Just the dudes. But look at that guy by that mobile home near the loading docks. It's the only one with no bike out front. Does it look like he's guarding it?"

"He's definitely standing like he's at attention. And he didn't make a move to—"

The last words caught in my mouth as Chucho stepped out of the mobile home we were referring to. He yelled behind him at someone. I had a good guess who, even if I couldn't see her. He shut the door. Not enough to call Gris, but enough to feel like my hunch was right. Either way, we had eyes on Chucho. If he was there, Julie was too.

"That Chucho?" Buck Buck asked.

Gabe answered for me. "Where's Julie, you fucking pendejo?"

"You fucked up our gate," Chucho said, as he approached.

"Were you with Julie while me and her were going out?"

"You ain't going out no more, so who gives a shit?"

"Not what I asked. Means she wasn't with that rich dude in La Quinta. She was with you."

Chucho shrugged, smirked. "I take what I want."

"You're about to take an ass-kicking. Unless you need your boys to do your fighting for you." Gabe waved his hands at the men around him.

"Let's go," Chucho said. Although the words were unnecessary, as his arms were already held out wide in the universal gesture for "let's go." He picked up his step and ran toward Gabe, a couple of bikers parting to let him into the circle. He made a leap toward Gabe, attempting to tackle him around the waist.

But Gabe (and everyone else) saw it coming. He sidestepped Chucho just enough to throw him over his thigh as he brought an elbow down on the back of his neck. Chucho ate shit on the hard ground, sliding a little on his face.

If I were Gabe, I would've jumped on Chucho's back, held him down with my knees, and whaled on him. But Gabe was more honorable than I'll ever be. He got in a boxing stance and waited for Chucho to stand. He wanted to humiliate Chucho properly. He didn't want an asterisk on the victory.

The problem was that when someone with honor fights someone dishonorable, the latter will always pull a dick move. More damage has been done by that bullshit Vince Lombardi quote about winning than can be imagined. Because dumbshits use it as license to cheat. If you believe winning is the only thing, you're an idiot.

Chucho got up on an elbow, his face scraped and dirty, and pulled a pistol from his jacket. It was hard to tell from that distance, but there was a good chance it was Bobby's gun.

Gabe was too angry to be scared. He screamed, spit flying in Chucho's direction. "Do it, you bitch." He turned to the crowd. "You going to let him pull a puss move like that? Not man enough to fight straight up."

One of the bikers stepped forward. He wasn't the biggest guy there, but he looked a little older than the others. He had that relaxed gait that told you he wasn't about to take any shit. "Put it away, Chucho."

Chucho hesitated for a moment, but only that. He had no interest in testing the seriousness of the request. He put the pistol away and got to his feet. "He attacked us, Goyo. Can't let that go."

Goyo took a step toward Chucho, which made him flinch. "You brought this here, so it's on you, too. You're the one going to be fixing the busted gate."

Buck Buck and I both ducked down when everyone turned to look at the damaged gate.

"But I was—"

"Cállate," Goyo shouted. He walked to Gabe, stopping a few feet in front of him. "You might want to fight Chucho, you might even got good reasons. That's between you two. But you broke our property, killed my buzz, and messed up my day."

Before Gabe could do anything, Goyo cleared the distance and dropped him with an explosive haymaker. I swear I felt the air buckle when it landed.

He turned to one of the other bikers. "Put him somewhere. Anywhere but with the girls. I want to talk to him. Flaco, Rubio, ditch the car. Strip it, dump it, let the desert bury it, just get rid of it."

Chucho did his best to blend in with the rest of the men, but Goyo wasn't having any.

Goyo grabbed Chucho's jacket. "We're Los Hermanos. Someone challenged you straight up, let you take the first shot, and you pulled a gun? I should fucking beat your ass out of principle."

"They're breaking up," Buck Buck said. "We need to make like the vice squad and get the fuck out of the neighborhood."

"We can't just leave the kid there."

Buck Buck and I watched a big, shirtless biker drag the unconscious Gabe toward one of the trailers, his boots scraping furrows along the ground.

"Got to," Buck Buck said. He booked it across the street.

I stared for a moment. "Fuck."

The biker took Gabe behind a storage container, out of view. That's when I saw it. Between the storage container and where I stood. Roughly drawn into the ground with a stick was what looked like a bird, the dark lines visible on the white surface. Or at least, I thought it was a bird. It was like that geoglyph out in the desert, hard to see except from above. I squinted my eyes trying to get a better look, until I realized that I was exposing myself for too long.

I hightailed it back toward the office trailers, joining Buck Buck and keeping low and out of sight. When we reached the edge of Plaster City, I looked at the expanse of open desert that we had to cross. I spotted Snout's van. A Border Patrol SUV was parked next to it. But that was an afterthought, really. Most of my attention was on the other Border Patrol SUV that drove over the dry wash straight toward us.

"Free ride," Buck Buck said.

The SUV stopped in front of us and idled for a long moment. The reflection off the windshield made it impossible to see the driver. After a moment, Little Piwi stepped out of the passenger's side. He pointed a big thumb to the back.

"Run or fight?" Buck Buck asked.

"There's nowhere to run. No reason to fight."

Buck Buck looked disappointed. "That's why you're a sidekick. There's always a reason to fight."

But we both walked to the SUV and climbed in the side door, sitting behind the mesh screen that separated us from the front.

The Border Patrol officer drove back to Snout's van. Little Piwi opened the door, letting Buck Buck hop out. As I was about to take a step down, Little Piwi shook his head and pointed back into the SUV. I sat back down. Buck Buck joined Snout, Russell, and two Mexicans in suits, who loaded the rocket equipment into the back of Snout's van. A Border Patrol officer leaned against his vehicle and smoked.

Little Piwi held out his hand to me.

"I don't know what that means. I don't have a weapon, if that's what you're worried about."

He made the phone gesture with his other hand, thumb and pinky sticking out, then opened his palm to me again.

I took out my phone and placed it in his big paw. He tucked it into his jacket pocket, slammed the door, and sat back in the passenger seat. He adjusted the rearview mirror so it looked at me. Our eyes met. The driver hit the gas and drove us over the wash and onto the dirt road. Little Piwi's eyes stayed on me for the whole drive. We were dropped off at a black SUV parked just outside of Seeley.

I had a ton of questions, but I knew better than to ask Little Piwi anything. I could get more information talking to my dick. I didn't test the theory though.

SIXTEEN

Tomás did not look happy, a disappointed parent staring at a teenager rolling in at three in the morning. My heart wasn't exactly filled with Sanrio characters and duckling kisses, so I matched his look with one of my own.

Little Piwi had driven me in the black SUV to Elvia's, a Mexican restaurant in the middle of the country between Holtville and Calexico. A family restaurant with a jungle gym and two seesaws out front, the place couldn't have been more isolated. While most restaurants relied on location, location, location, Elvia's food was so good that its remoteness didn't matter, bringing in people from all over the Valley.

But not that day. It was lunchtime and the place was empty except for Tomás. It might have had something to do with the half dozen intimidating Mexicans in suits standing around outside. Tomás sat with his back to the wall at a corner table. The waitstaff brought water and beer and food. We didn't order or talk to them beyond a nod and a *gracias* every time they brought something. After they brought enough food for ten people, they silently walked into the kitchen. I wouldn't have been surprised if they had walked straight out the backdoor, got in their cars, and drove away. Tomás had that effect on people.

Little Piwi had his own table near the front door. He had the same amount of food in front of him as the two of us, but since he consisted of ten people smashed together to make one giant person, the amount was more fitting. As he dispatched his chile rellenos, his eyes never left the front door.

A slight smile cut through Tomás's seriousness as he looked at my getup. "I like the pocket protector."

I looked down at my nerd disguise and shrugged.

"You keep showing up in places you shouldn't be," Tomás said, tearing off a bit of tortilla and smearing it in some mole sauce.

"I could say the same to you," I said. "There seems to be some overlap in our respective crusades."

"The only difference. You have no reason to be out there. I have a reason to be everywhere. What's your interest in Plaster City?"

"Same as in La Quinta. Bobby's girl is there. You?"

"You're done with that, I thought."

"Julie's not home yet, so no, we're not done."

"You're in the middle of something bigger than one girl."

"I was starting to get that feeling."

I hadn't been to Elvia's in a while and the food smelled great, but my appetite was all but gone. I picked up a tortilla chip, dipped it in guac, and took a bite.

"Help me make informed decisions then," I said. "What's your business in all this?"

Tomás shook his head. "You need to go home and forget about Plaster City."

"How long have you known me? I'm not doing that."

Tomás stared at me for a moment. He nodded to himself, took another few bites of food, and wiped his mouth with a napkin. "When Craig Driskell died, that should have ended the production of any videos on this side of the border. He was the financier and distributor. Like what a movie studio does. No Driskell, no studio. But apparently our biker friends found some brains. They went indie. And while I admire their entrepreneurial spirit, it interferes with my plans to fill the vacuum that Driskell's death was supposed to have created."

"You told me that you had nothing to do with Driskell's death."

"I tell you a lot of things," Tomás said. "You're my friend, Jimmy. But you have to look at this relationship a little more clearly. You have to see me for who I am."

"Did you kill Driskell?" I threw the chip in my hand down on the table, which admittedly didn't have quite the impact I was going for.

Tomás smiled. "You want me to confess to a murder? I wouldn't exactly be a criminal mastermind if I took credit for miscellaneous felony crimes. Doesn't matter how he died, he's dead."

I stood and turned to leave.

"Sit down." He didn't shout, but it was a command.

I sat back down. "So Driskell 'mysteriously' dies and now you're going to make videos of teenage girls fighting? That's the whole thing. The master plan. Christ, Tommy. Even for you, that's fucked up."

"'Even for me?'" Tomás repeated. "This is what I'm talking about. I appreciate that you think I'm some kind of good villain. I do. It's charming. But I'm not. I'm going to lift the hood and show you how this engine runs. These fights, they're nothing. Girls boxing? It's a Disney movie compared to some of the videos I've made. The things I've had people do. You have no idea."

"I don't want to hear any of this shit."

"I don't care what you want," Tomás shouted. "You need to know who the fuck you're talking to. Last few years, I've been making porno and playing the player, sure. Not no more. Over time and on the secret, I've gained information, contacts, power. I'm taking over. I've got the plaza in Mexicali. I own that city. And now I'm going to own this valley, too. The criminals, the law, the money, every fucking grain of sand. Nobody runs an operation without my say. Anyone gets in my way—innocent or guilty—they pay. Ass, cash, or the lash."

"Tommy," I said.

"Cállate," Tomás spat. "Don't call me that no more. Tommy ain't nobody. He was a guy you used to know. Not the chingón in front of you. I'm Tomás fucking Morales, motherfucker."

I watched him fume for a few seconds before speaking. "Okay, you're evil. I get it. Fuck."

"Always joking." Tomás glanced toward the front door and back to me. "You're the only person who doesn't fear me. You and Maves, but he don't scare. That has to change."

"You got that wrong. I'm plenty scared of you."

"Not enough," Tomás said. "Did you know I once had a guy eat a handful of broken glass because his count was low? Of course you don't. I've lost track of the number of body parts that people don't have anymore because of their poor judgment. I lit an innocent man on fire—did it myself—to make a point to some very guilty men. You ever seen pictures of those displayed corpses on the news? They make American

papers every once in a while. Page eight, if there are photos. Mexican papers, it's everyday front page. Bodies with no
heads sitting in lawn chairs. Hanging from overpasses. Torsos
along the highway. People now nothing but parts. And you
get mad at me for lying to you."

"There's such thing as right and wrong." It felt like a
stupid thing to say, but how do you respond to a list like that?

"So my priest tells me. Usually right before he buys a
disturbing variety of pornographic material from me."

I looked down at all the untouched food on the table.
The sweet scent of chiles and spices had disappeared. Only
the grease remained in the air.

"What happens now?" I said, beaten.

"You go home. You raise your son. Work in your fields.
Join the Rotary club. Go back to your life. Forget about whatever it is you were going to do."

"And what happens out there?"

"In Plaster City? I'm going to shut that down."

"I hate to ask. What does 'shut that down' mean exactly?"

"I hate to answer," Tomás said. "So I won't."

"There's got to be a way to let me pull Julie out without
affecting whatever Armageddon you're going to throw at
those bikers. She'll be in the cross-fire. She doesn't have to
get hurt. I can't let that happen."

"Sure you can. If she's with Los Hermanos, she's in danger right now. You think those girls are anything but slaves?"

"What if I can do it without getting in your way? When
do you release the hounds?"

Tomás thought about it. He took a long drink of water
and stared into space. I could only imagine the calculations
going on in his head.

"I am obviously not a sentimental person, but I appreciate the time you spent with me when I was a kid. I was younger and I know you hung out because you felt sorry for me. That's why you're sitting here and not facedown in an irrigation ditch. Loyalty is a contract for services rendered. But that debt has been paid with interest."

"I never said you owed me anything."

"Your word still means something to you, right?" Tomás asked.

I nodded. "Set the terms and I'll stick by them."

"You've been in contact with Griselda Villarreal."

"Have you been spying on me?"

Tomás shrugged. "She's the law. She can't know shit. I tell you anything, you have to keep her out. I'll know. Sheriffs don't go into the Yuha unless they get a call. If there's any police, there will be consequences."

"Consequences?"

"People might get hurt. People could even die."

"Are you threatening my friends?" I kicked the chair back and leaned in close to Tomás. Close enough to feel his heat. I saw Little Piwi stand in my peripheral vision. Tomás stared at me, silent, waiting.

He said, "The future hasn't happened. I don't know who, how, when. But accidents—and non-accidents—happen. I can't kill you, Jimmy. You're my friend. But someone you care about? Someone I don't give a shit about? I'd do that without thought or guilt. Hell, I wouldn't even do it. I'd have someone do it for me. You still want to try to save the girl?"

I turned and walked toward the front door. Little Piwi didn't stop me. With one hand on the knob, I stopped myself. I had no bargaining power. I let go of the knob and marched back to Tomás.

"I don't like threats," I said.

"Who does?"

"Okay, Gris is out. No cops. But I need Bobby and the boys."

"They kept their mouth shut about the other thing. Basically criminals themselves. Tell them if you want. But if Villarreal or any cop finds out from you or them, bad things happen."

I nodded. "Deal with the devil."

Tomás took the napkin from his lap and threw it on top of his plate. It soaked up the red sauce, darkening its edges. "I'm going to use Los Hermanos to send a message. It's a Mexican thing. Makeshift marketing. We like big displays of power. They help spread the word of one's magnitude and creativity among the circles I want to reach most. For that, I need an audience. The next time they have their fights, I'm going to let them have their fun, build a big crowd, and then bring the hammer down. Quickly, violently, and with enough people left alive to create legend."

"What about the girls?"

"They'll be absorbed into my operation. And if it eases your conscience, they'll get a better arrangement. No reason to waste talent."

"What in the fuck happened to you?"

"Opportunity."

"When are the next fights?"

"I don't know. That's why I have eyes on Plaster City. How my boys ended up catching sight of you. Did you really shoot a model rocket, dress up like that, and walk in there? That's the best plan you could come up with?"

"I had glasses on, too. Make fun all you want. It worked."

"Model rockets," Tomás shook his head and laughed. "I admire the originality."

"So I have until the next fights."

"And then you better not be anywhere near Plaster City. You're not a Bible reader, but you know how God would get all wrathful and take out a whole place? Like the Flood or Sodom and shit, wipe 'em from the map? When the smoke clears and the coyotes take the bodies, Plaster City ain't going to be much more than Bond's Corner or one of those other places that's nothing but a dot on an old map."

"Like Dixieland," I said without thinking.

"Exactly," Tomás said. "Little Piwi will drive you home. You should take some of this food with you. It would be a shame to waste it."

———————

When Little Piwi turned into my driveway, I saw Bobby's Ranchero parked behind my truck. The Mexican Gargantua handed me my phone and my leftovers, waited for me to get out, and then drove south.

Bobby came out the front door, his step a little quicker than that morning. He had color in his face and looked closer to his old self.

"Buck Buck gave me the haps. What the hell did Morales want?"

"We got to talk," I said. "A serious what-the-fuck-happens-next powwow."

Bobby nodded. "Then I better grab some beers."

I parked myself in one of the lawn chairs next to the sandbox and waited for Bobby to come back. I wanted to be careful how I framed this for Bobby. If he got the impression that Tomás had threatened Griselda—which he pretty much had—Bobby would go warpath.

Bobby handed me a beer and took a seat, showing some pain and leaning awkwardly toward his good side. "That was a mistake," he said. "Five bucks says I ain't going to be able to get back up without help. I feel like an old man."

I held out the bag of leftovers to Bobby.

He opened it up and smelled inside. "Elvia's?"

I nodded.

"Maybe later." He set down the bag between us.

"Angie's truck ain't here, so I'm guessing she's in town," I said. "You see her before she took off?"

"For like ten seconds. She was taking Juan to swimming lessons, I think she said."

"That's right." A few days ago, Juan's summer schedule had been etched in my brain. When he had to be dropped off or picked up. I should have remembered his lessons, but I couldn't even remember what day it was.

We sat and sipped our beers.

"Hey, man," Bobby said. "Are we okay? Me and you?"

I thought about it a moment and gave him a nod. "It'll take more than a difference of opinion, harsh language, and a few bruises to hurt this friendship. But some shit's got to change."

Bobby turned. "That so?"

"I've been one foot in and one foot out with this family stuff. I got to do it right. We're friends, but this is my last Mavescapade. Once Julie is home, I can't do this shit no more. I'll hang out, grab coffee, one beer, but no more crazy shit."

"You're retiring?"

"Hopefully on a win."

Bobby held up his beer, toasting that. "You got any other problems with me?"

"Tons. Your body odor, your bad breath, your love for the movie *Crank 2*."

"It's a classic."

"Also, your definition of the word *classic*."

Bobby laughed. "Okay, now that we're done with the marriage counseling, are you going to tell me what the fuck happened out in Plaster City? And with Morales?"

"I didn't see Julie."

"Yeah, Buck Buck said."

"But I saw one of her drawings. On the ground. I saw it, I'm sure. Pretty sure. Ninety percent. It was in that white shit out there, so it had to be recent. And Chucho was definitely there. I got to believe she's in there."

"Good enough for me," Bobby said. "You going to tell me how Morales fits into all this shit?"

I gave him the rundown of my conversation with Tomás.

"Did he say when the next fights would be?" Bobby asked.

"He didn't know. Or didn't say."

"Then, on your approval of course," Bobby said, "we gather all the violence we can rustle up and hit Plaster City with everything we got before Tomás goes Nagasaki on the place."

"The front door ain't the only way into a house. Didn't you learn anything from getting shot? We got to be cleverer."

"Lay it on me then. What's the plan?"

"I don't know," I said. "Hell, our last plan used model fucking rockets. It's not like we're good at coming up with plans. We're a desperate, dumbass bunch of dumbasses. See, I can't even insult us good."

Bobby adjusted his back in the beat-up lawn chair, one hand on his wound. He winced and immediately caught me reacting to his expression.

"It's fine. I'm fine," Bobby said.

"Peak of health. You got shot, stupid."

"Whatever slapdash high jinks, I'm coming along. Don't even open your mouth to argue, I'm going to be there. You went on your last mission to Plaster City without me and look how that turned out. You need my chaos. And it's my daughter, remember."

"First we have to figure out what the hell we're doing."

"What about ninjaing in there at night? Sounds like they're more posers than threats. Probably not that diligent about security. We shimmy in, get Julie out."

"There's too many of them to risk. We need a distraction. Something that will get Los Hos out of their compound. Then we could look around and avoid any head-on fighting."

"I know you prefer the backdoor, but I like head-on fighting. It's my forte."

"The *e* is pronounced at the end of *forte*," I said. "The best distraction would be the fights. They're on the factory grounds on the other side of the highway. That means the fenced-in area would be emptier."

"Didn't you just finish telling me that Tomás was waiting for the fights to go all Ragnarok?"

"He said he wanted a big display of power or something like that. So he'll wait until there's a good crowd and then hit the factory. We'll be safe on the other side of the highway."

"That's a lot of guessing and wishful thinking, bro. Plus, we don't know when the next fights are going down."

"That's what we got to find out. But that's the time to go. With all those people around, it's more likely they wouldn't notice some extra strange faces wandering around."

"I've always thought of your face as extra strange."

"The strangest."

"I hate to sound like I'm backing out of a battle," Bobby said, "but isn't that cutting it a little close?"

"No matter when we do this, we only get one shot. We got to take the best one."

"So we get Buck Buck, Snout, Gris . . ."

"We have to keep Griselda out of this."

Bobby turned to me, already shaking his head in disapproval. "Why?"

"I made a deal with Tomás. No police of any kind. Specifically Griselda. He called her out by name. She can't know anything. Besides, it puts her more in the shit if she knows what we're doing. This is going to get straight-up illegal."

"Bro, don't make me lie to her. I got this whole one hundred percent honesty thing going on. I told her I was going to be straight up from now on. That was like two days ago. You're killing me."

"I made a deal. It might be a bad deal, but it could've been worse. It's the one I made. You got to back my play. With Tomás, there's always an 'or else' attached to everything, even if he doesn't say it."

"Okay. I won't lie to her," Bobby said. "I just won't tell her anything."

I stood up and stretched my back. "I'm going to grab another beer. You want one?"

"No, I better not."

"Yeah, you're right. Maybe I shouldn't either."

"That was a joke, dumbshit. Of course, I want another beer."

―――――•―•―――――

An hour, the rest of the beers in the fridge, and a dozen bad ideas later, Bobby and I weren't any closer to constructing a decent plan. It mostly came down to waiting for the fights and then slipping into the compound, but the details never gelled. Tunnels, hang gliders, and smoke bombs were all discussed seriously.

My phone rang. Rudy. It occurred to me that I had forgotten to tell Bobby that I'd gone to see his father. I stood up, walked a few yards away, and answered the phone.

"Veeder, I got something that might help you. Been asking around to the locals. See who knows what about up the highway."

"And?"

"I want to see Bob."

I looked back at Bobby scratching at the edge of his bandage. He threw me a nod, curious about who was on the phone.

Rudy said, "I'm not threatening to hold back nothing, mind you. I'm not holding information ransom. I'll tell you what I heard. But I'd rather tell it to Bob in person. You coming out here got me thinking. I got fences to mend, sorrys to say. Bob's my boy. He likes it or not, that means something. And if a bunch of Mex thugs got my grandchild, I can't let that stand."

"Hold on."

I pressed the phone to my chest and walked back to Bobby.

"You ain't going to like this," I said. "I went to see your old man. When you were in the hospital, I was looking for any angle, asking all kinds of help. He's out by Plaster City, Coyote Wells, that part of the desert. Knows people out that way. Knows the area."

"Okay, so why's he calling?"

"He wants to see you."

"Yeah, fuck him."

"He says he heard some things. He wants to help get Julie back."

"And he won't tell us nothing unless I go see him? Fucking like him to put what he wants first."

"No, he specifically said the opposite. I know you two got issues, but if he honestly wants to help, it's you that has to put your shit aside, get in my fucking truck, and drive out there."

"You don't know him."

"Neither do you. At least, not who he is now. He ain't pulling some trick. There's no trick to pull." I shook my head. "You can't see the irony in all this? You're trying to save your daughter, who shot you, but you still want to save her, have her forgive you, or whatever the fuck. But you're not willing to forgive your own old man? Look at the hypocrisy of it."

Bobby stared at me, not hiding his anger. "The last time I saw him, I stabbed him in the hand with a fork. And that was our best Thanksgiving. I know he's not drinking or found

God or whatever the fuck, but he's still a mean son of a bitch who did a bunch of awful shit. Keep the silverware away from me, because I can't make any promises that my behavior has improved."

I put the phone back to my ear. "Rudy, you still there?"

"I'm here."

"We're on our way. It'll give you time to make us some Arnold Palmers. You still owe me from last time."

———————

Rudy made an entire pitcher. And just to be a dick about it, he had dug up some cocktail umbrellas and bendy straws and put them in the glasses. I didn't give him the satisfaction and ignored the flourishes, but it actually pissed me off how good my Arnold Palmer was. Most people make them too sweet.

At first, Bobby stayed in the truck. I sat with Rudy on the slanted deck.

"He going to just sit there?" Rudy asked.

"He wasn't exactly excited about coming out here. If he gets out of the truck, he has to talk to you, and I think he's concerned about what he'll say."

"What he'll say or what I'll do?"

"Look, I did my part. He's here. I need to know what you found out. You know what's at stake."

"Big party or something out in Plaster City on Friday. That's what I'm told. I'll give you the details when—Why ain't Bob getting out of the truck?"

"How do you know? What kind of party?"

Rudy gave Bobby a big wave. Bobby shook his head, but opened his door, got out, and slowly walked toward us.

I helped Bobby up onto the deck, doing my best to avoid aggravating his injury. Rudy stood not to shake or hug, but to avoid being at a disadvantage. Bobby and Rudy sussed each other out, circling each other, eyes locked. Curious and cautious. Two fighters prowling the ring. Protect yourself at all times.

"How's your shoulder?" Rudy asked.

"There's a hole in it."

"One in your head, too. But you never let that slow you."

"That's genetic."

Rudy nodded. "Don't matter the caliber, a bullet stings for days."

"A man of experience."

"In my long-past days."

I grabbed my drink off the small table. "You two got things to talk about and it's none of my business. If what you say is true, Rudy—and I still need to hear the details—Friday gives us time. But I'm going to admit, I'm concerned about leaving you two alone together. Should I be?"

"I'm busted up and he's old," Bobby said. "What are we going to do?"

"I need you both to promise that if I leave you alone for ten minutes nothing stupid is going to happen. Do I have to pat either of you down for weapons?"

"I'm trying to make amends here," Rudy said. "I got no bad feelings. Bobby's the one with the chip."

"I wonder fucking why."

"Ain't no swearing here," Rudy barked.

Bobby shouted a *fuck you* that if typed out would have at least thirty *u*'s. He stared Rudy down, his expression daring him to do something about it.

"Show some respect, Bob," Rudy said through gritted teeth. "Ain't no excuse for that language."

"Of course there is." Bobby laughed. "It's words. Every word's got a reason to be said. If it didn't, it wouldn't be a word. Just 'cause you're on God's good side now or whatever the fuck, don't mean you run the show. You may've asked and God may've forgiven you, but he ain't nearly as vengeful a dude as me. Give Mom her twenties and thirties back and we'll talk about forgiveness. For now, I'm trying to work my way to fucking tolerance."

They stared silently at each other for about five seconds.

"Okay, good," I said. "Closer to a Middle East cease-fire than a European armistice, but I'll take it. I'm going to wander the yard. Look at the animals. Don't kill each other. Yell all you want, but no fisticuffs."

I hopped off the deck—a good way to be reminded that I'd been mauled by a dog recently—and headed toward the graveyard of farm equipment, old cars, and scavenged satellite dishes. The animal smell rode the heat to the house. I was curious what kind of livestock could create that stench. I had money on a fusion of mule and sloth.

"Watch out for llama pies," Rudy called after me. "Haven't taught her to use toilet paper and Theresa thinks the world is her john. Very unladylike, even for a llama. And careful of Butthead. That goat can be a real hardcase."

Staying in the rough path that wound through the acres of rusted junk, I tried to remember the last time I had a tetanus shot. Did they give me one for the dog bite?

I hoped that some of the anger between Bobby and Rudy was for show and without me there it would settle down. Bravado and trash talk needed an audience. There was a good chance they would only stare at each other instead of talk, but for them that would be a step in the right direction.

Rudy's property was like other desert spreads. Nothing ever got thrown away. Or if it did, it got thrown out back. A junkyard of anachronistic farm equipment, gutted cars, a beat-up panel truck, fenced-in corrals, multiple sheds, and roaming animals. I was pretty sure I saw an iron lung. When you got all that space, it's easier to abandon large garbage than haul it away.

I kicked at the chickens that got underfoot as I strolled toward a barn in the distance. I wanted to get a closer view at what looked to be a DeSoto parked inside. Unlike the cars baking in the sun, a tarp half-covered the chassis and it looked clean. Black with suicide doors, Rudy's taste in vehicles was definitely better than Bobby's and his Ranchero.

I hopscotched through the minefield of diverse animal shits, some recognizable, some exotic. A pig snorted at me from its pen. It didn't bother to get up, lying underneath a slow running tap, letting the water drip onto its head.

"Hey, pig."

It snorted again.

When I looked back up, a goat stood in my path, maybe ten yards in front of me. I hadn't heard it or seen it, like it had appeared out of nowhere. Demonic creatures tend to do that.

"Hey, goat," I said. A regular Doctor Dolittle, I was.

The goat stared back at me with its creepy lizard eyes, projecting simultaneous hate and apathy like only a goat can. I walked forward, pretending that I wasn't intimidated. I wanted to take a look at that car and I was bigger than the goat was. I was higher on the food chain. Hell, I've eaten goat. I'd show no fear, demonstrate who was the evolutionarily dominant one, show that goat who was boss.

The goat was. The goat was definitely boss.

Within a few feet, the goat nut-butted me. Direct hit. He sunk my battleship. My own trademark move used against me. I leaned down, reflexively grabbing my groin, which only made it hurt more. The goat immediately tried to bite my face. I pulled my head away in time to avoid its teeth. It lunged again. I dodged, jumped onto the nearest fence rail, and leapt into the pigpen, my shoes sinking into what I hoped was mud, but was not.

The goat stared at me from the other side of the fence, calculating and patient, slowly chewing that way goats do. If there was a way to convince the goat to use his powers for good and not evil, I would have brought the goat along when we went into Plaster City. Unleash hell in goat-form on those bikers.

I never got a chance to see the DeSoto. Just another reason to hate goats.

Bobby approached from the house, quick-stepping toward me. The goat looked at him. Bobby casually shooed it with one hand and the bastard, son of a bitch, jerk goat walked away. Just like that. Walked away from a shooing. What the hell did I do?

"What are you doing to that pig?" Bobby asked.

I climbed the fence without answering and did my best to scrape the muck off my boots on a low rail.

"That was quick," I said.

"It's time to go."

"You guys work anything out? Reach any kind of peace?"

"This ain't a movie, bro. We're not going to talk for two minutes, reach some epiphany, and hug that shit out. We talked, agreed the past couldn't be changed. That we both got some work to do. But for the grandkids, if he was willing to make the effort, I'd meet him halfway."

"Did he tell you more details about what he found out? About Friday?"

My boots as clean as they were going to get, Bobby and I headed back to my truck.

"His buddy Lorenzo Silva runs Ocotillo Beer & Ammo, the only liquor store out in these parts. The closest other one is in Seeley. So Lorenzo's is where the desert rats stock up on booze. He told Rudy that some of them Hermanos bikers came in and ordered fifteen kegs for Friday. Got to mean fight night."

"Friday is two days away."

"Yeah, I understand time."

"We still don't got a plan."

"Rudy and I worked it out on this napkin." Bobby held up a ragged piece of paper covered in ballpoint. "The two of us might got our differences, but when it comes to mayhem we're of a same mind."

"I'm afraid to ask."

"You'll like it. It's clever and sneaky."

We walked past the house and Rudy sitting on the deck. He gave us a wave.

"See you on Friday," Rudy said.

I turned to Bobby. "Hell no."

"Yep. He's coming. If that old man wants to be the girl's grandfather, his first act of good fucking faith is going to be helping pull her ass from the fire."

SEVENTEEN

Friday.

The back of the panel truck felt like it was two hundred degrees. A steamy heat that drained my pores, slicked my skin, and made it difficult to breathe. Bobby and I sat facing each other behind the false wall at the end of the trailer nearest the cab. According to Rudy, it had been built by smugglers to sneak exotic animals from Mexico. I didn't believe him, but there were all sorts of used vehicles sold along the border with unique modifications. I had a buddy who got stopped on the border because the dogs smelled cocaine residue in the door panels of his recently purchased Vanagon. Caveat emptor, sucker. Carfax don't list that shit.

Having made an arrangement with Lorenzo at the liquor store, Rudy drove the truck to deliver the kegs to Plaster City. That would get us onto the grounds and, from there, everything would be improvised. The Maveses only plan to a point. Not really a plan if you think about it. More of a notion. But with all the random factors that could come into play, it didn't make sense to plan too far. That's how we ran. Slapdash, but not half-ass.

We had cut holes in the truck ceiling for air and light. The big bag of guns sat between us.

"Kind of ironical that we'd be in a truck full of beer," Bobby said, "but we didn't think to bring some back here to drink."

"I got water," I said, holding up my half-full bottle. "More I drink, the more I sweat."

Bobby shook his head. "I'm good."

"Are you? I really wish you would've let Buck Buck do this."

Bobby looked down at his arm. It was still in the sling, but to limit its movement he had secured it tightly to his body with a thick bandage. "With one arm tied behind my back."

"You already made that joke."

We hit a big bump, both of us lifting six inches off the truck floor and landing hard. Bobby winced and caught me looking.

"It's just pain, Jimmy. Me and pain, we're old pals. I only need one hand to shoot a gun. My main health concern is Gris. If she finds out about this, I'm a dead man."

"You didn't have a choice."

"I want good things for her, and I'm not a good thing sometimes. She makes me want to change, but I don't know if I can. This old dog ain't learned no new tricks. Wait, that's not true. I learned from an old guy how to open a wine bottle with a shoe."

"With a shoe?"

"I'll show you when this is over. It's pretty cool. I'm just saying, I don't want to, but I've fucked up and'll fuck up again."

"That sounds like an excuse."

"I'm out here, ain't I? Lying to her again."

Three loud knocks from the cab shut us up. Rudy telling us that we were pulling into Plaster City.

"They're waving me in," Rudy said, muted through the truck panel.

The truck slowed and took a right turn, which meant we were pulling into the factory and not the compound. That put us on the wrong side of the highway. He stopped, the engine idling.

"Ocotillo Beer & Ammo. I got your kegs. Where you want the bar set up?" Rudy asked.

A faint voice replied. "Drop the beer and ice over there in the shade. We'll take it from there."

"Didn't Lorenzo tell you? Had a problem with his refrigeration. No ice. Brought the Kegerators and a genny. It'll keep the beer cold longer and you'll be able to swap out kegs without having to pre-ice."

"We always use ice."

"If you want to run to El Centro and get ice, I don't care. Going to need a lot."

"No fucking ice. You're kidding me. It's ice."

"That's what Lorenzo told me. Talk to him. I'm the guy who drives the truck."

"Set the shit up. I ain't going to El Centro. Ice'll melt before I get back."

"This setup will work better," Rudy said. "Here's what I'll do. Looks like you're setting up for a heck of a party. Not only will I set up the bar, I'll bartend for you, work the keg. Since my divorce, my Friday nights are free. I might be able to make some tips on top. You got some bands playing?"

"Fights."

"Betting allowed? I just got paid."

"Definitely. Everyone bets."

"Sounds like fun."

"I'm going to have to ask about the bartending thing. Unpack the truck. Someone'll come over and talk to you, old man."

The truck crept forward, turned, and stopped. Rudy cut the engine.

"Not bad on his feet. I hope that wasn't too suspicious," I said.

"We'll find out soon enough," Bobby said.

Bobby and I reached into the big bag of guns and each took out a pistol.

"Guy walking toward us. Angry walk. Sit tight." Rudy's door opened and then it was quiet. There was some faint talk outside, but I couldn't make out the words.

Bobby and I waited. The back of the truck slid open and I could feel the weight of men climbing inside.

Rudy said, "Fifteen kegs, two Kegerators, a genny to run them, and enough diesel to keep the genny humming. Lorenzo threw in cups for the inconvenience."

"And you want to stay and be our bartender?"

"Man said it was fight night. I did a little boxing in my younger days. Used to go all the time to Mexicali, but the Indian casinos took all the good fights. Too expensive now. Nothing like a smoker on a Friday night."

"You pat him down?"

"No, Goyo. He was in the truck. I called Lorenzo. Said he was his guy. Look at him, hair like that, old dude, he's not a cop."

"Frisk him, cabrón."

"Cool with me," Rudy said. "I got a knife in my boot, I'll tell you right now."

There was some shuffling around and a few scattered comments. "Careful, son. My balls hang lower these days." "While you're down there, why don't you check my prostate?" "If I wore a wig, would my hair look like this?"

"He's clean."

Goyo said, "You know how to work all this shit? Set it up? Keep it running?"

"That genny's a little persnickety, but yeah, I can keep the beer flowing if that's what you're asking."

"Alright, old man. You're our bartender. I hope you ain't expecting no tips from this crowd. You'll be lucky they don't steal your truck."

"Are you serious? If anything happens to this truck, Lorenzo'll fire my behind. Only job anyone'll give me with my record."

"Yeah, they jam you up like that. After you unload the truck, Flaco will take it across the road."

"It'll be safe over there?"

"Yeah, it's all fenced in."

———◦———

After the truck was unloaded, someone—I assume Flaco—drove us across the road. Bobby and I kept as quiet as we could, even when the truck bounced hard and threw Bobby's shoulder against the wall. He bit his lower lip, but kept quiet.

Flaco parked and got out. We waited another fifteen minutes in silence before we removed the false wall. Out of the stale air of the compact space, the openness of the empty truck trailer felt fresher and cooler, even though it reeked of dust and sweat.

Bobby leaned down and looked through one of the peepholes we had put in the back of the truck.

"We're in. North side of the truck bays. Still some scattered Mexi-bikers strolling the grounds. I got to figure once things get going on the other side it'll clear out."

"We wait."

Because heat rises, Bobby and I laid down flat on the filthy trailer floor. We passed the remaining water back and forth.

"You'd think that raiding a biker gang's camp would be more glamorous, wouldn't you?" Bobby said.

"I don't do it for the fame. I do it for—well, mostly the stupidity. My gut says in short order, we're going to wish we were back here in the dark and quiet."

"You, maybe. You're all about stability and shit now. Family life. Home and garden. Quiet and responsible."

"You make it sound bad."

"For you, no. But you're you. All that gallivanting in your past led to life as a gentleman farmer. Me, I'm me. I can't wait to get out there and kick some fucking ass. Itching to wallow in the blood and guts of the thing. Fuck some shit up."

"And bring Julie home."

Bobby rolled his head to face me. "Fuck you. I didn't forget that. Don't change that I've been antsy for a fracas since the hospital."

An hour later, the compound cleared out. From what we could see, all the bikers made their way across the highway to the factory. Music blared, Spanish lyrics over what sounded like a video game soundtrack. The only bikers that we could see were two men shooting dice on a sheet of cardboard. While they weren't doing a good job of it, I assumed they were guarding the trailer they knelt in front of, most likely there to keep the girls in and not us or anyone else out. Who would be stupid enough to raid a biker camp?

The two guards looked up when two of their compatriots approached. One of them went into the trailer. Less than a minute later, he walked out with two teenage girls. One of them was LaShanda, the girl who had fought Julie in the video. The other one was a blonde, short with a thick neck. From the distance and through the peephole, it was hard to gauge their expressions, but their body language was surprisingly more invigorated than subdued. And while they didn't look like they disliked each other, they looked ready to fight. They walked with the two bikers out the gate.

"Ready?" Bobby asked.

"I'm never ready for shit like this," I said. "Which makes me wonder how I always seem to end up doing it."

"Soon as we're out of the truck, run to that shack thing over there. We can't make the distance to the trailer without being spotted, but from there we can wait for our moment. Don't shoot your gun unless it's life or death. No fear-firing."

I nodded.

Bobby walked to me and gave me a hard hug with his good arm. "I know what you're risking and how hard it is. Thanks, Jimmy."

"You would do the same for me. Hell, you have."

"It's different for me. You're scared and you're here. Says something, brother."

"Let's go get killed before I start crying."

I popped open the trapdoor (I'm telling you, this truck was tricked out full-on smuggler-style. I wouldn't be surprised if it had an ejector seat and smoke screen) and hopped down below the truck, immediately pressing myself against the back tire out of view. Bobby climbed down gripping with his one hand, but made it next to me without much problem. The open air and shade felt great.

Staying low to the ground, I scooted over to what was essentially a lean-to, a shed wall of corrugated tin leaning against a storage container. If the guards looked up in the three seconds I was in view, things would get shitty quick. They didn't and I slid into the room. My right foot hit something. That something groaned.

Gabe looked surprisingly happy to see me, considering that I had kicked him in the head. They had trussed him up like a calf, his arms and legs tied together behind him, bending him in a C. His mouth was duct-taped and I could see that he had spent some time chewing at it.

Bobby ducked under the wall next to me. I stared into Gabe's eyes and put my finger to my lips. He nodded. I tore the duct tape off Gabe's mouth and immediately covered it with my hand, feeling the gummy glue sticking my hand to his cheek. I waited a few seconds and then took my hand away.

Bobby had pulled out his knife. He sawed at the complex web of ropes that held Gabe. They tied him down the way I secure stuff, the bigger and stupider the knot, the better. When all you got is a granny, quantity beats quality.

"Thanks," Gabe said in a voice above a whisper.

"You seen Julie?" Bobby asked. "Julie here?"

"Ain't seen shit. Been in a container for days. I pulled a dumbass move coming here. Pretty sure they forgot about me. Then someone remembered and thought I was going to die, so they put me here. They're fucking idiots. Chucho comes in, kicks me a few times. No Julie. Sorry."

"Want to help?" I said.

"I'll fight every one of these motherfuckers. Tie me up? Fuck that."

Gabe's arms and legs fell to his side as Bobby finished cutting him loose. He rolled onto his stomach and shook the blood back into his hands.

"What do you need me to do?" Gabe asked.

"Make some noise," Bobby said. "Loud enough for those two fucks to hear."

Bobby took out his pistol and pointed it toward the entrance. I did the same, waiting for the space to fill. Gabe grabbed a pipe just to be armed, and then he screamed for help in two languages.

Both dice-rolling guards rushed into the space, the faster one almost running directly into my pistol. He stepped back, confused. Both men's eyes got huge when our presence and the presence of our pistols registered.

"Who the fuck are you?" the one with hair said.

He didn't get an answer. Unless pipe was an answer. Gabe dropped him, not unconscious, but to his knees. He put a hand to the visibly growing lump. I reached down and took his pistol from his belt.

"Don't got to hit me, man." The bald guard reached down with two very dainty fingers, plucked the pistol from his waistband, and dropped it on the ground. Gabe quickly picked it up, feeling its weight and examining it. The man held up his hands.

"What the fuck, Pelón?" Pipe Lump said.

"They got us," he said to Pipe Lump. "Why should I get hurt, too? And I know you been cheating at dice."

"You're out of Los Hos," Pipe Lump said. "When Goyo, Chucho, when they find out, you're done. These pendejos are just a couple of backward ass country fucks."

"You must like getting hit with a pipe," I said.

Bobby pointed at the men with the barrel of his pistol. "This is you, Gabe. We got to keep moving. Only got a short window. Got to go now. You watch these guys. Have Pelón here tie up fuckface. Then you tie him up. Keep them quiet. Got it?"

"Got it."

Pistol at the ready, I threw open the trailer door and rushed inside. Girl screams greeted me. Seven teenage girls, their ages ranging from fourteen to nineteen, lounged around the living room area of the trailer.

There wasn't much in the way of furnishings. Mattresses filled most of the floor areas against the walls. Water and soda bottles sat piled in one corner next to full garbage bags that stank of takeout Mexican and Doritos. Six fans blew the stench around, but did little to cool the stuffy space.

"Anyone else here? Is there anyone in back?" I shouted.

Bobby didn't wait for an answer, rushing into the back of the trailer, throwing doors and curtains open as he passed various alcoves. It only took him a few seconds to come back out with a young black girl, held by her skinny bicep. The girl didn't look scared, like she was used to being manhandled and told what to do.

"Back's clear," he said.

A Mexican girl with neck tattoos and serious chola eyebrows stood and put her hands on her hips. "Who the fuck are you? You don't look like no fucking cops. And what the fuck is up with that dude's hair?"

"Where's Julie?" Bobby shouted.

"She ain't here."

Bobby and I looked at each other. Could I have been wrong?

Bobby let go of the black girl and grabbed Chola by her shoulders. "What does that mean? Not in this trailer? Or not out here in Plaster City?"

"Get off me," Chola said, shrugging out of Bobby's grasp. She hit his bad shoulder hard, Bobby biting his lip to avoid shrieking in pain. "How the fuck should I know where she is? That bitch don't stay with us. Why you want to talk to her?"

"We came to bring her home."

"Are you like her daddy?"

Bobby turned to me. "What the fuck do we do now? If she's not here. Grab the truck and Rudy and go?"

"You got a ride?" Chola said. "That means you can prison-break my shit. Take me out of here with you."

A couple girls stood, shouting "yeahs" and "me toos." The others soon followed. They started to surge toward us.

"Hold on, hold on," Bobby said. "We came here for Julie. We can't take all these girls."

"We got the truck," I said. "They stay and Tomás comes in, he'll take them. Same game, new team. They're trapped for good."

"Fucking Morales."

"Tomás Morales? He's coming here?" Chola said, her face turning white. She looked around wildly, like a trapped animal. "You got to get us out of here."

The other girls whispered to each other, Tomás's name sparking fear in English and Spanish. The rising terror on the girls' faces made them look even younger, in need of protection.

"Damn it." Bobby waved me over.

I turned to the girls. "Stay there. Don't move."

"Don't leave us here," Chola said.

Bobby and I huddled near the door, heads close, whispering to each other.

"We can't take them," Bobby said. "Julie. That's it. We can't."

"She's not here. I say we have to. And officially it's still my show. They're all someone's daughters. But instead of having a dad to break them out, they got us."

Bobby looked at the girls. If he saw what I saw, in front of him were children forced not into adulthood, but into some purgatory where they were objects for amusement.

"Fuck," Bobby said. He broke the huddle and then one of the fans by kicking it. "For nothing, man. All this and no Julie."

A few of the girls started from Bobby's mini-tantrum, taking a few steps away.

"He's not going to hurt anyone," I said, trying to calm them. "He's just upset about his daughter."

"Julie really is his daughter?" Chola said. "Yo, she's probably in her trailer."

Bobby turned to Chola quickly. "You said you didn't know where she was."

"I don't. I said she's probably there. We don't leave this fucking trailer except to fight. I don't know where no one is."

"Which trailer is hers?"

"Once you're out the door, turn right. You'll see it. It has a bird painted on the side."

I barked orders to Chola. "Okay, you're in charge. There's a panel truck at the far end of the loading docks. You'll see it. Says Ocotillo Beer & Ammo on the side. There's a trapdoor underneath. If you climb under the truck, you'll be able to get in the back. Find water—a lot of it—wait for us, stay out of sight."

"You seriously did like a Trojan Horse to get in here?"

"I guess we did," I said.

"Do I get a gun?" Chola said.

"No," Bobby said. "Soon as we find Julie, we'll drive everyone the fuck out of here."

"Julie know you're coming to save her? She might've used to been like us, but she ain't got to be saved no more."

"And why is that?"

"She runs this shit, yo. She's the fucking boss."

"Of course she is," I said.

We found Julie for the second time in our long hunt, sitting at the kitchen table of her air-conditioned Winnebago. She sorted and uncrumpled different denominations of bills, stacking them in neat stacks and making a tally of the count on a columnar pad. When the door crashed open, she jumped in her seat and turned quickly to face us. Seeing me, she put one hand on the money and reached for her backpack with the other hand.

I brought my pistol up quickly. "Don't do it, Julie. Bobby might not have the heart to shoot you, but he's your father. Me? I'm looking for a reason."

Julie called my bluff and reached anyway. Of course, I didn't shoot her, but I covered the distance quick enough to grab her wrist before she was able to pull her weapon. I easily pried the small pistol from her girl fingers, wondering if this was the gun she shot Bobby with. It was small, compact, and deadly. Just like her.

The whole time, Julie screamed the entire Spanish/English dictionary of obscenities at me. Not in alphabetical order, but she was under duress. She definitely exceeded my limited vocabulary, making me curious as to what a *panocha* and a *joto* were.

Bobby watched from the doorway, stepped inside, and closed the door behind him. Julie stopped struggling when she saw him. As if out of reflex, her face took on that teenage girl face that every parent knows, the snide one that looked like she smelled bad yogurt.

"You didn't die," she said.

"Wow" came out of my mouth.

Bobby shook his head, looking at the ground. "What the fuck happened to you?"

"I'm sorry, okay?" Julie said.

I'd heard more convincing apologies from waiters telling me they were out of the chicken fingers.

"I got a load of things to say to you that need to be said, but we don't got time to dick with that now," Bobby said. "I'd give you the choice between the easy way and the hard way, but I know the fucking answer. Let's tie her ass up, Jimmy. We'll carry her out of here."

"You want to tie up your daughter?"

"Gag her, too."

I turned to Julie. "And that's why you don't shoot your father."

Even with all her wriggling, I was able to get her arms and feet bound in only a couple minutes. The big, chunky knot I used to secure her was pathetic even by my standards, but it did the trick. We couldn't find any tape, so we used a torn-up shirt to gag her ongoing barrage of original profanity.

Bobby and I looked at the money on the table.

"You never know," Bobby said. He threw the loose bills into Julie's backpack and slung it over his shoulder. He spotted something in the backpack and pulled it out. It was another one of Julie's journals. He put it back and zipped up the backpack.

Opening the Winnebago door a crack, he peeked out. "Looks good."

I threw Julie over my shoulder. And as hesitant as I was to leave the air-conditioned space, I followed Bobby, Julie's weight feeling like next to nothing. Small victories gave me strength.

But those victories never lasted.

As soon as my foot hit the ground, five Mexican bikers with drawn weapons walked out from behind the trailer. Chucho led the way, armed with Bobby's pistol. The smile on his still-busted-up face appeared to revel in the five-against-two odds. That guy had never won a fair fight in his life.

Bobby looked down at the pistol in his hand, thought about it for a moment, but let it fall to the ground. One of the bikers pulled the gun from my waistband.

EIGHTEEN

"Is that Julie?" Chucho asked me. I still had her draped over my shoulder. He bent to get a look at her face. "You fuckers don't give up."

He walked to Bobby and said, "I had dreams about seeing you again. Beating your ass."

Bobby smiled. "That's the thing about dreams. They're always about things that ain't never going to happen."

Chucho gave Bobby a hard right to the stomach, just below where his arm was tied to his body. Bobby took the punch, didn't budge. He showed no sign of pain or even that he'd been hit. His expression looked like he was waiting in line at the Post Office. I wondered if he remembered that he'd learned that move from me way back in junior high.

"That punch was so weak, if it was tea, it'd be Earl Gay." Bobby gave me a wink.

He did remember.

Chucho tried to stare Bobby down. Bobby looked back, bored. The scenario was not going as Chucho had planned. He couldn't risk hitting Bobby again, for fear of looking even worse, but he had to do something. He didn't get to make a decision.

Bobby gave him a hard open-hand slap to the side of the head. The blow sent Chucho reeling and crashing against the side of the trailer. The other bikers' guns came up, but thankfully nobody fired.

I remained as motionless as I could, knees shaking a little. But I chalked that up to still having Julie hoisted onto my shoulder. She wasn't heavy, but I couldn't carry her all day.

"You going to let him bitch slap you, Chucho?" a younger, heavily-tatted Hermano said. "Fucking embarrassing."

Before Chucho could answer, Bobby turned to the young biker and laughed. "What's embarrassing is that you need those fucking guns. There's five of you. Two of us. We're old and I only got one good arm. And you're scared of us." He turned to me, shaking his head. "Today's youth. Total pussies."

"I ain't scared of shit, bitch. Especially not some gray-haired pocho fuck." The young guy jammed his gun into the back of his pants and took off his shirt.

"He's taking off his shirt," Bobby said. "That's how you know he means it."

The other men didn't look as anxious to fight, but they put their guns away, too. Nobody wanted to look weak.

"We're supposed to get back," said a fat guy who—considering the originality of their nicknaming, I guarantee—was called Gordo. "Goyo said to drop off the money and get right back."

"If the five of us can't cripple these two in less than a minute . . ." the young guy said, not finishing the thought.

Chucho made his way behind the other four men. He didn't look like he had any fight left. He'd tangled with Bobby three times and none of those encounters went well.

When it came to messing with Bobby, most people stop at once.

"I'll wash. You dry," Bobby said to me, bringing up his good hand in a fist.

I dropped Julie from my shoulder a little harder than I meant to, but carrying a live person is an awkward thing. She grunted, but couldn't do much more than that. I raised my fists slowly, a weak attempt to delay the inevitable.

"I guess that means I rinse," Gabe said, walking out from behind a nearby tent, pistol held in front of him. When the Mexican bikers turned, Bobby quickly picked up his pistol and aimed it at the young Mexican. I stood there like a dumbass.

The young Mexican looked genuinely hurt. "What about all that shit you said? We were going to square up. Fight like men."

"Why would I do that when I got a gun?" Bobby said. "I could get hurt."

"You'll understand when you get older," I said. "When you realize all this posturing macho shit is what children do. You're young. That means you're still stupid. It's okay. We were too."

"Fuck you."

"Gabe, grab their guns. Then we're the fuck out of here," Bobby said.

After I got my pistol back, Bobby and I covered the five bikers as Gabe frisked them and made a small pile of firearms between us. When he got to Chucho, they stared eye to eye for a moment and then Gabe punched him hard in the liver, dropping Chucho to a knee. Gabe put his pistol to Chucho's head.

"Don't," I said. "Don't do it."

Gabe leaned in close to Chucho and grabbed his face, squeezing his cheeks.

"We were best friends," Gabe said.

Chucho pointed toward the pile of person named Julie. "It was her. She had these plans. Said the gang could make all this money. That we'd be rich."

"Don't blame her. Man up and admit the shit you did."

"Don't do it," I repeated.

We stood frozen for what felt like weeks, as Gabe pushed the barrel of the pistol harder against Chucho's head.

Bobby's voice calmly filled the silence. "You can kill him, but if you're going to do it, find a rock. Shoot him and they'll hear it across the road. If you want revenge, make it quick. And quiet. We have to get the fuck out of here."

Gabe nodded and pulled the pistol away from Chucho's head. Then he brought the pistol back down, pistol-whipping Chucho in the jaw and side of his head. Then twice more. Blood quickly covered his face, its lower half distorted and out of place.

Bobby stepped forward and pushed one of the men forward toward the truck. "The rest of you. Start walking."

Gabe gave Chucho a kick, but Chucho didn't feel it. He was already unconscious. Gabe started following Bobby.

I hollered after Gabe, "Finish the job or carry him. Can't risk him waking up and giving us away."

Gabe grabbed one of Chucho's feet and dragged him along the hardpack behind Bobby.

I picked up Julie and threw her over my shoulder. "Let's get the hell out of here."

Bobby turned and gave a sharp laugh. "You hear this kid? Heat of the moment, he finishes the catchphrase. 'I'll rinse.' You're making me feel worse about shooting your ear off."

"I still got most of it. What about kicking my ass?" Gabe said.

"No, I still feel pretty good about that."

We corralled the men into the empty storage container. It was going to get oven hot but we didn't have time to tie everyone up. Gabe dragged Chucho inside, his head bouncing off the lip of the container with a wet thud.

"Fatty said you had some money for us," Bobby said. One of the boys shook his head and handed two big rolls of bills to Bobby. He stuffed them in his pocket.

"We going to die you leave us in here," Gordo said.

"Not if you resort to cannibalism," Bobby said. And on that bon mot, he slammed the doors shut and locked them down. One of the men slammed against the door, causing Russell's rocket to fall from the roof where it must have lodged. Bobby and I looked at it and gave each other a smile.

I might have felt bad about the five bikers, but they gladiatored teenage girls for human cockfights. If you live in a world where that's acceptable, you deserve what you get. They could roast in hell for all I cared.

———— · ————

I popped my head through the trapdoor into the truck trailer. The girl nearest me jumped and screamed, causing a chain reaction of screams, mine included. When everyone calmed down, I dropped back down and then shoved Julie up through the opening, pushing her body away from the trapdoor as far as I could.

"Hold on, everybody. It might get a little bumpy."

I hopped back down. Gabe waited to climb in. "Those girls back there might not act scared, but they are. Make them feel safe. That's your job."

Gabe nodded and climbed into the trailer. I made my way to the passenger side of the cab. Bobby sat waiting in the driver's seat.

"Gabe, Julie, and the girls are in. Let's go," I said.

"No keys," Bobby said.

"You're kidding. Which guy drove?"

"I don't know. I was with you in the back, remember?"

"His name was Flaco."

"So we look for a skinny Mexican. Great."

"Fuck. Hotwire it."

"Don't you think I would've if I knew how? Mexicans aren't born with the genetic ability to hotwire cars, Jimmy. Why would I know how to hotwire a fucking car?"

"Because you're basically a criminal," I shouted.

"I'm a rapscallion. It's different."

"Gabe. He fixes motorcycles. A mechanic."

"And he's Mexican, too," Bobby said sarcastically.

I jumped out of the truck and shimmied underneath to the trapdoor. When I knocked, it opened immediately. I poked my head inside. "Gabe. We ain't got keys. Can you get this truck started without them?"

"Not without any tools."

"Swiss Army Knife do it?"

"Maybe."

"You guys are pathetic," Chola said. "Give me the fucking knife."

———•·•———

Bobby and I stood guard as Chola climbed underneath the steering column of the truck, knife in hand. There were dozens of cars and trucks parked on the factory grounds and along the road. We could see blurry activity through the fence, if not the specific action.

I climbed on the hood of the truck to get a better look around. "Oh, shit. We might have a problem."

A fleet of black SUVs sat parked in a line in the dry wash where we had fired our rocket. The dozen vehicles were still, but their cleanliness and precision were ominous. They could only be Tomás's men.

Bobby stood on the bumper to get a better look. "Shit."

As if on cue, the truck roared to life beneath us. I slid down off the hood. Chola hopped out and tossed me my knife.

"What took you so long?" I said.

She rolled her eyes. It reminded me that she was a teenager. No more than sixteen. And she knew how to hotwire a car. I let myself believe that she learned it in shop class. I lied to myself all the time.

"Let's go," I said.

But Bobby was staring at the factory grounds across the highway. He turned to me. "What about Rudy?"

"We got to get the girls and Julie out of here. Can't take the truck in there."

"You're right. Got to grab him and meet up at Rudy's ranch later."

"There's a whole slew of bad guys over there. That's beyond even our usual shitty odds. This was a sneak-and-snatch, not an attack-and-grab."

Bobby squeezed the bridge of his nose. "You can't just make up expressions. Seriously, bro. When it's just you and me, that's one thing. But there's people around. It's embarrassing."

"'Sneak-and-snatch' isn't an expression?"

"Not even in England," Bobby said. "I can't leave Rudy there. He'd never let me hear the end of it if he got killed."

"You know what? Chucho and Julie are the only ones who know our faces. What says we can't waltz in there like we want to see the fights? Get Rudy and go."

"Bro, you're not going. I was talking me, not we. You got to drive the truck."

"Gabe can drive the truck."

"You're done, man. Gone above and beyond. To the edge of the cliff. You don't got to jump off with me. I'll be okay."

"Said the guy with one working arm. No argument. I'm in."

I gave Gabe directions to Rudy's place. Told him that no matter what, he was not to untie or even talk to Julie. Get to Rudy's and wait. If we didn't get back by nightfall, he was to call Griselda. She'd take it from there.

Bobby chucked Julie's backpack into the truck. Gabe held out his hand to Bobby. They shook.

Gabe said, "I know you weren't here to save my ass, but you did. Thanks, Julie's Dad." He turned to me. "And whatever your name is."

"Jimmy."

Gabe climbed into the truck, Chola sliding over.

"They'll frisk you at the gate," Chola said. "Unless you want to fight your way in, you're going to have to leave your guns here. Or shove them really far up your ass."

Bobby looked at me. "No guns?"

"We're going in, grabbing Rudy, and leaving. We don't need them."

"If it were easy, it wouldn't be us doing it."

Bobby and I handed our hardware to Gabe. He stowed it all under the seat. I slammed the door and we watched Gabe back up, get a running start, and drive through the same gate he had busted through just a few days before.

"He hates that fucking gate," Bobby said.

Bobby and I turned to each other and said something at the same time, and then we both stopped, started again, and then shut up. I held up my hand.

"You first," I said. "What were you going to say?"

"It's stupid. I was going to say, 'Daddy's coming home.' What were you going to say?"

"'Father knows best—the best way to kick your ass.'"

I put in the call to Buck Buck and Snout. They knew what they had to do.

Bobby and I walked out of the mangled gate and headed across the street toward the factory grounds to get Rudy.

"'I hope you bought a new tie, because it's Father's Day,'" Bobby said.

"'Who's your daddy? Oh, that guy. Yeah, he's got nun-chucks.'"

"'Luke, I am your father. The father of . . .'" Bobby paused. "No. I thought I had one, but I didn't."

"That's okay. I didn't have any more either."

The chain-link gates stood wide-open leading into the factory. Two Los Hermanos dirtbags smoked cigarettes, drank beer, and—I guess—stood watch. But when you're pretty much letting in other dirtbags who pay to see teenage girls fight, you're less of a guard and more of a ticket taker.

While one of the bikers patted us down, the other one kept one hand on the gun in his belt. "Fifty bucks."

I looked at Bobby. It hadn't occurred to me to bring cash to a rescue mission. But Bobby didn't flinch. He reached into his pocket, pulled out one of the rolls of bills, found two twenties and a ten, and handed the guy their own money.

"Each," the biker said.

"Better be worth it," Bobby said, counting another fifty.

"It is, man. Beer's free. First fight's still going. Hurry and you'll catch the end. If you got five hundred more, you can fuck the loser. All the fight is out of them by then."

Bobby stared at the guy. If he was thinking what I was, he was concentrating entirely on not beating the punk to death. I grabbed Bobby's good arm and pulled him onto the factory grounds.

The entire ground of the factory area was bone white, even brighter than the rest of Plaster City and difficult to look at directly. It reflected the sun, causing a desert form of snow blindness.

The deafening Mexican techno soundtrack played a repetitious beat that I could feel in my chest. It seemed appropriate for fighting, but it was hard to believe that anyone on the face of the planet actually liked that shit.

The crowd that roamed the lot consisted of two distinct types. There were the bros, the same shitheads that had been at Driskell's party. The other group consisted of Mexicans in boots and cowboy hats, the kind of men who grew up on animal fighting and were looking for fresh action. Sifted within the crowd was the occasional Los Hermanos jacket.

The center of the action was deeper onto the factory grounds. A huddle of whooping and hollering men blocked our view of the fight that was under way. In the shade of one of the factory towers, Rudy worked the kegs, a line of men waiting to be served beer. It was nice to see that even at an event where pretty underage girls beat the shit out of each other, the spectators still honored the sanctity of the line. It is ingrained in us early that cutting is wrong. Is there anything more truly American than waiting in a line?

Bobby and I ambled nonchalantly over to the beer line, and not to raise any hackles, we waited. When we reached the front of the line and Rudy spotted us, his eyebrows raised.

Bobby leaned in, whispering to Rudy. "We got to go. Now."

"It's done? You got her?"

Bobby nodded.

"Thank God. This garbage they call music is killing me. I'm going to have to listen to six straight hours of Waylon just to antidote it." Rudy poured one more beer, smelled it, stared at the foam, and poured it on the ground. He started to walk away.

"Wait," Bobby said. "I didn't get my beer."

"Are you serious?"

"We waited in line. We're right here." Bobby reached over and filled up a cup himself, beer spilling and foaming everywhere. He took a swig and then refilled the cup to the top.

I turned to the line that had formed behind us. "Bartender quit. It's self-serve."

And immediately the line deteriorated and the crowd circled the taps. That's the thing about lines. They operate on a delicate balance. People respect them but hate them. First chance, anarchy triumphs.

Bobby, Rudy, and I walked toward the gate. But, of course, it couldn't go that smoothly. It surprised me that I was the one who made things more difficult. Fifty yards from the gate, I stopped and turned to look at the men watching the fights. Bobby and Rudy stopped abruptly.

"What about them? Those girls?" I asked.

Bobby stopped. He laughed loudly. "Why not? If it was too uneventful, it wouldn't be a satisfying Mavescapade."

Rudy slapped the two of us on the back. "Ain't nothing more satisfying than whooping a younger man."

So with six balls and no plan, we stomped toward the makeshift fighting pit. But who needs a plan when chaos intervenes?

Before we got there, I saw a familiar face staring at me through the crowd. Cold Sore. I had forgotten about him. But he hadn't forgotten me. His cold sore looked as angry as his expression. Campho-Phenique would only cure one of those.

Cold Sore yelled something, but I couldn't hear anything over the music. He looked around frantically, and then pointed and pushed the two bikers next to him toward us. They both pulled pistols, but in the thick crowd they kept them trained at the ground.

I took off in the direction of the fight, hoping to get lost in the mob of men. But I was alone. Bobby and Rudy weren't runners. Unless they were running toward a fight. Which is what they did. By the time I realized they weren't with me, they had met the two bikers halfway.

Bobby risked later ridicule for being a kicker by jumping feet first into the stomach of one of the bikers. The guy folded in half. Bobby twisted his body to land on his good shoulder, but still hit the ground hard. Rudy clotheslined the other biker in the neck hard enough to give me a bruise at this distance. That guy fell to the ground choking for air. Rudy hit him again just to make a point.

Lost in the immediacy of their violence, it took me a few seconds to realize that I wasn't doing anything.

Some of the spectators roaming around grew interested in the melee, maybe thinking it was part of the entertainment. Guys shoved other guys out of the way to get a better look. Shoved guys took umbrage and shoved back. And very quickly, a couple completely unrelated fights broke out. Violence begets violence. Go to an MMA match and see how many parking lot skirmishes start from the deadly cocktail of testosterone and beer and stupid.

Not literally. That would be a disgusting cocktail. I'd call it a Hot Couture.

I lost sight of Bobby and Rudy in the growing melee, but I did spot Cold Sore leading Goyo and a few of the remaining upright Mexican bikers to the mess that we had wrought. They tried to break up the fights, but they didn't seem prepared. They had no bouncer moves, mostly clumsy shirt-pulling and dragging men that were already out of the fray.

As a full-blown riot blossomed, I dodged a couple fists, got kicked in the shins, and barely missed getting puked on by a gut-punched drunk. When I broke off from the men, I ended up next to the two girls who had been the former center of attention. No longer fighting, the two bruised and bloody girls watched, confused and a little frightened. I held up my hands to show that I was harmless.

"It'll take too long to explain, but if you stay here, you're in danger. You want to get out of here? Come with me."

"Is there free cotton candy in your rape van, too?" LaShanda said. "Fuck off, creep." She rubbed at the side of her mouth, blood painting the back of her hand and wrist.

"We already escaped the other girls. Julie, too. I ain't fucking with you."

"Yeah, and I would trust you why?"

I remembered how Chola had reacted to Tomás's name. "Because Tomás Morales is coming here to fuck shit up."

The two girls looked at each other, the realization that there was danger in every direction. The other girl spoke up. "Where's your car?"

"About that. I don't have a car."

The fighting grew around us. I shoved at men as they crowded our space. It looked like all hundred-plus men in attendance had joined the free-for-all. Most of the fights had become divided along racial lines, the bros squaring up against the Mexicans. And for all the swearing and pea-cocking anger, there was definitely a contingent that was having fun.

"How you going to get us out without no car?"

As if on cue, the theme to the *A-Team* in car-horn form blared. I looked to the factory gate to see Snout's dumbass van bounce onto the grounds. It skidded to a stop before it reached the boiling pit of brawling men. Buck Buck sat in the open side door, strapped into a chair that Snout had welded to the floor. He pointed a shotgun wherever his eyes landed, trying to figure out who needed to be peppered with birdshot.

"Are you fucking kidding me?" LaShanda said.

"We couldn't get a Batmobile on short notice," I replied. "Come with me if you're coming."

The only way to the van was through the tumult. I put up my dukes and swung wildly, wading into the crowd. The girls followed. When one less-than-brave bro tried to tag the back of my head, the quieter girl kneecapped him with her heel.

I got hit a few times, but overall I gave more than I got. And with a torn shirt, slightly more blood on the outside than the inside, and an increasingly dimmer view of the male of the species, I reached the van with the girls right behind me.

Buck Buck pulled the cigar out of his mouth. "I love it when a plan comes together."

"Even the teenage girls think you're ridiculous," I said.

"Teenage girls think everything is ridiculous," Buck Buck said in his defense.

I looked at the two girls. They nodded in agreement. We all climbed into the van.

"Rudy and Bobby are somewhere in the mosh pit," I said.

"Oh shit, oh shit, oh shit," Snout said from the front.

We all looked out the windshield to where he pointed. It looked like a haboob, a huge cloud of dust coming at us from the northeast. I hopped out and climbed the ladder on the back. Standing on top of the van, I confirmed the worst. The fleet of black SUVs that had been sitting in the dry wash was now in motion. The vehicles drove toward Plaster City, four across and three deep.

"Fuck me," I said.

I slid down the front windshield, rolled off the small hood, and fell to the ground.

Snout screamed, "Hey, watch the paint!"

I ignored him. "We have to get the fuck out of here. Now. Right now. This place is about to get bloody."

A gun fired. A bullet pinged off the side of the van.

"The hell?" Snout said.

"Get down," I shouted.

I dropped to the ground and scanned the crowd. Finally, I spotted Goyo about twenty yards away, aiming his pistol and firing again. Buck Buck fired back. Goyo dove behind a low wall.

The gunfire stopped the fight. The crack of a gun had that power.

"Buck Buck! Fire a couple shots in the air," I said.

"Tonight long stick goes boom," he shouted.

The shotgun thundered. Men scattered from the sound. I caught sight of Bobby and Rudy, bloody and bruised, but still dishing punishment. Bobby's shoulder was saturated in blood, the bandages and sling frayed and torn. He finally caught sight of the van. I waved him over, pointing quickly to the dust cloud closing in. Bobby swore and grabbed Rudy by the collar, moving toward the van.

Goyo stood up and lined up his shot, aiming at the running Bobby.

Without thinking, I took off toward Goyo. He fired at Bobby. I didn't look to see if he hit his mark. By the time he caught sight of me, I was right on him. He turned and fired. I felt my arm get warm, but I didn't let it stop me, tackling him at the waist. We hit the ground hard. He tried to raise the pistol, but I grabbed his wrist with one hand and punched him in the ribs with the other.

He hit me with a shot to the neck that rocked me and relaxed my grip. He brought his knees up and pushed, knocking me off him. I rolled to a knee, but he was already standing and pointing his pistol at me. I closed my eyes and saw Juan's face.

He fired.

But I didn't die. I opened my eyes to see Goyo slump down onto the ground, blood pouring from what was left of his head. I looked around, confused.

The first black SUV had breached the factory grounds, men with rifles standing in the open sunroofs. Men with pistols pointing out windows. They fired into the crowd, men wearing Los Hermanos jackets falling.

"Come on," Bobby yelled from the van, shaking me out of my stupor.

Holding my bleeding shoulder, I scrambled to the van and jumped inside. Bobby, Rudy, the two girls, and Buck Buck yelled over one another. Buck Buck slammed the door shut.

Bobby screamed, "Make like cowshit and hit the fucking trail!"

Snout was way ahead of him, flooring it and heading away from the gate. Shots pinged off the back. The girls screamed, thankfully drowning out my surprisingly high-pitched yelp.

"Reinforced," Snout said.

He drove straight toward the panicked men running for their lives. Snout steered around them as best he could, but he clipped a few. Some men climbed onto the factory catwalks to get away. A few Los Hermanos men tore off their jackets, fleeing with the others. Many of the Mexican men chose to remain motionless on the ground, hands over their heads. Like they'd been to this party before. It was a war zone.

"We need to find another exit," I said.

"I'm on it," Snout said.

Tongue stuck out the corner of his mouth in concentration, Snout drove along the northern perimeter, parallel to the highway. A high chain-link fence topped with barbed wire lined the edge. A few men tried to climb the fence to escape, getting tangled in the wire. I dared to take a look out the back window of the van. More SUVs, gunfire emanating from every opening the vehicles provided. Los Hermanos fell. A few men fired back, but were soon facedown.

"Hold on," Snout yelled.

The van drove onto a hill of gypsum, tires spinning in the white powder, digging itself in, but kicking up a thick cloud of white behind us.

"You're going to get stuck," I yelled.

He tore hard right off the hill, the van sliding sideways. When he finally got some traction, he turned the wheel hard again and rammed into the fence, smashing the windshield, but breaking through. For a second, the van skidded and tipped onto two wheels, but Snout got control before we rolled. Just before. We bounced back onto four tires and, dragging a piece of the fence that scraped like nails on a chalkboard, we headed west toward Coyote Wells and Rudy's farm. Nobody followed.

"Everyone okay?"

Mumbles and nods, too much adrenaline and amazement to create cohesive thoughts.

"Fuckers were killing fuckers back there," LaShanda said.

"You're okay now," I said. "It's over."

She slid across the floor of the van and put her arms around my waist, squeezing me. I put an arm around her and held her tight. Her body shuddered as she cried against me. I held her for the length of the ride.

Bobby put his arm around the other girl. She looked up at him and smiled. "Thanks."

NINETEEN

Julie sat bound and gagged in Rudy's living room, surrounded by the people who loved her. Becky and Russell had held down the fort there while we terrorized Plaster City. Julie bored her angry teenage eyes into Bobby, who sat beside Rudy on his couch. They dabbed at their bloody faces with kitchen towels. We had dressed our more serious wounds. Luckily, Goyo's shot had only grazed me. I stood by the door, feeling like the odd man out, not part of the family. Buck Buck, Snout, Gabe, and the girls waited outside.

"What happens now?" I asked.

"Got to start talking at some point," Bobby said. "You ready for this, Beck?"

Becky nodded.

I walked to Julie and untied the shirt-gag from her mouth. Julie stretched her jaw, opening it wide and chewing on the air.

"I hate you all," Julie said. "You ruined everything."

"You're not going to get anywhere in life blaming other people," Bobby said. "We're going to start with some apologies. To your mother. To me. To everyone in this room, who went out of their way to save your ass."

"Where is my money?"

"I'm not hearing no 'I'm sorrys.'"

"And you ain't going to. Mom never wanted me. You don't count. I don't need any of you. I want to go back. When Los Hos finds out—"

"There's no more Los Hos. There's no back to go back to," Bobby said.

"What are you talking about?"

"If your ungrateful self would shut up, he'll tell you," Rudy said.

"Who the fuck are you?" Julie said. "I don't know you."

He rose out of reflex, but sat back down. I could see the wheels turning. If he told her not to swear, she would do it more. Children know a thing or two about torture and how to use one's annoyances as a weapon. You couldn't win.

"I'm your grandfather. Now shut your mouth and let the grown-ups talk."

Julie's face registered surprise, but she didn't say anything.

Bobby got down on his haunches in front of her. "Los Hermanos made an enemy of Tomás Morales."

She nodded her head, her confidence gone at the mention of Tomás's name. "I know who he is."

"A half hour ago, after we took you out of Plaster City," Bobby said, "Morales had an army go in there and wipe out Los Hos. We saw the beginning, but the end—I'm sure—was more complete. You can read about it in the paper tomorrow. Your biker friends, Chucho—" He turned to me. "Bro, we didn't let them out of that container. That's messed up." He turned back to Julie. "Los Hermanos, they're either dead gone, disappeared, or heading for the hills. What I'm saying is there's nothing left. Only place to go is home."

"That was my home."

"That's not true, Jules," Becky said. "Why would you say that?"

"All you do is yell at me. You don't treat me like a person. Like an adult."

"Because you're not," Becky said, her volume rising. "You're sixteen years old. You'll be grown up most of your life, but if you try to act like it too quick, that life will be a mess. I had you young. I know."

"Are you saying I messed up your life?"

"For Christ's sake," Bobby said. "That's not what she's saying."

"I'm more grown up than you two. Not some waitress. Some drunk. I was running things. We were making money. They listened to me. I showed them how to make money and they listened. They treated me like a woman."

"By making you fight?" Bobby said.

"Nobody made me fight. I would do it every day, but my face would get fucked up."

Rudy flinched at the profanity but only shook his head. Becky flexed her jaw and tears rolled down her face. I couldn't tell if it was anger or sadness. Her clenched fists sat in her lap, knuckles white. She tried to say something, but stopped herself. Russell put an arm around her.

"Reality check, daughter o' mine," Bobby said. "You shot me. You shot your fucking father with a gun. You know how fucked up that is?"

"Seriously, dude. I've watched TV. I know what a father is. You ain't it. You're a guy that fucked my mom. Why am I talking to you?"

"Okay, fair enough. Fuck the father angle," Bobby said. "But here's who I am. I'm the guy that will press charges against you for shooting me. I'll send your sassy, snarky ass to juvie or worse, and then get shit-faced drunk afterward. Maybe shed a tear in my beer. I got ten girls outside that'll— what's the word, Jimmy?"

"Corroborate."

"What he said. And I got a chance to take a look at your most recent journal. It's impressively detailed when it comes to your crimes. That means I can nail your ass to the wall for running Los Hermanos' operations. You're in deep shit, Julie. That's why you're talking to me. Because I'm so pissed off at you right now, I'm willing to fuck your life up before you get a chance to fuck it up yourself."

"Whatever."

Bobby turned to Rudy. "Where's your phone? I'm calling the cops."

Rudy pointed to the kitchen.

"Mom." Julie's voice got an octave higher, each syllable stretched out. "You're not going to let him, are you? I'm really sorry."

Bobby laughed loudly and for quite some time. When he caught his breath, he said, "At first, I thought this was like *The Searchers*. I thought the Comanche had brainwashed you. But I'm starting to see that you're the Comanche. You're diabolical."

Julie ignored him. "Russell, I've learned my lesson. You believe me, don't you?"

Russell shook his head. "I don't."

"We're going to make a deal," Bobby said, "or I'm going to call a deputy friend of mine. You got a decision to make. You ready to bargain?"

Gabe poked his head into the room. "I don't want to interrupt your family time or whatever, but shit's going down outside."

Bobby turned, but I waved him off. I wasn't adding anything to the conversation anyway. "I got it," I said and followed Gabe outside.

From Gabe's nonchalance, I was expecting a tussle between the girls or something equally banal. I wasn't expecting nine heavily armed Mexicans standing in front of three black SUVs. They blocked the dirt drive that led to the road. Facing them along the edge of Rudy's deck sat the ten girls. Some of them looked scared, but most looked more resigned to their fate. In the no-man's-land between, Buck Buck and Snout stood with shotguns pointed at the ground. They looked heroic.

Snout turned to me, smiling. "Hey, Jimmy."

"What's going on?" I asked.

"They said they're taking the girls. Buck Buck told them they weren't. That's about where we're at."

"Don't shoot no one. Let me get Tomás on the horn."

He answered on the first ring.

"Those girls are mine," Tomás said in lieu of a greeting. "They're part of the package."

"That wasn't part of our deal."

"True, but taking them with you wasn't either."

"They're people, not property."

"You still don't understand. It used to be cute, now it's irritating."

"They're nobody's property. They're teenage girls. Messed up, damaged girls. You're not taking them without a fight."

"If not them, I'll find others."

"And if those girls were in front of me, I'd stop you from abducting them too."

"What do I get in return?"

"Nothing. This isn't a trade and I'm not asking for a fucking favor, Tommy. I'm telling you that we will fight if your men try to take these girls. That's what I'm telling you. You can decide to do whatever the fuck you want with that information."

Tomás said nothing for a few seconds. He sighed. "It's so much easier in Mexico. I don't know why I'm so hell-bent on doing business north of the fence. More pain than it's worth."

"It'd make things easier for me, too, if you stopped."

"My abuelito would never talk to me again if something happened to you. Not that he's talking to me now," Tomás said. "Hold on."

Ten seconds later, one of the armed men answered his phone, listened, and yelled a few words in Spanish to the other men. They stowed their weapons, got in the SUVs, and drove away, kicking up dust and gravel.

Tomás came back on the line. "It's done."

"We're done, Tommy," I said. "I can't associate with you anymore."

"That makes more sense," Tomás said.

"I'll always be grateful for your help bringing Juan home."

"Raise him well. You're a good man, Jimmy. Even a bad man can see that."

Tomás hung up. And while it had been necessary to sever that tie, it still felt like I had lost a part of my past. But Tommy had been gone a long time. Only Tomás fucking Morales remained.

Buck Buck and Snout walked to where Gabe and I stood on the deck.

I slapped Snout on the back. "You looked good out there, Snouter. Like a real badass."

"I'm going to buy a cowboy hat," he said.

They hopped onto the deck. It collapsed under the combined weight. The girls jumped off the edge, a couple rolling on the ground. They dusted themselves off and laughed as we dug ourselves out of the wreckage. When Rudy came to the front door, he couldn't have looked more disgusted.

Before I went back inside to see how the treaty negotiations were going, I wanted to have a powwow with the girls. Chola had become their de facto leader, stepping up in the heat of the moment.

"Those narcos were here for us, yeah?" she asked. "What did that cost you?"

"A friend. But the friendship was dead. We just hadn't buried it yet."

"You going to turn us over to the cops? Social Services?"

"The responsible me says I should, let them sort it."

"You don't seem so responsible to me."

"If I let all you go on your own, some other bad shit is going to happen. I know you ain't lost kittens, probably more worldlier than me, but I'm thinking I shouldn't be letting you wander stray."

"You make that call, put us back in the system, they drop me back in foster care." Chola nodded at the other girls. "They send them back to their fucked-up houses, fighting off weird uncles, pervy fosters, or maybe their own dads. Parents who don't give a shit. We're not on vacation. We took off for a reason."

"If I let you on your own, where do you go? What happens? If all the choices are shit, what do I do with you?"

"They can stay here."

Both Chola and I turned to see Rudy climbing down from the stack of timber that was once his deck. "I can use help around the place. Fix this deck, for starters. Can't do much more than feed them, keep them alive, maybe find a few girls work in town. Clean out the old Airstreams out back, call in some favors. I got the room. Looks like they've been helping each other, even if they been fighting. That's more of a family than real family. Why break them up?"

"You ain't thought this through. Big responsibility," I said. "And you weren't exactly father of the year."

"You ain't the decider. They are," Rudy said. "Yeah, I was a bad father. My boy hates me. And's got every right to. The things I remember doing were bad, but the things I don't remember, they're the ones that hurt most. I still learn about bad I did when I was drinking. I can't fix the past, but I can do something right now."

"There're ten girls here. Can you handle that?"

"I can try."

Buck Buck and Snout stepped forward. Buck Buck said, "We can't take any of them in, but we can find work for a few of them. Decent pay. Irrigating's been getting in the way of our training."

I didn't ask.

Rudy said, "I ain't saying they live here forever. Most of 'em won't want to at all. Just give them time to figure things out. If it don't work, you can come up with something else then."

"Why would I trust some old dude out in Bumfuck I don't know? You could be a freak," Chola said.

Rudy walked to his truck, took something out, and walked back. He handed Chola his truck gun. "I get out of line. Shoot me."

The girl looked at the gun. "Okay."

"I only got one rule," Rudy said. "No swearing."

"Shit," Chola said. "It'd be easier if you just wore earplugs."

———

Becky climbed down the remains of the deck as I was about to go back inside.

"Do you have a cigarette?" she asked.

I handed her one and lit it. "How you doing?"

"Needed a break. Julie makes me so angry. I'm glad she's safe, but I can't help it. I'm wondering if someplace else is better for her. Not jail, but there's got to be places. I honestly don't know who that is in there and what I'm going to do with her when I got her back home."

"She knows how much trouble she's in. She's playing tough, but she knows."

"It's a messed up thing, threatening your daughter to come home. Like it's so bad. I feel like I lost my little girl the moment she ran away."

We smoked in silence. When I was done, I crushed the last cigarette underfoot that I ever planned to smoke, handed her the rest of the pack, and went back inside.

———

"Okay, so you'll go back home," Bobby said. "But how do I know you'll stay? That you won't leave again?"

The negotiations appeared to have reached a civil pitch during the Mexican standoff outside. It was nice to see some calm amid the chaos.

"Where am I going to go?" Julie said. "You said it yourself. You convinced me."

"You'll have to stay out of trouble. There will be rules and repercussions."

"And in a year and half, I'll be eighteen and I can do what I want."

"Exactly. That's all we're asking. And hell, you might find that being a normal teenager suits you."

"I don't really like what other teenagers do."

"What about your drawings? I've seen your art," Bobby said. "It's amazing. You could do something with that. Go to art school. Learn about painters and drawers and stuff."

"Artists don't make money."

"Are you kidding me?" Bobby said, "Picasso was like a gajillionaire. He'd pay for expensive meals and cars by drawing scribbles on a napkin. That's badass."

"You ever hear the expression, 'starving artist'?"

"Money ain't everything. You like drawing?"

"It's okay."

"Then keep doing it. Not everyone's got your talent. Maybe you can apply to colleges next year. You're smart."

"We can't afford college," Julie said. "We're poor. I told you. Every time there's something I want, something to do, we don't got the money to do it."

"That's all excuses. There's scholarships and loans. I went to college."

"Really?" Julie said with a smirk.

"Why doesn't anyone believe me?" Bobby said. "If college is what you want, we'll figure out a way."

"What about my money? The money I made?"

"You're splitting it with the girls outside. They earned it too. I'll keep your share safe until your eighteenth birthday. How's that?"

"And then I get it back and can do whatever I want?"

"That's right. You will be released from your rigid sentence of staying with your caring mother in a safe and loving home. Life is so hard for you."

"We could've made so much more," Julie said, more to herself.

"It's time to go home," Bobby said. "You don't have any other choice."

TWENTY

Real life doesn't come beautifully wrapped with a bow on top. Most events usually look more like a three-year-old's attempt to wrap Mommy's gift. Crinkled and torn paper, too much tape, and covered in glitter and stickers. But it isn't for the lack of effort or the love put into the thing. Some people just can't wrap for shit. No matter how hard people try, there will always be limits beyond our control, a ceiling to our influence and our ability.

Julie returned home to Indio without any more struggle or drama. Becky and Russell established strict ground rules and kept a close eye on her. From what Bobby told me, it looked like Julie was making an honest effort at both school and home.

Gabe brought Angel over regularly so they could draw together. And so he could hang out with her, I'm sure. Love made us all do crazy things, including not giving up on the people who betrayed us.

I got invited to Julie's seventeenth birthday. It was a quiet affair. Julie didn't invite any new friends. She stayed reserved, but friendly, most of the night. None of the nastiness, but a distance that made me wonder where her mind was.

Three weeks after her birthday party, Julie ran away for good. Bobby and Becky never heard from her again.

Becky contacted the authorities and went through the motions to get her back, but I think she had had enough. There wasn't any chase left in her. At seventeen, Julie had essentially emancipated herself and as difficult as it was for those that cared, she was where she chose to be.

With the money from Plaster City, we were able to hire tutors so the girls could get their high school diplomas. Not all of them hung around, but the remaining six worked hard, inspired by the realization that this was their shot.

Bobby surprised everyone by taking in Lety—formerly known as Chola. He acted like it was no big thing, he had the space and maybe he could learn some things about teenagers to help him when his other daughter reached that age. It was a good deal for both of them. Lety got a place to stay where she could concentrate on her studies. It kept Bobby's drinking in check as he played the part of the responsible grown-up. And with a couple of the other girls helping with the land, he was able to get to Riverside more often to see his daughter.

He was making the effort, but he wasn't perfect. A Mavescapade arose now and again, back to the more manageable monthly schedule. I only heard about them later. True to my word, Plaster City was my last Mavescapade. And while Bobby and I saw each other—morning coffee, baling hay, the Holtville Carrot Festival—we both had become homebodies, much more focused on the real lives we had built for ourselves.

Bobby played it straight with Griselda. He told her everything that had happened. She got understandably pissed, but admitted that if we had told her, she would have shut us down. Griselda seemed genuinely impressed that Bobby took in Lety. A lot of girlfriends would be suspect of their boyfriend taking a sixteen-year-old into their home. Bobby's new attempt at honesty must have been working.

The Riverside County Sheriff's Department never found Craig Driskell's killer. They never would.

In the week after our rescue, the front page of the *Imperial Valley Press* had stories about the massacre in Plaster City. Five bodies had been found hanging from the catwalks of the gypsum factory towers. The speculation played on the public's fear that the drug wars had made their way to the Valley. Almost no truth in any of the articles, but that sold a lot of papers. And while it was investigated by every branch of law enforcement, to the best of my knowledge, nobody was ever charged.

But the Spanish whispers in Morales Bar and the underside of the Imperial Valley told a more complete story. The rumors and theories about Tomás Morales and his death squad skirted far closer to the truth than any legit news source.

I went back to Plaster City two weeks after our adventure to look around. The entire area had been cleaned and scoured. Back to its blinding white purity.

With five bodies displayed publicly, I wondered what happened to the others. Maybe one day, some hiker or gold prospector in the North Yuha would stumble on some mass grave. But it would be hard to associate them with Plaster City. There are thousands of bodies in this part of the desert, from drifters to illegals. Like Buck Buck had said, when you're walking in the desert, you're walking in a graveyard.

When I went to Morales Bar, I was always tempted to ask Mr. Morales about Tomás. But I don't think he would've known anything. Tomás was no longer a part of either of our lives.

Russell took me and Juan back out to the dry wash east of Plaster City to shoot off rockets and look for shells. The look of sheer joy on Juan's face as he pressed the button and the rocket launched in the air will be forever one of my fondest memories. It reminded me that I didn't feel wonder nearly as often as I did as a child.

Juan still had a lot of questions that he wasn't ready to ask. It frustrated him. We talked about it in brief installments, him absorbing his short, but dramatic past in small bites. Someday I hoped it would all make sense to him.

———————

One night after putting Juan to bed, I found one of Pop's old bottles of wine in the cellar. Nine times out of ten, they turned out to be vinegar. Surrounded by irrigated fields, the basement regularly flooded, the moisture rotting the corks. But this time, the gamble paid off. The wine was perfect.

I brought Angie a glass and we sat outside staring at the view from our backyard, rows and rows of lettuce. It's actually prettier than it sounds.

"It's good to be home," I said. "I can't think of anyplace I'd rather be right now."

"Me neither," Angie said, and then her voice got serious. "But there's something we have to talk about."

"Uh-oh. What?"

"Is there something you want to tell me?"

"No. I don't think so."

"I found some butts in the ashtray of your truck when I was looking for some change. Were you smoking when you were in Indio?"

I was caught and I knew it. So instead of answering Angie's question, I countered with a question I had already planned to ask.

"Will you marry me?"

When she stopped laughing, I got my answer.